TO ERR IS HUMAN

SHORT CREEK MYSTERIES

TO ERR IS HUMAN

BOOK THREE
SHORT CREEK MYSTERIES

By
Amy Rognlie

MBI

To Err is Human
Published by Mountain Brook Ink
White Salmon, WA U.S.A.

The website addresses recommended throughout this book are offered as a resource. These websites are not intended in any way to be or imply an endorsement on the part of Mountain Brook Ink, nor do we vouch for their content.

This story is a work of fiction. All characters and events are the product of the author's imagination. Any resemblance to any person, living or dead, is coincidental.

Cowman, Mrs. Charles E. *Streams in the Desert*. March 9, quote of unnamed poem by Mary Butterfield. Public domain.

Hopkins, Gerard Manley. "The Wreck of the Deutschland". Public domain.

Martyn, Henry. *Selections from the Journal and Letters of Henry Martyn*, excerpted in *Listening to the Saints,* copyright 1962 by The Upper Room, Nashville.

Wolfe, Humbert. "The Uncelestial City". Public domain.

Wordsworth, William "To A Butterfly". Public domain.

All scripture quotations taken from the Holy Bible, New International Version®, NIV® Copyright ©1973, 1978, 1984, 2011 by Biblica, Inc.® Used by permission. All rights reserved worldwide.

ISBN 978-1943959-74-7
© 2019 Amy Rognlie

The Team: Miralee Ferrell, Nikki Wright, Cindy Jackson
Cover Design: Cover design by Ken Raney
Mountain Brook Ink is an inspirational publisher offering fiction you can believe in.

Printed in the U.S.A. 2020

Dedication

Soli Deo Gloria

Acknowledgments

As always, thank you to Vicki Burtchell, Autumn McMurry, Jan Spano, and Danny Rognlie for your insightful comments and enthusiastic encouragement.

Thank you to Miralee Ferrell and the MBI staff. You're the best!

CHAPTER ONE

Three weeks. Three weeks until the wedding. I breathed out a happy sigh in the bright May morning air as I left the house. We'd been planning Aunt Dot's wedding for months now, and it was almost time. Even my parents were coming in from out of the country for the big event. And then the weekend after that, we had the long-awaited grand opening of Hope House. To say I'd be busy the next month would be a major understatement.

"Come on, Annie. Let's go to work."

My German shepherd, Annie, hopped into the delivery van for the short drive to my florist shop and bookstore, C. Willikers. Annie was a beautiful girl—Todd's dog, really—but he had been traveling so much lately with all the extra classes he was taking we decided Annie should stay with me for now, an arrangement that suited me fine.

I hummed along with the radio as I drove, checking off the items on my mental wedding checklist as I pulled up to the shop. Cake ordered. Check. Dress altered. Check. Menu finalized. Check. Roses—

Where were my rose bushes? My prized rose bushes, the focal point of my shop's cottage garden, were gone. And why was my best friend Mona pacing around in my yard?

"What in the world?" I jerked to a stop in front of my small store and flung open the door of my delivery van. "Come on, Annie. What's wrong, Mona?"

Mona bustled over and threw her plump arms around me, a cloud of perfume enveloping me. "Callie! Thank God! I've been trying to get a hold of you. Houston is going to be okay, I think, but you're going to be really mad, and I don't blame you. The sheriff is on his way over after he gets done with his coffee, because it wasn't really an emergency, he said. But I think it is an emergency because it's not every day someone almost gets killed in his friend's yard."

She paused for a breath, and I peered over her head to see our friend, Houston, pastor of the church next door, lying on my lawn. "Houston?"

He waved weakly. "I'm all right. Just a little bump. Almost saw who it was."

"What? What's wrong? Who what was?" I was confused. "And who almost got killed?"

Mona was not known for accuracy of detail, so someone "almost getting killed" could mean pretty much anything. Except that someone did, once, almost get killed in the back yard of my store. Ack. I preferred not to think about that. I blew out my breath. "Will one of you please tell me what is going on before the sheriff gets here?"

I wished Mona would have waited to call the sheriff. I would have rather told Todd Whitney first, a local deputy and my soon-to-be-fiancé, if things went as we both hoped.

Houston sat up, holding his head. His tie was askew, but other than that, he looked like he always did—ready to step into the pulpit. "I think it was probably an accident—"

Mona snorted. "That wasn't any accident."

"What happened?" I directed my question to Houston.

"I don't know. I got to the church a little early this morning, and well, you know, decided to take a walk."

"*You* were taking a walk?"

"Yeah, well, I'm trying to get into better shape." His face flushed red. "Anyway, I was headed past your shop, and I noticed something seemed off. I started up the walkway into the yard, and that's when it hit me."

"That the rose bushes were missing?"

"No, the branch." He bent his head down so I could see the top of his head.

"Ouch." I glanced around, just now noticing a rather hefty branch lying beneath the pecan tree. "This branch fell on your head?"

He nodded. "Fortunately, I heard it creaking a bit and moved out of the way before it hit me full force. But that's when I noticed your bushes were gone. Who would dig up someone else's roses?"

I trudged up the brick pathway, mourning the sight of the bare trellises that, only yesterday, had been filled with buds. I reached the black wrought-iron gate, my friends beside me. We all stared at the two enormous holes on either side of the walkway. My heirloom Eden rosebushes hadn't been destroyed—they'd been stolen.

"What kind of nut job digs up other people's plants?" Mona poked at the dirt clods with her foot, her rhinestone-covered flip-flops sparkling in the morning sun. "These were probably super special ones too, huh?" Mona didn't share my love of all things growing, but she knew how much time and energy I'd put into my garden here at the shop.

I nodded. I had no words. How had my morning gone from wedding-day happiness to falling branches and stolen roses? And not regular old roses. No, these were my prized roses that I had been babying and coaxing along since the very first summer I lived here in Short Creek. The roses I had schlepped all the way down here from my mother's garden in Ohio. The focal point of my carefully cultivated cottage garden look.

"They were just starting to look how I wanted them to." I sighed. "I know you already reported it to Sheriff Wayne, but I suppose I should talk to him about it, even though he probably won't take it seriously."

The local sheriff and I were not the best of buddies, mainly because he claimed he didn't like me poking my nose in where it didn't belong. Or something along those lines. But still. Someone had stolen my roses!

Houston ran his hand down the trellis. "Wasn't there some story on the news about this kind of thing recently?"

I shrugged. "I never watch the news. Was there?"

"Yep. Something about people's bedding plants being stolen from their yards. Never caught who did it, though."

"That's ridiculous." What was this world coming to? "I can only think of one person who would stoop so low."

Houston raised his eyebrows. "Oh, yeah? Let me guess."

"Ginger Slayton," we all said together.

Ginger, president of the local garden club, had an overblown sense of propriety about what went on in our little Central Texas town of Short Creek. If a person didn't keep her yard up to Ginger's standards, she'd give the poor soul a tongue-lashing like you'd never heard.

"She can get pretty nasty, but do you really think she'd go as far as digging your roses out?"

I shrugged. "She's always been mad about them for some reason. Said they were scraggly, and I should have planted something native. Really, I think she was mad I didn't purchase them from the garden club sale or her landscaping company in Temple. I tried to make her understand that I had a vision for this property, and I had sentimental reasons for planting these particular bushes."

"Ginger Slayton has a landscaping company?" Mona swatted at a gnat. "She doesn't seem like the business-woman type to me, clumping around in those ugly old garden boots of hers all the time."

I shrugged. "It was hers and her husband's. I heard she still has a stake in it, even though they divorced a few years back."

"But why would she care so much what you wanted to plant in your own yard?" Houston shook his head. "That seems so petty."

"Right?" I sank down onto the front porch step and stared out at Main Street. I had moved to Short Creek several years ago from the big city, hoping for peace and a "normal" life. Ha. Since I got here, I'd helped solve two murder cases, been involved in creating a ministry home for sex-trafficking victims, and witnessed the romance between my Great Aunt Dot and her beau, Harry. Life certainly wasn't boring, though I would have preferred it to be a little less exciting sometimes.

Of course, on the flip side, I had also opened the shop I'd always wanted, fallen in love with a great guy, and made a host of new friends. I'd also gained a lot of insight into God's ways and learned a great many lessons. One thing I was still working on was speaking up for myself when I needed to.

In fact...

I stood, almost knocking over a huge pot of Pink Symphony caladiums. "I'm going to talk to Ginger."

Houston made a choking noise. "Ha! I'd like to witness that conversation."

"If she had something to do with this, I'd like to know

why." I started sweating, just thinking about it. I really, really hated confrontation. Maybe Mona would go with me for moral support. She loved a good, emotional scene more than anything. And she certainly would never lack for words.

"Let's do it. We need donuts." Mona pushed her sunglasses up on top of her head. "And coffee. Let's go, y'all. No use standing here barking around the wrong bush. Let's find out what ol' Ginger has to say."

We both blinked at her, unmoving. *Barking around the*...what?

I caught Houston's eye, then looked away, pressing my lips together to keep from giggling. I could always count on Mona to mangle the English language at the most opportune times.

"What are y'all waiting for?" She made a scooching motion. "Shoo. Head toward the Donut Hut. Ginger is always there on Wednesday mornings, stuffing her face."

I never ate donuts. And I didn't do confrontation. But here I was, strolling into the Donut Hut behind my friends. The tiny place was packed as always at this time of day. I waved at Todd's partner, Jay, over the heads of Ginger Slayton and her garden club friends who were taking up all the available tables and most of the available air, too. I tugged at the collar of my blouse. Jay nodded to me before refilling his industrial-size travel mug with what must have been half the coffee in the pot.

Houston wended his way through the women to talk to Jay while Mona and I perused the donut selection. Nothing looked good except the apple fritters, but I knew I'd later regret eating so much sugar and grease. Especially if I had a run-in with Ginger first. I sighed, trying to turn my attention elsewhere as I braced myself to approach her.

"I think that's the new dentist," I whispered to Mona, nodding at the handsome, fifty-something guy in front of us in line. His salt and pepper hair was perfectly combed, and even from the back I could tell this guy was a fastidious dresser.

"Yep. Griffin something-or-other." She stuffed a wad of napkins in my hand, then leaned toward me to whisper loudly.

"Don't look now, but Ginger and her peeps are all staring at you."

Awesome.

"Mona—"

The man turned around as if on cue, extending one hand while he clutched a water bottle in the other. "I'm Dr. Smythe. Still trying to meet everyone in town."

I shook his hand briefly, noting the unnatural whiteness of his teeth as he gave me a wide smile.

"Callie Erickson. I own C. Willikers up the street." I tried to extricate my hand, but he held onto it.

"Toy store?"

You can let go of my hand now.

"No, full-service florist and used books, with some yarn thrown in." I pulled myself free and inched backwards.

His grey eyes lit up. "Oh, you're the one. Penny told me about you."

This guy was creeping me out. "I'm not sure what she would have told you, but—"

Mona snorted. "Penny Vaughan? She has a lot of room to talk."

"Mona!" I gestured with my head to where Penny was sitting eight feet away, smiling at Ginger like she was slated to be the next president of the United States.

Just then, Penny stood to lead the garden club women in a rousing rendition of "Happy Birthday," apparently to their fearless leader, Ginger. Sigh.

I watched Penny hand Ginger an oversized gift basket of what looked like soaps and lotions. The ladies oohed and ahhed as Ginger made a show of admiring every item.

Maybe I should talk to Ginger a different day. Besides, I didn't love the idea of making a big scene with her in front of all her friends. In fact, maybe it wouldn't be a good idea to talk to her at all.

"Let's go, Mona," I murmured. "I'll talk to her some other time."

Mona looked up from digging in her purse. "Nope, you need to do this, girlfriend."

I realized Dr. Smythe was still watching me, wearing a curious expression. I forced a smile in his direction, realizing I had dropped the conversation with him. "Uh, what exactly did Penny tell you about me?"

"She said you've been involved in two murder cases since you've lived here." He leaned toward me, smiling that toothy grin, and I stepped back again, bumping into the person behind me.

He made it sound like "being involved" in murder cases was an exciting thing.

"Uh..." I glanced at Mona, hoping she would bail me out.

Mona, not the most perceptive at picking up on social cues, slipped her arm through mine, beaming. "Yep. Callie's our president detective here in Short Creek. She already sent a bunch of criminals to jail. Didn't you, Callie?"

I groaned.

Dr. Smythe wrinkled his brow. "A what detective?"

"Resident. She meant resident detective. But I'm not really." Surely it should be our turn to order soon, right? I cleared my throat. "It's been so nice to meet you, Dr. Smythe, but I won't take up any more of your time. I need to speak with Mrs. Slayton now, if you'll excuse me."

I fled toward Ginger's table, feeling Dr. Smythe's gaze beating onto my back. Yikes. I wouldn't go see him even if I was dying from...from gingivitis. Even talking to Ginger Slayton wouldn't be as bad as hanging around that guy any longer.

The garden club ladies quieted as I smiled at Ginger. "Good morning, Ginger. I hope I'm not interrupting anything."

She pulled her reading glasses off to stare at me, her silvery-reddish hair bobbing over her ears. "Deciding to join the garden club now, Ms. Erickson?"

What? "No, ma'am. I'd like to sometime, but life is a little too busy right now. But I was wondering if you knew anything about my rose bushes?"

Mona made a disapproving noise. I knew she thought I was being too polite, but I wasn't a very assertive person. And besides, I didn't know for sure that Ginger had anything to do with my missing roses.

Ginger barked a laugh. "What do you mean, do I know anything about your roses?" She glanced around at the other women as if to gauge their reaction. "Of course, I do. I know everything there is to know about roses, and yours don't belong in Short Creek."

I fought the urge to roll my eyes. "Mrs. Slayton, my rose bushes are gone. Someone dug them up and took them."

She pushed herself to her feet, her double chins quivering. She was wearing her green rubber gardening boots under her skirt. "Are you insinuating something, Ms. Erickson?"

"No, I—" I felt sweat prickle under my armpits.

"I think you are." She pushed Penny aside to stand in front of me. "You think you can barge into this town and do whatever you want. Well, we don't like outsiders here. Especially from up north."

I gulped. What did that have to do with anything?

"Ever since you came here, trouble has followed you. And if you think I'm going to stand by and let you slander me, you have another think coming."

"Just a doggone minute." Mona shouldered her way in front of me, her favorite Texas-shaped earrings quivering in indignation. "Callie hasn't done anything except help our town. She's captured criminals, opened Hope House, and brought our town a lot of money 'cause of her shop. And she's a super nice person who would give anyone the shoe off her foot."

The shoe off my foot? I would have laughed if I wasn't so distressed. Even so, I would not stoop to this woman's level. I kept my tone polite while sweat soaked through the armpits of my shirt. "Ginger, I'm sorry you feel—"

She sneered. "It's not only me. But I'm bold enough to say it to your face. And I don't know anything about your stupid rosebushes, but if someone stole them, it serves you right. You think because you are friends with the mayor, you can get away with anything."

What? What did being friends with the mayor have to do with anything? I grabbed the back of Mona's blouse to stop her from lunging at the older woman. "I'm not trying to get away with—"

"Oh, yes you are." Ginger's voice rose until she was shrieking. "You think people don't know what's really going on at your store?"

My jaw dropped. Was this woman a psycho? "Ginger, I don't know what you're talking about, but this conversation is over." I grasped Mona's arm and pulled her away with me toward the door, ignoring the whispers.

The mid-morning heat blasted me in the face as I yanked the door open. I marched out and stood in the middle of the sidewalk, trying to make sense of what had taken place.

Mona and Houston pushed through the door together.

"I'd say you caught her in a bad mood," Houston ventured.

I was still trembling. "That would be the understatement of the year."

"What a ridiculous person." Mona fanned herself with a sheaf of paper napkins. "You should report her to Sheriff Wayne."

I shrugged. "Not much to report that he hasn't heard before. She's just an all-around nasty person, I guess."

I tried to go about my business as usual the next day, but I was still bothered by the loss of my rosebushes, not to mention Ginger's crazy accusations. In a way, I felt sorry for her. She must be a very unhappy, angry person to lash out at someone else like that. Especially someone she barely knew. At least she hadn't shown up at my shop today. I kind of thought she would.

I shook my head as I locked the shop for the evening and headed home. Annie and my two pugs, Purl and Intarsia, greeted me enthusiastically at the door of my little house. I let them out into the front yard and sank onto the porch steps while they did their thing.

I threw Annie's ball for her a few times until she tired and flopped down next to me. Why was I still thinking about the deal with Ginger so much? I ran my hand along the wiry black fur of Annie's back, forcing myself to relax. Taking a deep breath, I focused my attention on a flock of house sparrows who twittered and pecked at the ground under the pecan tree. They startled and rose as one when Purl ambled over near them, but soon settled again, busily searching for their next meal. Pugs aren't much of a threat, I guess. But still. She didn't need to be wandering toward the street.

"Come here, Purl."

She glanced at me over her shoulder and headed toward my neighbor Sherm's yard. I sighed. At least Purl was old and fat now, so I could easily grab her if she strayed too far. Intarsia, the black pug, trailed after her, picking her way through fallen pecans.

"I suppose we should go get those pugs, Annie." Before I could stand, I heard the familiar reeech-bang of Sherm's front screen door.

He wobbled down the front steps, clinging tightly to the handrail, then squinted in my direction. "Oh, hey there, Callie. Saw them dogs out my window and thought they were loose."

"Sorry about that, Sherm. I was headed over to get them." I could have saved my breath, because Sherm was nearly deaf. Annie ran ahead of me to greet our elderly friend.

He patted her head as I scooped Purl up and tucked her under my arm. "Still got this big ol' police dog, I see."

"Yes, Todd's traveling a lot, so Annie's staying with me."

"What's unraveling?"

"Traveling!" I shouted. "Todd travels a lot."

"Rattles a lot? That don't sound right for a p'liceman." He scratched his head and spit into the boxwood bushes. "Dadgum it. I heard some rattling myself t'other night. Did y'all hear it? 'Bout midnight. Woke me up, it did."

It would have had to be some pretty loud rattling for Sherm to hear it. I sighed and shifted Purl to my other arm. Sherm was a dear man. I should be more patient. "No, no rattling at my house," I yelled. "Only pugs snoring." I grinned at him.

"No ma'am. Not in the mornin'. It was durin' the night."

Oh, dear. This conversation was going nowhere fast. "Well, I hope you sleep better tonight. I'll see you tomorrow." I waved to Sherm, then nudged Intarsia in the direction of my yard and headed toward the mailbox.

I set Purl down and grabbed two days' worth of mail from the box. I riffled through it, then glancing up a minute later, I noticed Purl making a beeline for Sherm's yard again. What was so interesting over there today?

"Annie, round up these pugs for me. Isn't that what German shepherds are supposed to do? Herd things?"

Annie trotted beside me as I strode toward the pug. Purl turned up the speed when she saw me coming, but I snatched her right before she disappeared under the boxwood hedge behind Sherm's house. "Got you." I turned to head back to my own yard. "Now where's Intarsia? You two are a handful today."

I scanned my front yard. No little black pug in sight. Maybe she had strayed behind Sherm's house while I was collecting the mail. Purl squirmed, and I held her firmly as I peeked over the bushes. Was that a curly black tail poking out near the trash cans? What was she doing over there?

"Intarsia. Come!"

She gave an answering yip but didn't appear. I sighed. I didn't have the energy for this today.

Annie pushed past me, making her own path through the hedge. I edged around to a break in the shrubbery, then sidled through, feeling like Peter Rabbit wriggling under Mr. MacGregor's fence. Not that Sherm would mind me popping into his backyard to retrieve my dog, but—

"Aaaahhhh!" I froze, horror washing over me in hot waves. A woman lay face down on the lawn near Sherm's trash cans, her legs bent at an odd angle. She didn't move, but I could see she was clutching a peach-colored rose. The dogs sniffed her body but didn't touch her. I gulped.

Was she dead?

I'm no expert, but she looked dead to me. And her neatly-paired garden boots sat next to her, as if she—or someone else—had placed them there.

Another wave of shock washed over me as I stared at those boots.

Ginger Slayton.

CHAPTER TWO

The gaping holes in the yard of C. Willikers greeted me as I pulled up early the next morning. "Well, Ginger. Whether or not you stole my rosebushes, I'm sorry you're dead," I said out loud. I still couldn't believe it. I had talked with the woman a couple of days ago, and now she was gone. I shivered. I guess none of us know when our appointed day was. *That's why we always have to be ready to meet God*, my dad always reminded us kids when we were growing up.

I smiled despite my lingering shock of finding Ginger. I hadn't seen my parents in three years, but they were coming home next week on furlough in time for Aunt Dot and Harry's wedding. I couldn't wait for them to visit my shop and meet all my friends, especially Todd.

The store looked nice. Hiring Sharlene O'Dell as my assistant a few months ago had been one of the best things I'd ever done. My favorite things—plants, books and yarn, were all artfully arranged by Sharlene's talented design. I could take a few minutes and breathe in the peace of this place I loved.

I hadn't slept well last night after all the ruckus over Ginger's death. And why did Ginger have a rose with her when she died? Was it one of mine? From my missing bushes? If so, why? It was the same vibrant peach color as my roses, with the same unique bunchiness typical of Eden roses. Of course, I'm sure I wasn't the only one growing these roses, but I'd never seen any others like mine in town. On the other hand, it seemed odd that Ginger would be carrying around one of my roses, but—

My door chimed and I turned to see my friend Lonnie push through the door, carrying a huge box. Lonnie was the leader of our weekly prayer group and long-time friend of my Aunt Dot.

"Hey, Callie, I got the bows done." She plopped the box down on the counter. "I can't believe the wedding is next week."

"I know. I'm so excited." I opened the box of bows that

Lonnie had volunteered to make for the wedding reception. "I think Harry is more nervous than Aunt Dot. It's so cute."

"Adorable. I'm so happy your parents will be able to be here for it too." Lonnie patted at the moisture on her round face with a tissue. "How are you? I mean, with this thing with Ginger Slayton?"

I shrugged. "It was kind of traumatic to be the one to find her, but I'm doing all right. I didn't know her well. Do you know if they figured out what happened? Heart attack?"

Lonnie's eyes widened, and she dropped her voice to a whisper. "No. Rick says Wayne told him that he suspects foul play."

"Oh, no." My heart sank. Lonnie's husband, Rick, was the mayor of Short Creek, so I knew Lonnie wasn't spreading idle gossip. Anyway, Lonnie wasn't a gossiper. I stared at her. "Like, they think someone killed Ginger? On purpose?" Please, no. Not another murder. Not in Short Creek. And literally in my back yard. What was this world coming to?

"Yes. But who would want to kill Ginger? She can be kind of prickly, but I can't imagine anyone hating her enough to take her life." Lonnie wrinkled her nose.

I blew out a breath. "I know there's no love lost between her and Wormy over that fuss they had last year. Remember the craziness with the city council elections?"

"Yeah, but Wormy? The owner of the Donut Hut? He's a great guy."

"Well, I think most people think so. But he was furious with Ginger when she started the smear campaign against him in the election last year. He won anyway, so I guess people forgot about it."

Lonnie shook her head. "I still can't picture him doing something so terrible. Isn't he a member of Houston's church?"

"I think so. But that doesn't guarantee anything."

"No, but still. What about that guy who lives next door to Ginger?" She fiddled with one of the bows. "We've tried to reach out to him, but he is, shall we say, not receptive at all."

I struggled to put a name with the face in my mind. "You mean the guy who moved here about the same time I did?

Wasn't his name J. P. or J. D. or something like that?"

"J. T. Culpepper."

I frowned. "Why would anyone suspect him? Have he and Ginger had run-ins?"

"Not that I know of, but he is a felon, Callie."

My face grew hot. My own brother, Jason, had recently been paroled from prison, and he would be the last person I would suspect of killing someone else. "Having a police record doesn't mean J. T.'s a murderer." It bothered me when even well-meaning people—my friends—lumped everyone together into a category like that. I know it was hard to understand unless you'd had a family member in trouble with the law, but not everyone sitting in prison is guilty of the crime he was accused of. And even if he was, it didn't automatically mean he was a violent criminal or would be willing to take someone else's life.

"I'm sorry. I wasn't thinking about your situation. I just meant that...that the police might suspect him because he served time before."

Yeah, the police and everyone else. Poor guy. From what I knew of him, J.T. was minding his own business and trying to make a new start. I sighed. "Well, I hope they figure it out quickly. It's a little scary to think there might be a killer running around."

Lonnie made a face. "Yeah, kind of creepy. I bet you'll feel better when Todd gets back into town."

"We're going out to dinner tonight, hopefully. You know how the traffic can be in Dallas."

"We usually avoid going that direction if we—"

"Hello there, ladies." Sheriff Wayne barged through the door and clumped over to the counter. He looped a thumb through his belt loop. "Y'all wouldn't be discussing the Slayton case, would ya now?"

I fought back the urge to roll my eyes. Sheriff Wayne was a decent man and a good sheriff, but he was a little bit lacking in the social skills department. I figured he'd be around sooner or later to get my report on what happened since I stumbled on Ginger's body. "Can I get you a water bottle, Sheriff?"

"Nah, I don't drink that stuff." He pinned me with a stare. "Miz Erickson, I don't care if you are Todd's girl. I'm putting you on notice. You need to stay out of this case more'n you're already in it. Do I make myself clear?"

How was I *in* the case? I merely found the woman. I didn't kill her. "What do you mean, *in* the case?"

"I mean," he leaned toward me, "don't poke your nose in where it doesn't belong." He gave a mighty sniff. "And, half the town saw y'all two having an argument at Wormy's donut place over there the other morning. That don't look too good for you, so if I were you, I'd lay low and focus on knitting."

What? I gaped at him. Surely, he wasn't insinuating...

"Now wait a minute, Wayne." Lonnie drew herself up. "I hope you're not accusing Callie of having anything to do with this woman's death."

"I'm not accusin' anyone. Yet." He spun on his heel and stomped back out the door.

Lonnie and I stared at each other.

I opened my mouth, then shut it again. I had no words. How in the world could the sheriff even suggest that I could— my brain refused to finish the thought.

"We need to pray big-time." Lonnie grasped my hands in hers.

"Auntie, we need to pray." I echoed Lonnie's words as I walked into my Aunt Dot's apartment at the Willowbough Assisted Living community.

"Well, darlin', you came to the right place." Aunt Dot closed her laptop and smiled up at me from her wheelchair. She reached for my hand and squeezed it tight for a long moment—her customary greeting—then frowned. "Did you hear about that Slayton woman? Such a shame."

I should have known Auntie would know about it before I told her. My Aunt Dot might be in her eighties, but she was a smart cookie and still wrote her weekly advice column, *Just Ask Dot*, for the *Temple Daily Star*.

"Yes. You do know I was the one who found her?"

"Callie, no!" Her hand flew to her throat. "I'm so sorry. Was it bad? Are you okay?"

I sank down onto the overstuffed chair across from her. "It wasn't gory, if that's what you mean. In fact, I figured she'd probably had a heart attack or stroke or something."

"But?"

"But Wayne told Lonnie that the police are suspecting foul play."

"Oh, my." She cocked her head. "Why?"

"I don't know."

"Well, you're right. We need to pray that whomever did it will be caught soon. Do they have any suspects?"

I squirmed. "Well, that's what we need to pray about." I cleared my throat. "Wayne was in my store this morning and, uh, more or less insinuated that I am a suspect."

Aunt Dot froze. "I don't think I understand what you said, darlin'."

I picked at the seam of the chair cushion. "Lonnie and I were talking about it, and Wayne came busting through the door all official. He said he hoped we weren't discussing the case and that I should keep my nose out of it."

"That was rude."

To say the least. I nodded, surprised to feel tears gathering.

"He's just jealous that you're the one who solved the Blackman case last year." Her eye-rolling left no doubt of her thoughts about the matter.

I had to smile. Aunt Dot, my great-aunt really, had always been my biggest fan and loyal supporter through everything life threw at me. And she wasn't going to stop now, sheriff or no sheriff. "I could have handled that. But then he said everyone in town saw Ginger and me arguing at the Donut Hut the morning before it happened. And that things quote, 'didn't look good' for me because of that."

"Oh, brother. He's throwing his weight around. I wouldn't put any stock in that nonsense." She raised her eyebrows, the hint of a twinkle appearing in her blue eyes. "You and Ginger had a public disagreement? What about?"

"My rosebushes. She hated them."

"Your gorgeous Eden roses?"

"Yes. And someone dug them up and stole them a couple of days ago. That's why I was talking to Ginger in the first place."

"What? Why would someone do such a thing? What is this world coming to?"

I sighed. "I don't know. But since we were going to use some of them in your bouquet, we'll need to come up with another idea. I'm so sad about that."

"Me too. Those rose bushes have been in our family since my dear departed sister planted those little slips in the garden at your folks' house, way before you were born. And they were thriving down here too. Putting out more bloom than I expected in this heat." She twisted her engagement ring around on her finger. "Harry will be so disappointed. But— wait a minute." She flipped her laptop open. "All of this makes me think of an email to the advice column a few days ago...hmm."

I glanced down at my phone while she perused her emails, noticing I had several missed calls from a couple of different local phone numbers. I didn't recognize the numbers, so I deleted them. I sure didn't want to talk to anyone about Ginger's death, if that's what those were all about. I'd had enough of speculation and nosy reporters in the last couple of years to last me a lifetime. Anyway, Todd should be getting into town any time now. He would help me navigate through this mess.

Are you almost home? I miss you! I texted him, adding a red heart emoji at the end of my message. It was so amazing how God had brought Todd into my life at just the right time. We knew we were headed toward marriage, but it would be a second marriage for both of us, so we were fine with taking things slowly. One of these days, though, he was going to pop the big question, and I was ready to say yes. I smiled to myself. We'd better get through Aunt Dot and Harry's wedding first, though.

"Ah. Here it is. I get some strange letters, but this one felt kind of plaintive.

'Dear Dot,

I'm very lonely and am getting older. I don't have a family and am tired of my job. No one ever brings me roses or takes me to dinner. I've tried to get to know people, but I can't seem to make friends very well. Do you have any advice for me?'

She took her reading glasses off. "Isn't that sad?"

Definitely sad, but what did that have to do with her wedding? Or Ginger's death? "Yes. I know many older folks in our community probably feel the same way. Are you going to answer it?"

"Maybe. But that's not why I read it to you." She gave me a pointed look. "Don't you think it could be a clue?"

I wasn't following. In the last few minutes, we had gone from Ginger to my roses to an advice column letter. "A clue to what?"

"To your new mystery, of course." She grinned at me. "Clearly, you didn't kill Ginger Slayton, but someone did. And God has given you a talent for figuring these things out."

"Oh, no." I held my hands up. "I'm not getting involved in anything like the Blackman affair ever again."

She sat back. "I don't think you have a choice."

CHAPTER THREE

I stared at my aunt. "What do you mean?"

"Look at this headline that popped up on the newspaper's website a minute ago." She turned her laptop so I could see it.

"'Foul Play Suspected in Death of Short Creek Businesswoman.'" I groaned. "I still can't believe Wayne would even suggest I'd be capable of such a thing. I'm a normal, nice person."

"It's unbelievable. But if he's going to point the finger at you, then you're going to need to do what you can to find out the truth."

"That's his job, not mine. And we only have two weeks until your wedding. And my parents are arriving in a few days. Do you have any idea how much stuff I still have to do in the next two weeks? Besides, how would I know who would want to kill Ginger Slayton?"

"It's crazy to even consider it, but you know how seriously Penny Vaughan always takes the annual Short Creek Lawn and Garden prize."

I rolled my eyes. "Yeah, I've heard. She comes into the store all the time for new houseplants because she always kills hers. She told me all about the contest last summer when Ginger won for the third time in a row."

"Penny's yard is pretty amazing with her gorgeous caladium bed under the live oaks. I guess it's only indoor plants she kills. But I can see where she thought she should have won." Aunt Dot picked up her crochet hook. "And it is a little weird for the president of the garden club to win three times in a row, if you ask me. Just looks bad."

"Still. I can't imagine Penny being mad enough about that to kill Ginger. Aren't they friends? They were sitting next to each other at the garden club meeting at the Donut Hut the other morning."

Aunt Dot shrugged. "I know Penny's the vice-president of the club. Or she was when I belonged to it years ago."

"Hmm. Maybe she really, really wanted to be the president

of the garden club? But is that worth taking someone's life?" I shook my head. "I can't believe we're sitting here discussing this like it's some sort of story on 20/20 or something. This was a real person in our own community." The enormity of the situation was starting to sink in. I blew out a breath. "Todd will know what's going on. We're supposed to get dinner tonight."

"Oh, is he back in town?"

"On his way. He was going to swing by and pick up Chad after his meetings. It's Todd's weekend to have him." Chad, Todd's teenage son, lived with his mother in Dallas. "I'm excited to see Chad. It's been a few weeks."

"Such a sweet young man. Will he be able to stay for the wedding?"

I shook my head. "I don't think so, but Todd's trying to make it happen. Have you heard from my parents lately?"

"No. I was going to ask you the same thing. Usually your mother at least texts me, but I haven't heard from her in a couple of days. Of course, you know how spotty their cell phone and internet availability are there." She finished crocheting a row and turned her work over to begin the next. "I'm so thrilled it worked out for them to be starting their furlough now so they can attend the wedding. It wouldn't be the same without them."

"Yeah." I had mixed feelings about seeing my parents again. My parents were coming here, to my little town, to live. For a year. I should be happy about that. But I wasn't.

I loved my parents. But to have them move here, to the place where I'd made a new start and finally found some peace...it was hard to explain. It was like they were part of my old life. And of course, they were. They were my parents. They had given me life, for crying out loud. Had loved me and my brother Jason the best they knew how, and still did. But I couldn't ignore the fact that all the pain and ugliness of my past was also intertwined with them—not their fault, exactly, but still, it was there. It was a paradox, and I hadn't figured out yet how to separate all the strands. How to "be" with them.

"You're going to have to forgive, Callie." Aunt Dot's tone was gentle.

I stared unseeingly out Dot's kitchen window. "I thought I had. But when I think of having heart-to-heart conversations with them, I freeze up. Light and friendly is easier, you know? Especially when we're half a world away."

She reached for my hand. "God didn't call us to easy, darlin'. He called us to obedience."

She was right. I squirmed in my chair. "I know. It's just—"

My phone dinged, sparing me from any more soul-searching. I read Todd's text. "Todd's going to swing by here to pick me up in a few minutes, he says." I stood and roamed over to her kitchen windowsill. Huge, salmon-pink blossoms covered the geranium I'd brought in from my garden last fall. "Looks like this thing is happy."

She nodded. "Yes, you'll need to re-pot it before you take it back to C. Willikers for the spring." She hesitated. "I know you don't want to talk about your parents, but I want you to know I'm praying for you. Have been praying. Harry and I both."

"Thank you, Auntie." I truly was grateful for her prayers. And, if I knew what was good for me, I would give in now and do the hard work of on-purpose forgiveness, because once Aunt Dot started praying for something, she was like a three-year-old with a new toy. Ain't no one going to convince her to let go of it before she was ready.

It had been convenient to be an ocean away from my parents, knowing they were, apparently, happy in their new life's calling of foreign missionaries. It was me who had the problem, because I wanted more from our relationship, but I didn't know how to fix it. Even if I forgave them, it still wouldn't fill the hole that had opened in my heart as a teenager.

I picked a spent blossom off the geranium. It was easier to pretend everything was fine. At least we weren't ugly to each other, right?

I jumped as a quick knock sounded on the door.

"Housekeeping!" A thin woman, her long grey hair pulled back into a ponytail, stuck her head into the room. I felt her gaze sweep over me before she spoke to my aunt. "Do you need anything, Miz Dot?"

"No, thank you, Veronica. Bernadette was already in this morning."

"Yes, ma'am. I'll be here until nine if you need anything."

Aunt Dot smiled at her. "Veronica, this is my niece, Callie Erickson. I think you've met before? Maybe at Callie's shop? She owns C. Willikers in town."

Veronica stepped into the room, holding out a work-worn hand. "Can't afford anything in that store, but it's nice to meet you. You have a real sweet aunt."

"It's nice to meet you too, Veronica. Yes, I do. Aunt Dot is pretty special." I took the woman's hand briefly, feeling a little embarrassed at her obvious discomfort. Was it me?

She slipped out of the room, and I raised my eyebrows at my aunt. "That was awkward."

"I think she must have had a difficult life." Aunt Dot pulled a skein of lavender yarn out of her bag. "I don't know her well even though she's worked here at least as long as I've lived here. I've tried to talk to her about the Lord, but she shuts me down as soon as I say anything about Him. I know she has a couple of kids. And a dog. She shows me pictures of them all the time."

My aunt had such a tender heart. "I'm sure she'll come around. Surely she can tell you care about her."

Aunt Dot sighed. "I hope so. So many people are hurting these days. If only they knew God loves them and would forgive them if they turned to Him. How do people live without the comforting presence of the Holy Spirit?"

Good question.

We fell silent until Todd's tall frame filled the still-open doorway a minute later. "How are my two favorite ladies?"

I turned from the window and smiled a welcome as he pecked Aunt Dot on the cheek. He looked weary; his sunglasses pushed up into his dark, rumpled hair. He reached for me and I walked into his embrace, my senses filling with the warm, cinnamon-gum-and-aftershave scent of the man I loved. "Long day?"

He held me tightly for a long moment and rested his chin on the top of my head. "Long week."

"And about to get longer," I murmured against his chest. I hated to burden him with any more stuff, but he probably already knew about Wayne's crazy accusations, anyway. I mean, the guy was his boss.

He pushed me away enough to give me a quick kiss. "What? Wedding plans going awry?" He grinned at both of us.

Maybe he didn't know. "No, still the deal with Ginger Slayton."

He made a face. "I hear Wayne's got his tail in a knot over it. I'll calm him down."

Aunt Dot and I exchanged glances. "Uh, it's more than that." I pushed my glasses up further onto my nose. "He more or less told me I am a suspect in the case."

Todd stared at me, then closed his eyes and squeezed the bridge of his nose for a moment before sinking onto the couch. "You're kidding, right?"

"Nope. He came into the shop this morning and told me to butt out, basically, and that he wasn't accusing anyone yet, but that it didn't look good for me because Ginger and I had had a public argument a few days before it happened."

"Unbelievable. Who hasn't had a public argument with Ginger Slayton?" He shook his head. "Wayne's a good man, but he jumps the gun too often before having all the facts."

"Then you don't think Callie should be concerned about it?" Aunt Dot looked relieved.

"Nah. I'll talk to him. He needs to learn to keep his mouth shut and not make wild accusations. What possible grounds would he have to accuse Callie?" He rolled his shoulders and stood. "I'm sure it can wait until after the weekend, though." He tugged on my hand. "Let's go eat, Callie. I'm starving. And Chad's waiting in the car with a headache. He says he'll see you soon, Dot."

We both hugged Aunt Dot. "I'll call you tomorrow," I whispered to her. "Thanks for praying."

She reached up to squeeze me around my shoulders, her silvery hair brushing my cheek as she whispered for my ears only, "I'm feeling a caution in my spirit, darlin'. I think this is more serious than it seems."

Great. Despite Todd's assurances, I had been sensing the same thing as Aunt Dot, but hoped it was only me. I sighed. "I guess I'll find out."

And find out I did.

After a lovely dinner at our favorite Italian restaurant, Todd and I swung around to Willowbough to grab my car.

"Will you and Chad come over for lunch after church on Sunday? I was planning to put a chicken in the crockpot. And Annie misses you dreadfully."

"We'd love to. Hopefully Chad will feel better by then. I don't think he's been sleeping well lately." Todd frowned. "Something is bothering him, but he won't tell me what. Anyway—"

Todd's phone rang. "Whitney here. Whatcha got?"

I folded my arms and leaned back against the side of his pickup truck, watching him frown. I was pretty used to him having to take calls even when he was off-duty, but that didn't mean I had to like it. Hopefully he would be able to go home and rest now instead of running off to rescue someone who'd locked his keys in his car or some other dumb thing.

He finished the call. "That was Wayne."

"What's up?" I didn't like the look in his eye.

He rubbed his hand down his whiskered cheek. "Just a bunch of hooey. How could he even think—"

My stomach dropped. "Is it about the Ginger Slayton deal?"

"Yeah." He blew out a long breath. "Apparently someone else has come forward with some accusations."

"Accusations about me?"

"Yeah. Someone said they saw you out in your yard the night that Ginger died."

"This is ridiculous. I can't be in my own yard?" Surely Todd wasn't having doubts about me too. "You know I'm out in my yard all the time, especially with the dogs."

"I know." He cleared his throat. "But this person reports he or she saw you with a weapon."

"What?" I don't even own a—well, actually, I did own a

pistol at Todd's insistence, but I don't take it out in the yard with me. "The news reports don't even say how she died. Who told Wayne I was out in my yard with a weapon? That's a flat-out lie."

"Were you out in your yard that night?"

I thought back. "I always let the dogs out before bed." Had I gone out later that night for any reason? Maybe that was the night one of the pugs had an emergency and needed to go out in the middle of the night? I shrugged. "I don't know. Surely it would take more than someone's accusation for Wayne to seriously think I was a suspect."

He sighed deeply. "You'd be surprised. In a case like this, no lead is too small."

"Are you saying that you guys are seriously considering the idea that I could have somehow been involved in Ginger's death?"

"Ah, Callie." He tried to pull me into his embrace, but I pushed him away.

"No, really." I stared at him, anger seeping through my thoughts. "I can't believe this."

Todd cupped my cheek in his hand. "I want you to hear me. I don't believe you had anything to do with Ginger's death."

"Well, I hope not." I glared at him. It took a lot for me to become angry, but when I got there, I was there. At least for a little while. "But your stupid boss thinks I was involved, which means you probably have to report anything I say to him."

He cocked his head. "Let's just say it would be a conflict of interest to be involved in this case in any way, shape or form."

"And so?"

"And so, I will do my best to stay out of it. And you and I—" here he folded his arms around me and pulled me tight against his chest. "You and I will pray that the truth be revealed quickly, and all false accusations will be proven untrue."

Well, okay, except for one thing, I realized later as I unloaded my dishwasher. Todd had never told me who my accuser was. And it rankled that other folks in the community, besides the sheriff, would not only think me capable of such evil, but accuse me falsely.

What if everyone in town started believing I was guilty? What kind of evidence, false or not, would it take for Wayne to come arrest me? I imagined myself sitting in a jail cell. How could I get everything done for Aunt Dot's wedding if I was in jail? Surely Todd would bail me out, but—

"Stop it, Callie." I slammed the dishwasher shut. "This is not helping."

I took a deep breath and whispered the words I had learned long ago. "Jesus, I trust You." I drew another breath and blew it out slowly. "Jesus, I trust You. God, I know you are in control. Please give me Your peace, Holy Spirit."

I knew from experience that when in crisis, it helped to do normal, everyday things. I'd water the plants. Focus my mind on mundane tasks for a few minutes.

I started with the African violets on the windowsill above the kitchen sink, then paused. What was that big old crow doing in the yard again? At least this was the other side of the yard, where I didn't have to see the crime scene tape still circling my neighbor Sherm's back yard.

I loved watching my "bird friends," as I called them, but usually I had cardinals, chickadees, wrens—all the regular little birds. The last few days, I'd noticed a crow hanging around the side yard near the bird feeder. Did crows even eat birdseed?

Hmm. Maybe he was injured. I moved closer to the window. He crouched underneath the birdbath, one wing held out awkwardly, his other wing tucked against his blue-black body.

I wasn't a big fan of crows, but neither did I want to see any creature suffer. He was looking a little more ragged than when I had first seen him the other day. Poor thing probably couldn't fly up to reach the water very well. And it was hot out these last few days. Record-breaking hot.

I grabbed a cereal bowl and filled it with water, then

slipped my phone into my back pocket.

"You stay here, dogs." I was positive neither Annie nor the pugs would hurt the bird, but I didn't want him to try to fly away and injure himself more. I slipped out the kitchen door into the stifling garage. What did crows eat?

I pictured a scarecrow in a garden, crows perched on his outstretched arms. I hadn't planted a vegetable garden this year, and even if I had...hmm. I spied the tub of dog food. I bet a crow would eat dog food. Especially the cheap kind made with corn. I grabbed a handful, then made my way to the yard, trying not to spill the water.

The large bird shuffled his feet as I came nearer, turning his head to see me.

"I won't hurt you." I set the water dish and the dog food on one of the flat paving stones. "There you go. Now you don't have to try to fly up to the feeder."

He cocked his head, and I sighed as my heart lurched. I could only divert myself so long from the ridiculous uncertainty of my situation. Surely this would all be okay soon.

CHAPTER FOUR

But it wasn't. I woke in the morning, my heart heavy. I lay on my back in the quiet, half-thinking, half-praying.

Who would have accused me of prowling around with a weapon in the middle of the night? And why would he or she do such a thing? I was sure Todd couldn't tell me who it was, but I needed to know.

Or did I? I grabbed my Bible and propped it on a pillow on top of my lap. Scriptures flooded my mind before I even opened the well-worn cover. *Do good to those who persecute you... Bless those who curse you... Forgive others, just as Christ forgave you...*

"Okay, Lord. I get it." Right when I thought I was doing well and life was going to settle down and be "normal," I had another huge lesson to learn. Of course, isn't that how life always is? Hadn't I read something along those lines recently? I flipped back to the January 1st entry in my devotional. Ah, here it was.

"If life were all one dead level of dull sameness it would oppress us; we want the hills and valleys. The hills collect the rain for a hundred fruitful valleys. Ah, so it is with us! It is the hill difficulty that drives us to the throne of grace...the bleak hills of life that we wonder at and perhaps grumble at, [that] bring down the showers... We cannot tell what loss and sorrow and trial are doing. Trust only."

It is the hill "difficulty" that drives us to the throne of grace. I knew that. I know that. But in the last few months of peace, I had forgotten. How quickly we humans are to revert to self-reliance. "Forgive me, Father God." I recalled the verses I had read only moments ago from Psalm 61. "You alone are my rock and my defense. You are my refuge, my Defender, my strong tower against the foe."

But who was the foe? And was my foe, my accuser, the same person who killed Ginger?

I opened the blind and stared out the window where only a few weeks ago, small leaf buds had begun to bulge on the branches of the old mulberry tree. Now it was arrayed in its full summer greenery. A squirrel hung from the back birdfeeder, gorging himself on black oil sunflower seeds. Everything out there seemed so peaceful, yet only a few feet away in my neighbor's yard, a woman had lost her life. I couldn't wrap my brain around it.

My phone dinged and I grabbed it up. It was a text from Mona.

Good morning! I know you're up because you're always up early, LOL!!!! Three smiley faces. *I'm stuck on my crotcheting project. HELP!!!* Five praying hands emojis.

I laughed out loud. I know she meant her crocheting project, but I couldn't help giggling at Mona's constant mangling of the English language. I didn't even want to think about what a crotcheting project might be. Ha.

What's wrong? I texted back. After several years of claiming she would never try needle arts, Mona had asked me to teach her to crochet a few weeks ago. It wasn't going well. I had never met anyone who had such difficulty with one hook and one skein of yarn. Good thing we hadn't started with knitting.

The edges of the frog scarf are all bumpy. Frowny face, frowny face, frog emoji. *And it looks like it's getting smaller at the top!!!!! I need to have it done in time for C. J.'s birthday.* Frowny face, birthday cake emoji, praying hands emoji.

I snickered, picturing some of my first attempts at crocheting. *Bring it over and we'll eat lunch here if that works for you. I took the day off. 11:30?*

Ok, sounds good. Heart-eyed emoji. Five yarn ball emojis and a taco emoji.

I sighed. Life was never dull, at least.

A few hours later, after Mona had unraveled half her frog scarf, we carried our tuna sandwiches out on the back porch with us. Annie joined us, giving us her best I'm-adorable-and-can't-you-see-I'm-starving look.

"Annie is a very sharing dog," I said as she settled between us. "Very sharing. Especially when it comes to tuna."

Mona nodded. "Rob always yells at me for giving Bubbles snacks, but she loves people food so much."

I pictured Mona and Rob's tiny poodle. "I can't imagine her eating much of anything."

"That little thing can really put it away." She sipped her iced tea, then made a face. "Uck. I forgot you like unsweet tea. How can you stand to drink this stuff?"

"I'm used to it." I had discovered that Texans like their tea sweet. Over the top sweet. Like tea syrup. I couldn't do it. "I'll grab the sugar for you."

She waved her hand. "Don't get up. I'll get it when we head in." She leaned back in her seat, then popped up again. "Oh my goodness. I can't believe I forgot to tell you."

"Tell me what?"

She shot me a mischievous grin. "I found your wedding dress yesterday."

What? I choked on my sandwich. Did she know something I didn't know? Had Todd—no, he wouldn't tell Mona before he told me, would he?

"You should see your face. It's super red." She laughed. "As soon as I saw it, I said to Rob, 'That's Callie's dress.' He said he liked it okay, but you know men."

I squinted at her, still confused. "You mean you found me a bridesmaid dress for Aunt Dot's wedding? I already bought it."

"No, not that one, silly. *Your* wedding dress. For when you and Todd decide to stop dilly-dallying and tie the knot." She raised her eyebrows.

I gulped, then cleared my throat. "He's the one dragging his feet."

"Mmm-hmm." She offered Annie a piece of bread crust. "You could speed the process up, you know. Drop some more hints. Start talking about honeymoon spots. Buy the dress. Stuff like that."

Right. Mona might go out and do something like that, but— "What does it look like?"

She smiled at me. "Wanna go see it? I asked the lady to hold it for you."

"You what?"

She shrugged. "Someone needs to get the ball rollin'. Y'all are dragging your feet."

"One wedding at a time is enough."

"Uh-huh. Whatever you say, Callie. How are you doing with all of this ginger stuff?"

"Ginger stuff?" I wasn't eating anything with ginger—oh, Ginger. As in Ginger Slayton. I should be used to Mona's abrupt topic changes by now, but the wedding dress discussion had me flustered. I groaned. "You don't want to know."

She raised her eyebrows. "Really."

"Wayne thinks I had something to do with it." I couldn't bring myself to say the word "suspect."

She laughed hilariously, as if I had told the funniest joke in the world. She fanned herself. "Whew. That was a good one."

"I'm not kidding." I made a face.

She snorted. "He knows you're smarter than he is."

Whatever. "What does that have to do with anything?"

"He prob'ly doesn't like being shown up by a woman." She used her napkin to dab a blob of mayo from the front of her leopard-print blouse. "I wouldn't even listen to him, if I were you."

"Easy for you to say." I slumped back in my chair. Annie nudged my hand, and I offered her my last bite of sandwich. "And if that wasn't bad enough, apparently someone reported seeing me out in my yard with a weapon the night Ginger died." I rolled my eyes.

"You? Right." My friend stared at me. "Who said that?"

I shrugged.

She squared her shoulders. "It had to have been Penny. She drives around in the middle of the night all the time."

"Penny Vaughan? Why?"

"I don't know. But she lives down the street from us, you know? Rob says he sees her leaving her house at like 1:00 or 2:00 in the morning, then she comes back like half an hour later."

I chose not to ask why Rob was spying on their neighbor in the middle of the night to begin with, feeling like we were already skating perilously close to gossiping.

"Well, I can't imagine why Penny would accuse me of anything. Maybe it was a random person who saw someone that night and was trying to be helpful by reporting it to the sheriff." I watched the crime scene tape around my neighbor's yard flutter in the breeze. "I feel like looking around in Sherm's yard myself."

"That's the spirit, Nancy." Mona grinned at me. "I don't see anyone here telling us we can't."

I stood and stretched, grabbing Annie's ball-thrower. "And besides, if I'm being accused of something, I need to know as much as I can, right?"

We smiled at each other.

I held the yellow tape up so Mona could duck under, then followed her, Annie dancing at my heels with her tennis ball in her mouth. I surveyed Sherm's yard, then glanced at his house. Sherm always kept his blinds closed, even in the middle of the day. And even if he saw me in his yard, he wouldn't mind. "I found her over here on the lawn near the trash cans," I said, striking out across the grass.

"That must have been creepy," Mona muttered. "I would have started screaming."

I had never been much of a screamer. "At least there was no blood."

Mona shuddered. "What do you think happened to her?"

"I don't know. But I wonder..." I looked at the spot I had found her body, the grass trampled from the activity of the last couple of days. "I guess I thought she died right here. But maybe..." I studied the thick shrubbery at the back of Sherm's yard, where the cardinals were darting in and out of the branches. "What if someone killed her somewhere else and brought her here to make it look like it happened here?"

Mona fiddled with her bracelets. "Who would do that? And who would want her dead? I mean, she was kinda a pain, but a lot of people are. Of course, I know she and Dr. Smythe were not on the greatest turns."

Terms. Not turns. I suppressed a smile as I poked around under the shrubbery with the thrower. I didn't know what I was looking for, but maybe I'd find something that would, as the police would say, "be of interest." I idly raked through the mulch under the bushes, turning up nothing but an old gum wrapper and what looked like a yellow airsoft BB. Nothing suspicious about that. The teenage boys in our neighborhood ran around shooting each other with the dumb things all the time. I was constantly finding the colorful little BBs in my lawn. "Dr. Smythe hasn't even lived here long. What, a few months?"

"Uh-huh." Mona swatted at some gnats. "But apparently Ginger went to him for a root canal and he botched it. She threatened to burn down his dental office."

I shook my head. "Of course, she did. Apparently, she always said the first ridiculous thing that popped into her head."

"Hey, Callie. Mona too. Isn't this so sad?" Boranda Stiegler, my neighbor from down the street, let herself into Sherm's gate. She looked like a model, with her stylish sunglasses pushed up on top of her head and an enormous bouquet of roses in her hand. "I know Ginger didn't die right at this spot, but I thought I'd bring some flowers for her."

I jumped up, glancing at Mona. Boranda was a nice enough person, but I didn't know her very well. The only time I had talked with her at length was the first and last time I let her cut my hair. "That's thoughtful of you, Bo. I didn't know you knew Ginger well."

She laid the flowers on the lawn near the trash cans and then straightened, pushing her bleached-blonde hair behind her ear. "Oh, yeah. I cut her hair for years. She cracked me up."

"Ah." I wasn't sure what else to say.

Bo scrutinized me, and my hand instinctively leapt to my hair. "I'm surprised to see you here, Callie."

"Oh, why is that?" I awarded her my best fake smile, not liking the look in her heavily-lined eyes.

"I heard you and Ginger had a big fuss right before she was killed."

She watched me like a cat cornering a mouse, and I struggled to keep my face neutral. "I wouldn't say it was exactly a 'big' fuss—"

"And anyway, Callie would never do anything so horrible."

Mona drew herself up to her full height, which was still a good six inches shorter than both Bo and me. "I can't believe you'd even incite something so insensitive."

"Insinuate. Incite means to—oh, never mind." I sighed. Was Bo the one who had reported supposedly seeing me outside in my yard the night of the murder? "Bo, I'm as sorry as you are that Ginger is dead. Believe me. But I had nothing to do with it."

She had the grace to appear shocked. "I certainly wasn't accusing you. The way she always talked about her ex-husband, it's a wonder he didn't off her before now." She pulled her sunglasses from the top of her head and put them on. "And that neighbor of hers, J. T., was definitely not on her happy list, either. He's a convicted felon, you know."

I gritted my teeth. "Well, Mona and I are heading back to my house." I scooped up Annie's ball and chucked it far into my own backyard, hoping Boranda would take the hint.

She didn't. "You know, Ginger did have a lot of enemies, now that I think of it." Boranda ran her fingers through her hair, spreading it out across her shoulders. "Did you hear she was accused of embezzling money from the school district back in the day?'

Mona bristled. "Boranda Stiegler. You need to shut it. The poor woman is dead, and gossiping about her is not going to help anything."

I hid a smile at the look on the hairdresser's face. "Thank you for bringing flowers. It was very thoughtful, and I'm sure Ginger would be happy to know you thought of her."

Bo sniffed and glanced at her designer watch. "I have to run now anyway. Hope things work out for you, Callie."

Annie dropped her ball on my foot while Mona and I watched Bo saunter away.

"That was pretty brazen," I said.

Mona was still upset. "I know, right? I can't believe she actually accused you to your face of killing Ginger."

"Well, she didn't actually go that far, but she might as well have." I bent to pick up the bouquet Bo had left at our feet. "These are my roses."

CHAPTER FIVE

I caressed the silky peach petals of the roses. "Or if they're not mine, they are the same variety as mine."

"You mean your roses that were stolen?"

"Yep."

Mona squinted at me. "Why would Boranda Stiegler have stolen your rosebushes? And if she did, why would she be dense enough to bring a bouquet of them for Ginger? Especially when she saw you standing right here?"

I raised my eyebrows. "That, my friend, is the question of the hour." Along with all of the questions of all the previous hours. But one thing at a time, right? "Come on, Annie. It's time to go home."

She grabbed her ball and trotted ahead of Mona and me, her tail held high.

"Apparently, folks are going to continue to question my innocence in this situation until I prove differently." We ducked under the crime scene tape into my backyard. "As much as I hate to think about it, I can't rely on the police to solve this. Especially since Wayne believes I *am* capable of murder."

"Anyone who knows you would never believe that, Callie." Mona smoothed the soft fur between Annie's large ears. "But I'll help you any way I can, Nancy. You know that."

"Thanks, Bess." Ever since the time I found a body on the doorstep of C. Willikers a few years ago, my friends had teasingly called me Nancy Drew. "I guess the first step is to find out how Ginger actually died."

Mona made a face. "And you think Wayne will tell you that?"

"Probably not. But it's worth asking."

"Could Todd find out for you?"

I pulled open my back door for Mona and Annie, and we all filed into the house. "I'm sure he's been filled in on the details of the investigation. But things like this are always a fine line for him, you know?" I glanced at my watch. "I've got to run. I told Sharlene I'd be in to the shop before two, and it's one-thirty. Want to come?"

"I'd love to, but Rob is comin' home this afternoon and I promised him I'd have his ribs ready when he got there. My man loves him some beans and ribs."

I imagined so. Rob was an over-the-road trucker, and when he was home, Mona was stuck to his side like glue. "Okay. Give him a hug for me. We'll see you at church tomorrow."

As it turned out, I didn't have to wait long to talk to the sheriff. He was waiting for me when I pulled up in front of C. Willikers. Great.

I parked my silver delivery van behind the patrol car where he stood, arms crossed.

"Hey there, Sheriff." I grinned at him, hoping he was in a less-surly mood than usual.

"Ma'am. Headed inside?"

I sighed. "Yes, sir."

He gestured for me to walk ahead of him, then clumped along behind me on the walkway. I peeked over my shoulder to see if he had his handcuffs out, ready to arrest me. He couldn't really arrest me merely because someone had accused me, could he?

I pushed open the door. "Hi, Sharlene."

"Oh, hey, Callie." My assistant appeared from the back room, then turned to Wayne. "May I help you, sir?"

He rolled his eyes. "I'm talking to Miz Erickson, not patronizing your store."

Sharlene and I exchanged glances.

"Thought you should know we're still waiting on the toxicology report. Some evidence shows Miz Slayton might have been poisoned, but I suppose Todd already blabbed that to you." He frowned at me. "Got anything to say about that?"

What a ridiculous, rude—I gripped the counter, returning his steely gaze. "I know you don't believe me, but I had nothing to do with Ginger Slayton's death. I already told you how I found her and every other detail I could remember. And Todd has not divulged anything of the sort. He takes his job seriously." I took a deep breath. "I think it's very unprofessional of you to come into my place of business and make snide accusations. And if you think you can come in here and try to intimidate me or harass me, I'll tell Rick and we'll see what he has to say about that."

Wow. My self-assertion lessons were paying off. Of course, it helped that Rick, the mayor of Short Creek, was a close friend and fellow church-member of mine.

Sharlene moved next to me and slipped her arm through mine, her eyes wide.

The sheriff hooked his thumb on his belt loop. "Easy now, ma'am. You're talkin' to an officer of the law." He lowered his hostility level a notch. "If you don't know anything about it as you claim, suppose you tell me who you think might have done it."

Was he testing me? I could feel Sharlene trembling, and squeezed her arm close to my side. "I don't have any idea."

"Why would you accuse Callie of something so terrible?" Sharlene's voice was thick with tears. "She's one of the best, most honest and loving people I've ever known."

He shrugged. "Be that as it may, we have to follow the leads we have." He fixed his eyes on me again. "Sure you don't have any idea who would have wanted Ginger dead?"

"Oh, come on, Sheriff." I was tired of his little mind games. "You've lived in this town long enough to know Ginger made a nuisance of herself all the time."

Did I see him almost smile?

"Suppose you tell me who you think would be annoyed enough to kill her." He smoothed his mustache, waiting.

What an exasperating human being. And what if I told him some of my suspicions and he falsely accused some other innocent person?

On the other hand ... the face of Griffin Smythe, the creepy new dentist, popped into my mind. "I've heard Ginger recently threatened to burn down Dr. Smythe's office," I reported reluctantly.

He snorted. "She did more than threaten. Had to pull her off the man before she tore his hair out by the roots."

Oh, my. Maybe Ginger was a nastier person than I had realized. "I don't know anything else."

He cleared his throat but didn't move. What was the man waiting for?

Tell him about the roses.

Oh, no.

Lord, do I really have to? Talk about murder. The man would kill me when he found out I had crossed the tape line.

"I, uh, have one other idea."

He motioned for me to continue.

"Boranda Stiegler brought roses to put on the spot where I found Ginger's body."

"When was this? How do you know it was her?'

I swallowed hard. "This morning. She, uh, told me what she was doing."

"What do you mean, what she was doing? Where did this conversation take place?"

I felt like I had that time in fourth grade when I pretended to be sick so I didn't have to go to PE. "I was, um, in Sherm's yard and she came in through the back gate with the flowers. We, uh, chatted, uh...for a while."

His already red face darkened. "Y'all were in Sherm's backyard this morning."

"Yes, sir." I watched the artery on the side of his neck pulse.

"I will say this one more time." He leaned close to my face and enunciated each word. "Stay out of this investigation. Do you understand?"

I took a step backward. "Yes, sir... except, you did ask who I thought did it. And I also understand that you already think I'm guilty and don't honestly want to hear what else I have to say. However... there's one more thing."

"Right." He composed himself, stroking his graying mustache again. "What else, Miz Erickson?'

"Uh, the roses that Boranda brought to the, uh, crime scene this morning? I think they're mine."

"I don't understand what you're getting at."

"Remember that someone dug up Callie's rose bushes and stole them?" Sharlene piped up, picking at her thumbnail.

He rubbed his temple. "So yer sayin' that Bo brought your roses that *somebody...*" he inflected the word with heavy sarcasm, "...that somebody stole from you right before Ginger was killed?"

"Yes, sir."

He squinted at me. "And why would she do that?"

Wouldn't we all like to know?

"I don't know, Sheriff." I sank down onto my stool near the counter, suddenly exhausted. "Could we please be done now?"

He stuck his hands in both pockets and rocked back onto his heels. "For now, Miz Erickson." He stomped toward the door, then turned. "But don't think you're off the hook. You're still on my short list."

Sharlene turned to hug me. "I can't believe he is so hateful to you. What a jerk."

I hugged her back briefly. "Thanks, Sharlene." I knew this must be particularly upsetting to my young assistant, who had had a few brief brushes with the law, including some jail time, in her past. "I'm praying the truth will be revealed soon."

"I'll pray that, too. Do you need me to stay this afternoon?"

I knew Sharlene could use all the hours she could get. She had recently moved into her own place at the trailer park just down Main Street from the shop and was thrilled to be supporting herself. And with all this craziness going on, I was behind on my to-do list for the wedding. "Yes, I'd love for you to stay. We need to work on the small arrangements of artificial flowers for the reception tables. Then once we finish those, we'll—"

"Oh, Callie! I'm so glad you're open today!" Penny Vaughan, Ginger Slayton's garden club groupie, pushed through the door, her nasal-toned voice loud in the quiet of the shop. She skidded to a halt by the counter, fanning herself. "I thought maybe y'all would be closed today because of..." she leaned closer and dropped her voice to a whisper, "...because of all the hullaballoo over dear Ginger."

Dear Ginger?

CHAPTER SIX

I disliked being so suspicious of everyone all of a sudden, but still, things were crazy right now. Was Penny a true friend of Ginger's? Should I try to question her about their relationship?

"I guess you and Ginger were pretty close." I gave her what was meant to be a comforting smile.

She dabbed at her eyes. "It was all so sudden. I still can't believe she's gone."

I noticed she hadn't answered my implied question. "My Aunt Dot was wondering if you're still the vice president of the Garden Club?"

"Yes, of course. I've been the *vice*-president for years. It's quite a lot of work." She walked around the counter to the African violet display. "My, you have a nice selection today." She fingered a fuzzy leaf. "I'm terrible with houseplants. Not the same as growing things outside. Of course, I'll be taking over Ginger's role as president now that she's gone, bless her heart."

"Ah, I see." I felt kind of bad fishing for information, but my own reputation was at stake. And, if I ruled out Penny as a suspect, that was one less person on my growing mental list of possible culprits. "I imagine such an important role in the garden club will take up a lot of your time. Will you still continue to work for Dr. Smythe?"

She whirled toward me, clutching a potted miniature violet. "Most certainly. Why would you think I wouldn't?"

Oh, dear. I didn't say she wouldn't. Why was everyone so touchy these days?

I shrugged. "Just asking. I met him for the first time the other day. Is he a nice person to work for?"

"He's amazing." She beamed at me. "And he says I'm the best receptionist he's ever had."

Probably the only receptionist he's ever had. I shuddered. "That's great."

Penny was only warming up to the topic of her new boss. "I've only worked for him for a little while, and he's already given me two raises. One right after the day Ginger assaulted him. I was shocked at her behavior. Could you believe it?"

"Uh, no. No, I couldn't." And if I didn't know better, I would think that sixty-something Penny was smitten with her younger boss.

"He was so brave, standing up to Ginger like that, even when she said such terrible things to him. And you know what he said to me after it was over?" She took a deep breath and started whispering again. "He said he wished she would go away forever and leave us alone."

Wait. What?

I must have missed something. Were we talking about the same incident? "I thought Ginger was angry with him because of her root canal so she threatened to burn down the dental office."

"Well, she *said* that's what she was mad about when the sheriff came." Penny giggled. "But what she was really on fire about was that Dr. Smythe turned down her invitation to attend the annual Garden Club Canoodle Doodle with her because he had already invited me to go with him."

I resisted the urge to smack my forehead, feeling like I'd suddenly been transported back to seventh grade. "I can see why she might be upset about the situation," I said, once I had successfully tamped down my overwhelming desire to laugh.

"She said some pretty awful things to me that day too." Penny set two African violet plants and a rabbit's foot fern on the counter next to my cash register. "But I forgave her."

I rang up her purchases, aware of Sharlene bustling around in the back workroom. "That's great you were able to patch things up with Ginger before she passed. Were you at work when it happened?"

"When what happened?" She handed me her debit card. "Oh, you mean when she was killed? I guess I don't know when that was. Do you?"

She seemed a little too nonchalant for my tastes. "The news reports say sometime early Thursday morning."

"Oh." She stuffed her card back into her wallet. "No, I don't work on Thursday mornings. I can't remember exactly where I was. Maybe grocery shopping?" She shook her head. "That's terrible, isn't it, to be grocery shopping while one of your close friends is strangled?"

Strangled? Whoever said Ginger had been strangled?

"Yes, a very sad situation all the way around." I popped her plants into a box and handed them to her. "Remember, don't overwater."

"I'll do my best. See you at Dot's wedding unless I kill these plants before then."

Or another person, I added darkly.

I watched her as she minced down the walkway to her Buick. Penny sure hadn't done anything to remove herself from my possible suspect list. In fact, she had moved her little self and her boss right up to the top.

"Did you hear that?" I called to Sharlene as Penny drove away.

"Yeah. Gross." Sharlene set a stack of ribbon spools on the counter. "How could Dr. Smythe want to be with her? She's, like, old."

I shook my head. "That part was bad enough. But did you hear her say something about Ginger being strangled? I sure haven't heard that, and I'm a—" here I made air quotation marks, "a 'suspect'."

"Ooh, that's weird. Maybe she just assumed that's what happened?"

We stared at each other.

"Or maybe she did it." I pulled my electric teapot and favorite mug out from under the counter. "I can't think about this anymore right now. I've got to call the people at the Pfieffer Building back about the menu for the rehearsal dinner. And then I need to try on my dress because the seamstress messed up and had to alter it again." I filled the tea kettle with water and switched it on. "And my supplier left me a message about the tulips for the Taylor/Bessmer wedding. That can't be good. Do you want a cup of tea?"

"No thanks." Sharlene patted my shoulder. "You'll get everything done, boss. What can I do that will help you the most?"

I smiled in spite of my throbbing headache. I doubted Sharlene even noticed she had called me 'boss,' as she had teasingly referred to me the last few months. Sharlene had come into my life as a broken young woman, searching for secrets from her past. Now, she was an eager new follower of Christ and someone who I was proud to call a friend.

"You can pray for me." I poured hot water over my tea bag.

She popped a stick of gum into her mouth. "I am. You and Dot taught me right."

Her words struck me like an unexpected shower of cold water, bringing perspective into what had seemed to be an overwhelming situation. Why had I allowed myself to get so worked up about everything? God was in control, and He was not taken by surprise by any of this. "I'll be right back," I murmured.

Alone in the tiny, stuffy bathroom, I sat down on the closed toilet seat. "All right, Lord. I'm sorry I have been trying to figure all of this out on my own." I sat in the dim quietness for a few minutes longer, rounding up every crazy, worried thought I'd had in the last couple of days. I pictured myself heaping them up in my cupped hands, then handing the whole mess over to Jesus. I imagined Him taking it with a smile, then handing me an exquisitely-wrapped gift in exchange.

"What is this?" I murmured.

My peace. My presence with you.

I hugged it to my chest, my throat tight. "Thank you. I receive it." I drew in a deep breath. I didn't have to figure things out on my own. "Please lead me to the truth, Father God. Let evil be exposed and the truth come to light."

CHAPTER SEVEN

I pulled into the parking lot at Willowbough Monday morning, feeling a little better about things. Going to church yesterday with Todd and Chad helped. It also helped that everyone there hugged me and no one accused me of murdering anyone.

I grabbed my phone to text Todd and noticed I had a missed call from my mom. That was unusual enough that I listened to her voicemail immediately, then laughed when I heard her message wishing me a happy birthday. It was my brother's birthday this week, so she must have accidentally called my phone instead of Jason's. I wondered if she had realized her mistake.

Maybe I should call her back.

Nah, I could call her later. Or better yet, I'd text her. Their internet and phone service were often spotty or nonexistent, so texting usually worked best, anyway. Plus, I wasn't sure how much my aunt had shared with her about my current situation, and I wasn't in the mood to answer a billion questions. Besides, they'd be here next week for the wedding. We'd have lots of time to talk then. And with the seven-hour time difference, it was dinner time in Zambia and I knew they often had meetings or other duties at that time.

After sending Todd a quick text, I headed into Willowbough. It would be good to decompress with Auntie for a few minutes before I headed to work. I needed to double-check with her about the rehearsal dinner menu anyway, now that I had finally been in touch with the caterer.

Lost in my thoughts, I ambled down the hallway toward my aunt's suite, nearly knocking over a woman who was standing outside Aunt Dot's door.

"Oh, I'm so sorry." I backed away, realizing it was the same employee who had popped into my aunt's room the other day. The one with the long, grey braid who didn't want to hear about God. I groped for her name and came up empty. Monica? Anika?

"No worries." She smiled at me. "I thought maybe you'd be

in jail today."

What?

I gaped at her. "Excuse me?"

She shrugged. "I heard you killed Ginger Slayton."

"Veronica!" Aunt Dot's door flew open and her soon-to-be husband Harry towered in the doorway.

Aunt Dot wheeled her chair up behind him in the doorway. "That was entirely uncalled for."

I cringed as other employees stopped to watch the show. I imagined them accusing me with their eyes. "I had nothing to do with Ginger's death."

Harry laid a protective arm around my shoulders and spoke loud enough for his voice to carry down the hallway. "It is a terrible thing that a woman in our community was murdered. But we need to work together to find the killer, not blame innocent people with unfounded, preposterous accusations."

Veronica shoved her hands into the pockets of her scrubs and stared at me, as if Harry had not spoken. "Y'all were arguing at the Donut Hut the other morning, and then Ginger was dead the very next day. And your friends were with you. Did they help too?"

When would this end?

I sighed. "Ginger Slayton has probably had a disagreement with every single person in this town over the years. I'm sure other people had more reason to harm her than I did. And—" I felt my blood pressure rising. "Leave my friends out of this. They had nothing to do with my conversation with Ginger."

"Except that they were at your store before you were that morning. Maybe they stole your rosebushes. Did you ever think of that?"

What?

"No, I did not think of that. I know my friends and they would never do such a thing." I glared at her.

"Callie, you should not be dignifying her accusations by answering them." Harry tugged me toward Aunt Dot's door, then turned to Veronica. "I will be speaking to your supervisor about your conduct."

She paled. "I'm sorry." She turned to me. "I have a big mouth sometimes. I didn't mean to sound like I was accusing you."

Could have fooled me. "No worries. I just hope the police find the real culprit soon."

"You should be able to help, seein' as you're a detective and all," she called after me as I closed Aunt Dot's door behind me.

"Right." I sank into my favorite chair at Aunt Dot's kitchen table. "This is unbelievable."

Harry paced around the small room. "I'm shocked at the response of this town to your involvement, Callie."

"My non-involvement, you mean?" I shook my head. "I think I'm mostly bothered that people would think me capable of such a thing."

"I'm more than bothered about it, darlin'." Aunt Dot shook her head. "It's such a shame for folks to be going on and on about you, while the real murderer is getting away with it."

Wait a minute. I hadn't realized the whole town was talking about it. "Who is spreading this around?"

Aunt Dot shook her head. "You know how it is. Everybody talks about everything. Probably no one single person."

An image of Penny Vaughan yakking her head off to every patient who came into Dr. Smythe's office popped into my head. I groaned. "This is so dumb. All I did was ask Ginger if she knew anything about my rose bushes, and suddenly I'm a suspect in her murder."

Harry planted himself in front of me. "This needs to stop."

"Amen!" Aunt Dot nodded vigorously. "The enemy is trying to distract you from what you need to be doing right now."

I rolled my head, trying to loosen my neck muscles. "I need to be making the arrangements for your wedding right now. And I need to call my mother. And I need to talk to Sherm about the whole incident."

Harry shook his head. "No. You need to be focusing on those girls who will be arriving at Hope House in the next few weeks."

"That, too." Ack. How would I ever accomplish all of it?

"We need to pray." Aunt Dot scooched her chair closer to mine and reached for my hand. "Harry, will you lead us off?"

"I'd love to." He sat in the chair next to mine and grasped my free hand. "Father God, we come to You in the strong name of Jesus Christ. We ask You to uncover things that are hidden. We plead the blood of Jesus over Callie's mind, heart, soul, spirit, and body. I speak peace to her in the name of Jesus. God, You are the revealer of mysteries, and I pray You will give us and the law enforcement folks supernatural knowledge to be able to apprehend this criminal quickly. God, we pray You will bless Todd as he walks a fine line between the duties of his job and his love for Callie." He paused for a breath. "And God, we pray nothing will hinder the opening of Hope House. Give Callie and the rest of the board the wisdom we need as we make decisions about these girls and their care. Our hope is in You alone, God. We pray Your will be done in each of these situations, as it is already done in Heaven. We trust you to bring justice to this situation that seems insurmountable to us."

Yes. Yes. Thank you, God.

I wiped my eyes. "Thank you, Harry." I squeezed his hand before letting it go. "Only this morning I read a poem by Mary Butterfield that said something like 'Within His word is found the key which opens His secret stairs...alone with Him...we mount our loads and rest in Him.'"

"That's beautiful." Aunt Dot sniffed. "I think we ought to pray for Veronica too. I can't imagine what got into her. She's usually such a quiet person."

"Who knows? Maybe she's having a rotten day." I stood. "I suppose I should be heading for the shop. I haven't gotten much done lately, needless to say."

Harry and Aunt Dot glanced at each other. "Callie, dear..." Aunt Dot twisted her engagement ring around her finger. "Harry and I think perhaps we should postpone the wedding."

I sank back onto my chair. Were they having second thoughts about getting married? After all these months? "Why?"

"Just for the time being." Harry patted my hand. "It seems

too much to ask of you right now while you're having to deal with this unforeseen situation."

I blew out a sigh. "I'm relieved to hear that's the reason. For a moment there, I thought you two lovebirds were getting cold feet."

"No, ma'am." Harry leaned over and gave my aunt a loud smack on her cheek. "This little lady said yes. It's a done deal."

I loved how my aunt blushed. "Well, I appreciate your concern, but I'm sure we'll get things straightened out with the Ginger deal soon. I'd hate to change the date, especially since you have already waited this long so my parents could be here for it."

Aunt Dot pulled her reading glasses on. "Yes, but once they're here, they'll be here for a year. Really. It's too much for you right now."

I stood again and gave each one a hug. "Absolutely not. The wedding goes on."

Harry laughed his booming laugh. "I told you that's what she'd say." He clapped his western hat on his head. "I have a date with my golf clubs this morning. Y'all two work it out and let me know."

"You're marrying a smart, smart man, Auntie," I said, winking at Harry.

"And I thank the Lord for him every day." She reached for my hand again and squeezed it. "At least consider our idea. Please?"

I pulled up to C. Willikers and parked, leaving the engine running, and stared at my empty rose trellises. How had things gotten so crazy again? I had felt better after Harry prayed, but now it seemed like everything was descending on me again. I blew out my breath, feeling the anxiety mounting. I needed to do something to get my mind off everything.

I wrenched the keys from the ignition, slammed the van door closed, and marched up to the front door. I would tackle the stack of invoices I'd been meaning to get to for the last week.

An hour later, I stared at my computer screen. I'd been trying to focus on invoices, but it wasn't working. I stood and stretched my arms over my head, wishing I was lying on a sunny beach somewhere, with nothing to worry about. Better yet, lying on a sunny beach somewhere with Todd, on our honeymoon. Maybe I'd run past the bridal shop later…

Right. I snorted. I had to get my head together. I was planning Aunt Dot's wedding, not my own. And it wasn't fair to Aunt Dot and Harry to postpone their wedding because of some absurd accusations. On the other hand, the local law enforcement seemed to be taking their good ol' time.

"These things are not quick, Callie," Todd had said to me this morning. "Every single little lead and detail has to be followed up on. And the toxicology report hasn't come back yet, either, so we're not one hundred percent sure what we're even dealing with."

I was trying to be patient, but it was getting ridiculous to have to deal with accusations everywhere I went. I sighed. As much as I hated to think about it, I needed to take matters into my own hands. After all, hadn't I been the one who solved Sister Erma's case last year?

Mona would help me.

I texted her. *Can you meet me at the store after work?*

I turned my computer off and texted her again. *Scratch that. Can you take the afternoon off and come over now?*

That was the beauty of owning my own store in a small town. I could close my shop and slap a "Back Soon" note on the front door whenever I felt the need.

So I did. I hadn't had one customer all morning, anyway. Maybe people didn't want to shop in a store whose owner might be a murderer. Really? That was the part that hurt the worst—that folks in this little town I had come to love would even consider I could be capable of something so evil.

Mona still hadn't texted back, so I hopped in my van and drove across the parking lot to Houston's church, where she worked as the receptionist.

She poked her head out the glass doors and gave me a thumbs-up before retreating inside.

I leaned my head against the headrest. God, please help me. I know there's someone out there who knows something. Or saw something. And why would Boranda Stiegler have stolen my roses? The woman couldn't keep a patch of weeds alive if she tried, judging from the brown square that passed as the front lawn of her beauty salon.

Mona popped out the door and bustled over to my van, her flowery blouse and skirt billowing around her plump figure. She hoisted herself up into the passenger seat, her cloud of scent preceding her. "Hey, friend. Everything okay? Are we going on an adventure? I didn't feel like typing up the bulletin this afternoon anyway, and the women's ministry president hasn't gotten me her blurb about the Memorial Day deal. Are you hungry?"

I breathed in the musky scent of her perfume and sneezed. And sneezed.

"Bless you. The cedar pollen is still thick this week, isn't it? Are you hungry?" She peered up at me over the tops of her favorite purple glasses.

Not pollen. "I hadn't thought about it, but I guess I am hungry." I don't eat when I'm anxious.

"Let's go to the taqueria and get lunch. I'm starving." She pulled her lipstick out of her purse and carefully applied a thick layer of fuchsia to her lips, squinting at her reflection in the visor mirror through her reading glasses.

I was always amused by the amount of forethought that must be required to go into matching one's outfit, lipstick, purse, and in Mona's case, western boots or flip-flops, depending on the season. I owned one shade of lipstick and was lucky if I remembered to put it on before church. And I wasn't fond of the taqueria, either. I made a face. "I don't think my stomach can take Mexican today." I pulled out of the church parking lot. "Let's grab something to eat at my house. I need to check on the dogs anyway."

Mona heaved a sigh. "That's not nearly as fun. I was all set for a big ol' enchilada with their amazing green sauce. I never can figure out how they make it so yummy. Do you have anything decent to eat at your house?"

"As in, 'non-healthy'?" I grinned at her.

"Well, at my age, I don't feel like eating bread with twigs and nuts in it. Or that nasty kale instead of regular ol' lettuce." She sniffed. "Rob and I are done with diets for good. We like each other exactly like we are, and we like our food the way we like it."

At her age? She was only in her fifties. I decided to leave that topic alone. "I do happen to have a loaf of white bread, since I knew Chad would be around some. He doesn't like twiggy bread, either."

She snorted. "Smart kid. I'll have a grilled cheese, please."

An hour later, we pulled onto Ginger Slayton's street. "I haven't been over here in a long time. These are pretty nice homes."

Mona nodded. "Yeah, older and kinda small. But it's a nice neighborhood. Penny Vaughan and her ex-husband used to live over here." She pointed at a tidy white house with an immaculate lawn. "I think it was that one."

I nodded. "Probably. Look at those flower beds." I slowed down. "No wonder she was mad about not winning the lawn and garden show. When did she move?"

"I don't remember. It's been a while, but that one across the street is Ginger's."

"Oh, fudge." I glanced at Ginger's house as I stepped on the gas, not keen on giving anyone fodder for more accusations. I'm not thinking it would be the best for folks to observe me casing Ginger's house.

We drove around the block and I pulled into the little park at the end of the street. "Now." I pulled my gardening gloves on. "We're going to go do a little reconnaissance."

Mona laughed. "Seriously. You're going to wear your gardening gloves? To spy out Ginger's house?"

"Most certainly. I don't want to leave fingerprints."

Her eyes widened. "I thought we were going to sneak around her yard or something. You're not planning to go inside her house, are you? Todd would be so mad."

I'd worry about that later. "Let's just say if the opportunity presents itself, I might have a little peek inside."

Mona reached for the door handle. "You are going to be in so much trouble if Wayne catches a sniff of this."

"A whiff."

She paused and glanced at me over her shoulder. "What?"

"Never mind." I grabbed my phone and slid out the door. "Ready?"

"As ready as I'll ever be. I don't know how you talk me into these things." She slammed the door. "At least I didn't wear my heels today. What are you looking for, anyway, Nancy?"

Good question.

I led the way across the street and onto the grassy easement behind Ginger's street. Lined with trees on both sides, it would provide some protection from spying eyes. "I'm not sure. But I bet there's some clue to why someone would want Ginger dead."

"Like what? Slow down." She panted along behind me. "And if we're sneaking around, why are we doing it in the middle of the day?"

I pushed through a patch of dewberry bushes. Thank God the chiggers weren't out yet, or I'd be one sorry girl tomorrow. "Because we're not doing anything wrong, exactly, and if we were caught sneaking around at night, we'd be in more trouble."

"And we're not going to be in trouble if we're caught in the daytime?"

I sighed. "No one's going to care that we're poking around Ginger's yard."

Yeah, right.

I stuck my phone in my back pocket and climbed over Ginger's back fence. Good thing she didn't have any neighbors back here. "Anyway, I'm the one being accused of murdering her. You don't have anything to worry about."

Mona rolled her eyes and picked a twig out of her silvery, spiked hair. "If Rob has to bail me out of jail, I'm gonna tell him it was your fault."

"It will be fine, Mona. All we're going to do is look around a little bit."

"You mean you're going to look around. I'm not climbing that fence. I'd get stuck, and then we'd really be in trouble." She crossed her arms over her ample bosom, her rhinestone cowboy-boot-shaped earrings bobbing. "Go on, but hurry. I still can't believe you sucked me into this. I'll be your lookout."

Not a bad idea. "Fine. But don't scream or anything. I've got my phone on vibrate, so text me if you see anyone coming."

"Yes, ma'am. Now hurry up. I need to go to the bathroom."

She was still muttering as I slunk through the oleanders and around the birdbath. "Shh!" I glanced back at her.

She smiled and waved.

Oh, brother. I had to focus on what I was doing. I was sure it was mildly illegal to be in someone else's back yard, but surely I wouldn't be in too much—

"Oh, boy." I stopped in my tracks and sniffed. Someone had been burning something recently. I glanced around the yard, spotting one of those portable fire pits on the back patio. Why would someone be having a fire in Ginger's fire pit a few days after her death, except to get rid of incriminating evidence?

I sidled toward the fire pit, then froze. The back door to Ginger's garage stood partially open.

Was someone in there? I stepped behind the enormous Texas sage bush near the corner of the house and waited. I couldn't hear anything.

My phone vibrated and I jumped. Was someone coming after me? I held my breath, easing my phone out of my pocket while glancing around the best I could. I didn't see anyone.

Hurry up! I have to go bad!!!! Smiley face, smiley face.

Really? My hands were trembling so bad I didn't even try to text her back. Okay then. I took a deep breath. I really, really wanted to see what was in the fire pit.

"Here goes," I whispered. I strode across the patio as if I had every right to be there, then stood staring down into the still-smoking pile of what looked like years' worth of paperwork. Tax documents, from the looks of the few that were not totally burned. I took my gloves off and snapped a few pictures, pretending I didn't see Mona's frantic arm-waving out of the corner of my eye. If she had to go that bad, she could find a tree. Or walk back to the van without me.

I stuffed my phone back into my pocket. The garage was next. I slipped in through the door, waiting a moment until my eyes adjusted. Wow. There sure wouldn't be any clues in here. This had to be the cleanest garage I had ever seen. Sunlight streamed through the small window onto a floor that was painted gray and swept to a shine, and every tool had its own place on the pegboard walls. I scanned the ceiling. The attic door was closed tightly, the ceiling painted white. Newly-painted, if my nose wasn't deceiving me.

Ginger's car, a big blue sedan of some sort, was parked on the far-left side of the two-car garage—as far to the left as one could get and still squeeze out the driver's-side doors. That seemed a bit odd. Why would Ginger have parked like that? Unless, of course, it wasn't Ginger who parked it there at all. Maybe whoever killed her had needed room for—for what? To drag her body out into a different vehicle? Or maybe she was still alive when the murderer—I shuddered. Stop it, Callie. It's not helping to freak yourself out. I drew a long breath in through my nose and out through my mouth before I stepped around the rear of the car for a closer look at the tools hanging on the wall. What if someone had used one of these tools to—

My phone vibrated at the same time I heard the sound. Someone was entering the garage. I dropped down on the floor next to the car. Who would be in Ginger's garage? Had someone followed me in here? I scrunched down near the front driver's side tire, my heart pounding. Why had I thought this was a good idea?

I held my breath and hunched down further. I could see someone's feet on the other side of the car. A man's feet. Well-worn flips-flops. Nasty-looking toenails. Hairy calves. Just … standing there. Eek!

CHAPTER EIGHT

What was he doing? Was he the murderer?

I gulped.

Did he know I was in here and was trying to psych me out? I pressed myself against the tire, waiting.

God, please protect me. I realize now this was an idiotic idea. I'm so sorry. But please...and don't let Mona text me again.

If my phone vibrated while the guy was still standing there, right on the other side of the car, I'd be sunk. Could I pull it out and turn it off without him noticing?

No, I didn't dare move. Plus, I was still wearing the stupid gardening gloves. Why had I come into the garage by myself?

I breathed as quietly as I could, hugging the tire while the strong rubber scent penetrated my consciousness. Odd, what one focuses on in extraordinary situations.

The feet moved.

I resisted the urge to try to squeeze underneath the car.

"Hee-haw! Hee-haw!" The guy's crazy ring tone blared out in the silence.

I stifled a gasp as I almost lost my balance. Why would he have his phone on? Maybe his partner was late and that's why he was waiting to kill me. He was waiting, so they could both—

"Dagnabbit!"

I jumped. But...*dagnabbit?* What kind of criminal says "dagnabbit"? I really, really wanted to stand up enough to see over the car. Maybe this wasn't Ginger's killer. Maybe he was a—

"Yoo-hoo! Anybody home?" Mona's flowery self appeared at the door, fuchsia-colored purse in hand. "J.T.? Is that you?"

Yikes. J.T.? And what was Mona doing? She was going to get herself killed.

The feet turned toward the door. "Yeah."

I blew out a long, silent breath. So now I knew who was in the garage with me. J.T. Culpepper, Ginger's neighbor, the convicted felon. Great. But why was he in Ginger's garage? And what was Mona's plan? I listened to her fuchsia and rhinestone boot-clad feet clack over to J.T.'s and imagined her slipping her arm through his. He must not have a weapon, at least one that was visible, if she was willing to cozy up to him.

"I was out taking a walk and saw you in the yard. Everything all right? I mean, with Ginger's death and all, I thought maybe everyone should keep an eye out for anything unusual, you know? I remember you help with her yardwork sometimes, and I've always admired her flower beds. I wonder if her family is going to sell the house or what? It's such a crying shame about what happened, but hopefully she's in a better place right now. Did you know her very well? I mean, I get that you haven't lived in Short Creek very long, but it's a great place, don't you think? I mean, except for a few murders every now and then, but other than that it's fine. Rob says you make a mean chili. Are you going to enter it in the Catfish Association Chili Cook-Off this year? It's coming up in a few months, you know, and..."

Mona kept up a steady stream of chatter, which was impressive even for her, as the two walked out the door. Poor J.T. must have been stunned into silence by the sheer volume of words. Or maybe he was rendered unconscious by the perfume cloud. I could smell it all the way over here.

I drew a deep breath. Okay, then. I cautiously rose from my cramped position, hoping I didn't have tire tread marks on my face. My t-shirt snagged on something, and I bent to unhook it from where it had caught on the edge of the bumper. But what was this? I dislodged a small, shiny item from under the very edge of the front tire with my gloved finger. Flat and round with a little ring at the top, it appeared to be a charm from a bracelet or necklace, though the ring was bent open as if the charm was forcibly removed from whatever it used to be connected to. Was it a charm from Ginger's bracelet? Or someone else's? It probably didn't mean anything, since I assumed the police had already searched her home and car thoroughly and would have taken it for evidence if it was important. Still, it was worth giving some thought to. I stuck it into the small resealable baggie I had brought with me, feeling more like Nancy Drew by the moment.

Hmm. Maybe there were more charms or even the entire bracelet somewhere. I shone the flashlight from my phone under the car, then ran my hand across the floor for good measure. Nope, nothing there.

"Callie! Come on! He's gone." Mona's stage whisper startled me.

I popped my head up over the car hood. "Be there in a sec."

"Hurry up! I'm doing the potty dance and I can't hold it much longer."

We drove the few blocks back to C. Willikers and Mona dashed to the bathroom.

"I still can't believe you followed J.T. into the garage," I said as she came out.

"Well, you were in there a long time. And he wasn't sneaking around. Just popped in through the side gate with a rake in his hand and started poking around in the flowerbeds like it was nothing. He's harmless, if you ask me. Did you notice all those bird feeders hangin' in his yard? We had a great ol' time discussing the fish fry coming up next week. He and Rob are both entering their recipes in the contest." She tugged at the waistband of her skirt and wiggled around. "There. So much better. What were you doing in the garage all that time, anyway?"

"I was only in there a few minutes. But look what I found." I held the baggie up for her to see.

She squinted at it, then pulled her reading glasses out and put them on. "What is it? Eww, who would wear a charm of a big ol' eye?"

I was wondering the same thing. I turned over the dull silvery disc and rubbed my thumb over the raised image of an eye, complete with eyelashes and brow. "So weird. Did Ginger even wear jewelry?" I pictured the somewhat dowdy Ginger clumping around in her skirt and gardening boots, bless her heart. "Or maybe it belonged to the person who killed her."

"People who kill other people don't wear charm bracelets. Nose rings, maybe." Mona scoffed. "Probably Ginger dropped it before she got into the car for the last time. Or one of her friends. Penny wears a lot of jewelry."

True. Hmm.

"Speaking of Penny, I need to have my teeth cleaned. I'm thinking maybe I'll try out Dr. Smythe."

"I thought he gave you the creeps."

"He does. Majorly. But I'll have to deal with it. It's worth it to see if either he or Penny react to seeing the charm."

Mona folded her arms. "You're serious. You really think one of them could have killed Ginger? What about Todd?"

"What about Todd what?"

"Don't you think you should show him what you found?"

Probably. But then he would be mad at me for going into the garage alone.

I stuffed the baggie into my pocket. "I will show it to him. Just not right now."

"Have you prayed about this?" She glared at me over her reading glasses.

Her words stopped me cold. I was usually the one asking her that question.

"Because if you didn't, you better. Remember when Houston was kidnapped that time and God gave you a dream to know where to look for him? You're trying to figure things out on your own too much, and it's gonna backlash."

Backfire. And she was probably right. But how was I ever going to clear my name if I didn't take some action? "I'm not going to do anything stupid."

Famous last words. *I'm not going to do anything stupid.*

Looking back on it now, I can see that it was not my best idea ever to let Dr. Smythe anywhere near my mouth, especially when I was lying in his chair between him and Penny with the charm displayed prominently on a sparkly silver chain around my neck.

"Where did that man geth hith dentist degree? On the internet?" I stretched out on my couch now, holding an ice pack to my cheek.

Todd sat on the floor in front of the couch, one pug on either side of him and Annie practically sitting in his lap. "Thank God it wasn't worse. I've heard some horror stories. No wonder Ginger threatened to burn down his office."

I groaned. "Thath not why."

"What did you say?"

I tried again to make my numb lips cooperate. "Penny saith that Ginger wath jealous because she wanted Dr. Smythe to take her to th' Canoodle but thath he had already asked her." I slurped through my teeth. How had I gone in for a cleaning and come out with one less tooth in my head?

"You lost me, sweetheart." Todd turned around to look at me. "Who went to the Canoodle with who?"

I slurped again. "Penny and Dr. Thmythe. Ginger wath jealous."

"And so you decided to wear the charm and see if you'd get a rise out of them." He shook his head. "What am I going to do with you?"

"Well, it worked, didn't it?" I sat up and moaned, steadying myself with a hand on Todd's shoulder. "You should hath seen Penny's eyes pop out of her head when she saw the charm. Then she told me she didn't know I was Catholic and thath Ginger hath one juhst like it."

Now it was Todd's turn to groan. "If that charm truly belonged to Ginger, you shot yourself in the foot, sweetheart. You now have a piece of jewelry in your possession that very likely belonged to a murder victim. And on top of that, you snuck into her garage. If Wayne catches wind of this—" Todd threaded his fingers through mine. "Please let Wayne and the detectives handle this. I know it's not fun, but you can live through some accusations for a few more weeks. No one who truly knows you would believe you were involved in something so heinous, anyway."

I knew he was right, but it still rankled. And I didn't want the wedding to be postponed. "And what doth being Catholic have to do with anything? The betht part was when Penny asked me where I got it, and I thaid I found it. You should have seen the look she gave Dr. Thmythe when I said that."

He sighed. "Callie. Look at me. What if, God forbid, Penny truly did kill Ginger? Don't you think she'd realize what you were trying to do?"

I hadn't thought that far. Ack. "You mean she might try to come after me too?"

"I don't want to speculate, but if she is involved in this situation in some way and she thinks you have figured it out, that's not a good thing for you. Will you please lay low and let the professionals handle this? I don't want to have to come visit you in the hospital or in jail on our anniversary." He looped my hair back over my ear. "A nice, relaxed, romantic dinner sounds better, doesn't it?"

Anniversary?

Wow. How could I have forgotten that next week marked the second year of our relationship already? And maybe I should let this thing go. It was eating me up, and I knew God was aware of the whole situation. I should leave it in His hands. In fact, I had already left it in His hands. But then I pulled it out again.

"Okay. You win." I slithered down onto the floor next to him, and he wrapped his arm around my shoulders. "But I need a few kisses. And not just the chocolate ones, either."

CHAPTER NINE

I hunkered down at my kitchen table the next morning, still in my cozy robe, with my Bible, my journal, today's newspaper, and a mug of tea. It was rather freeing, actually, to choose to let go of this whole Ginger Slayton situation. Todd had promised he'd keep me updated, and I knew he would keep his word. And God, through the Scriptures, had promised me peace. I knew He would keep His word too. The hard part, as I realized last night, was leaving everything in His hands and not trying to snatch it out again when I became anxious.

I glanced at my devotional again, re-reading words that had been written more than three hundred years ago, but still had the power to bring comfort and encouragement to my heart this morning. "Believe God's Word and power more than you believe your own feelings and experiences. Your Rock is Christ, and it is not the Rock which ebbs and flows, but your sea," wrote long-ago pastor Samuel Rutherford.

It was not God who changed in the midst of difficult circumstances. It was my own emotions and fears that caused me to stress and doubt. Sunshine streamed through the lace curtains over my kitchen window, warming more than the room. I sat in silence, waiting for God's promised peace to come.

God, please help me have the faith to believe in your Word and your power, no matter my emotions or questions. You are my Rock. I trust you, Jesus. I believe. Help my unbelief.

I rested in the quiet for a few more minutes, sensing His comforting presence surrounding me. He loved me. What did it matter what others thought of me?

"Good thing I asked Sharlene to open for me this morning," I said to Annie. "I needed time to regroup."

She raised her head from the floor to listen to me, then laid it back down with a sigh.

"I feel that way too. Exhausted. And it's only nine o'clock." I sipped my tea. At least my mouth had stopped throbbing from my tooth-pulling folly. "And look at those pugs. They don't even know it's morning."

I turned my attention back to the newspaper. I didn't always have time to read the whole thing every day, but I enjoyed reading it when I could. And I tried not to miss any of Aunt Dot's weekly advice columns.

Tap. Tap. Tap, tap, tap.

I sipped my Earl Grey, then lifted my gaze from the newspaper. A tufted titmouse perched on the window feeder, demanding my attention. When I didn't move, he tapped the glass again with his stubby black beak.

"Demanding little thing, aren't you?" I pulled my bathrobe tighter around myself as I stood, mug in hand. Both pugs stared at me from their bed across the kitchen. "I'm supposed to be having a relaxing morning after all the craziness of the week."

I shuffled into the garage and scooped sunflower seeds from the bin. "I might as well feed you guys too, while I'm at it," I called to the dogs. "Want your breakfast?"

Annie leapt up and trotted after me into the garage. The pugs followed at a more sedate pace. All three of them stared at me as I headed out the door.

"Okay, then. Let's all go out to fill the bird feeder. Come on, everyone."

I squinted in the morning sun as I detoured to the side yard to check the soil under the camellia bushes. I'd reluctantly transplanted them to a shadier spot this spring after we lost a huge shade tree during the winter. I looked forward to their bright pink blooms every winter and didn't want to lose them to the early May heat. I fingered a glossy leaf, then jumped as a flurry of black wings erupted near my feet.

"Well, hello there." It was the old crow again. Was he still hanging around?

He fixed one beady eye on me and did a little sideways hop.

Purl gave a half-hearted woof but made no attempt to chase the poor thing.

"I suppose this bird is as hungry as you are, girls." I opened the side door into the garage and scooped dog food out for the bird. "Here you go, crow."

I flung a handful of dog pebbles onto the mulch under the middle camellia bush and refilled the cereal bowl with water while the dogs looked on. The crow strutted over to the bush and snatched a pebble before gulping it down whole.

"He says 'thanks for sharing,'" I informed the dogs as I herded them into the kitchen. "You guys are all getting a little chunky, anyway. Probably time for a diet."

And speaking of a diet, I remembered I had volunteered to grab donuts on my way into work this afternoon. It was Houston's birthday, and that was enough reason for Mona to plan a party.

I pulled up in front of the Donut Hut an hour later, wishing I was still at home in my robe. The last time I was here was the day of the infamous conflagration with Ginger Slayton. I turned the engine off and sat there, thinking. How had such a relatively small thing turned into such a big mess? And why, until this moment, had I forgotten what Houston had said on the morning of the missing roses? He had been lying on the ground rubbing his head where the branch hit him, and he said something like, "I almost saw who did it."

Did what? Stole my rosebushes? Or hit him on the head?

I started to text him, then remembered I would see him in a few minutes. I rushed into the Donut Hut on a mission to get in and out as soon as possible. This could be the key to the whole thing. If Houston had seen someone...but if he had, surely he would have mentioned it by now.

I sighed, taking my place in line behind two elderly ladies and a dark-haired woman with a poodle on a sparkly leash. I didn't recognize any of them.

But Wormy, the proprietor of the Donut Hut, obviously did. He paused mid-joke to point at me. "Here's Callie Erickson now, ladies."

The three women turned to stare at me.

Awesome.

"These folks were asking about your store, Callie." Wormy beamed at me. I had long wondered how he could own a donut shop and still remain skinny as a rail. "They're doing a feature on Short Creek businesses for the *CenTex Courier*. I told 'em I thought you'd be happy to talk to them."

The younger woman smiled at me and extended her hand. I noticed the violet-blue of her collared blouse exactly matched the color of her eyes. She was stunning. "I'm Carly Richards with the CenTex Courier. It's so nice to meet you."

I shook her hand. "You too. I'm always happy for more publicity. Are you interviewing Wormy, as well?"

"Already did. I gave her the whole scoop on the history of the Donut Hut." Wormy winked at me, then handed one of the older women a large, white bag and nodded at Carly. "The way y'all were talkin', I thought y'all knew each other."

The grey-haired woman shook her head. "No. We came to look at some property and thought we'd stop and get some snacks for our drive home. Hard to pass up a donut shop." They both giggled and stepped around us.

"Thank you. Come again," Wormy called after them.

The reporter, Carly, placed her order, then stepped over to the coffee machine.

Wormy swiped the counter with a rag while I deliberated over apple fritters and chocolate glazed donuts. "Not much property up for sale around here that I know of. Unless they're talkin' about Ginger's house," he drawled.

My ears perked up. "Her house wouldn't be up for sale yet, would it? I wonder if she has kids or someone to get it ready to sell?"

"I don't know, but my wife is gonna be the first in line to buy it, I'll tell you that much. She's had her heart set on that house for a long time."

Really.

I eyed Wormy with more interest. I had pretty much crossed him off my mental suspect list, but—hmm. Would coveting Ginger's house have been enough motive to kill her?

Stop it, Callie. You're supposed to be letting Wayne take care of this.

Still.

"It is a lovely home. I had never been by there until the other day." Oops, should have kept my mouth shut about that.

But the temptation to see if he'd say anything else was too great. "The lawn and gardens are fabulous."

His eyes lit up. "Aren't they amazing? That house used to belong to my wife's relatives when it was first built, and she had her heart set on buying it when it went up for sale a few years ago. We put a darn good bid in on it, but Ginger got it."

Hmm. Sounds like a motive to me.

"That's too bad. Did you know Ginger well?" I pointed to the apple fritters. "I'll take a half-dozen of those and a half-dozen of the raspberry-filled, please."

Should I try to ask more questions? Wormy was a nice guy by all accounts, but he was also on the city council. If he thought I was trying to connect him to Ginger's murder, he might get upset. What if he decided to be vindictive and lodged some complaints about my business or worse, Hope House? We'd been down that road before, and I didn't want to go there again. Also, I reminded myself for the hundredth time, I was not supposed to get involved anymore.

He handed me the box of donuts. "Nah. The most I've ever been around Ginger was when she tried to mess with me during the election last year. Got her pants all in a wad about that one, didn't she?"

I laughed. "Truthfully, I didn't pay much attention. That was all going on during the time I was dealing with June Blackman and that mess."

Carly stepped over to the counter again, coffee cup in hand and laptop case slung over her shoulder. "Sounds like Short Creek has all the regular small-town drama."

"And then some." I grinned at her as I dug my keys out of my purse. "Did you want to see my shop? I'm headed over there now."

❦

Sharlene smiled at us as we came through the door.

"Sharlene, this is Carly Richards from the *CenTex Courier*. She's interviewing me for an article she's writing on the businesses in Short Creek." I gestured toward Sharlene. "Sharlene is my only employee, but she does the work of two people."

I was dying to tell Sharlene what Wormy had said about his wife wanting Ginger's house, but I had to wait until after I gave Carly the tour of the shop and a run-down of my history with it. Clearly, she had done her homework, because she asked me about the time I had discovered a body on the back steps of C. Willikers. She also already knew I was president of the Hope House board, and asked me several pointed questions about my involvement with the organization before she finally closed her notebook.

"If she uses all of that information, she'll be writing, like, one long article," Sharlene said as we watched the reporter climb into her shiny red sportscar. "It would be pretty cool for C. Willikers to be featured, though."

I shrugged. "At least she wasn't as nosy as the reporters from the TV station who kept bugging me for an interview last week. You'd think after I'd said, 'no comment' about a billion times, they'd get the picture."

"Yeah." Sharlene pulled the box of donuts over to the middle of the counter and peeked inside. "Yum. Hey, before everyone gets here, I've been meaning to ask if you'd pray for me."

"Of course. What's up?"

"Well, you know how we're supposed to be telling other people about Jesus?"

"Mmm-hmm." Sharlene was a fairly new believer, and I'd never seen someone so eager to learn and grow in her faith.

"Well, I finally met my neighbor. She lives in the trailer, like, right next to me, but she doesn't seem to be home very often. Anyway, I can tell she needs Jesus." Sharlene swiped her white-blonde hair from her face, her gaze earnest. "She's not very friendly, but I'm gonna try to be friends with her."

My heart melted. "I'm sure that's the kind of prayer God delights in. I'd be happy to pray for both of you."

"Thanks, Callie. Her name is Roni." She popped a piece of gum in her mouth. "Aren't Mona and Houston supposed to be here soon?"

"Yep, and Lonnie and Rick too. Todd said he'd swing by for

a few minutes if he wasn't swamped. And Harry will bring Aunt Dot. Rob is out of town." I pulled the electric tea kettle out from under the counter. "But guess what? Wormy said he and his wife wanted to buy Ginger Slayton's house."

"Who's Wormy?" She wrinkled her nose. "Oh, Donut Hut Wormy? Is the house for sale already?"

"Not that I know of. But I mean they wanted to buy it before Ginger bought it. But she outbid them and they didn't get the house."

Sharlene pulled a pack of water bottles out of the mini-fridge. "Yeah?"

"Couldn't that be a murder motive?"

"You're supposed to be staying out of this, aren't you?"

I held my hands up in front of me. "I'm not getting involved. I'm just saying."

"Right. I know you better than that." She twisted the lid off her water bottle and took a sip. "You think Wormy could have killed Ginger? He seems too, like, jolly or something."

"I know." The guy was hilarious. And how could anyone nicknamed "Wormy" be capable of a serious crime? "But sometimes it's someone nobody would suspect. I really can't see Boranda Stiegler doing it, even though she did show up at the crime scene with some of my missing roses." I straightened a stack of "Happy Birthday" napkins. "I still can't figure out what that was all about."

"Right? What motive would Boranda possibly have to off Ginger? Ginger didn't like her haircut and yelled at her?"

"The one time I let Bo cut my hair, it was bad enough I might have considered killing her over it." I pushed my glasses up on my nose. "Just kidding. But I do know Ginger accidentally scratched Boranda's truck one day not too long ago. Mona still lets Bo cut her hair for some reason I can't fathom, and Boranda gave Mona an earful about it. You know how particular Bo is about her pickup."

Sharlene chewed on her thumbnail, then caught herself and stopped. "That would be a dumb reason to kill someone."

"Yeah, but you hear about stuff like that on the news all the time."

"What about Penny and the weird dentist dude? Do either of them have a motive besides Ginger running off at the mouth about burning the dentist's office down?"

"I don't know, except it seems they are romantically involved, as you heard when she was in here the other day." I made a face.

"Gross."

My sentiments exactly. "And when people aren't pointing the finger at me, they're pointing it at poor J. T."

"What reason would he possibly have to kill Ginger? Solely because she was his annoying neighbor?"

I shrugged. "It seems like the fact he's a felon is enough for most folks to be suspicious of him. What people don't understand is not everyone who has spent time in prison is violent. He could have been sitting in there for stealing a car. Or embezzling money. Or maybe he was even falsely charged and was totally innocent? Who knows?"

"Uh, Callie? Don't look now, but your best friend Sheriff Wayne is coming up the walk."

CHAPTER TEN

"Fabulous." The one person I didn't want to talk to today. Unless he was coming to inform me the case was solved, in which case I'd invite him to stay and join the birthday party. I moved behind the counter and pretended I was working on my computer while Sharlene disappeared into the back room. Smart girl.

Wayne barreled through the door, and I winced as it slammed behind him. Um, it didn't seem likely that he was the bearer of happy news.

"Hey there, Sheriff," I sang. Might as well try to be upbeat, right?

"Miz Erickson." He stomped up to the counter, his beefy face red. "You're lucky I'm not cuffing you right now."

My throat constricted. *Uh-oh.*

"I heard you been snooping around Ginger Slayton's property. Is that accurate?"

Oh, boy. I don't want to go to jail today. "Um, sort of."

He hooked his thumb in his belt loop and glared at me. "You either have or you haven't, and I know you have. I have a mind to cite you for trespassing, but that would be too nice."

"I'm sorry, sir. I was only trying to be helpful. You did ask me who I thought did it."

He leaned toward me until I could smell the coffee on his breath. "Helpful would be to stay in this shop and knit or plant things or whatever you do in here until this thing is over. Didn't I already tell you that once?"

"Yes, sir. But I...it seemed like y'all haven't been doing much." Did I really say y'all?

He growled. "We've followed up on all the leads we have, Miz Erickson, and we are still waiting for toxicology. Would you like to suggest another course of action in light of your vast experience in law enforcement?"

Actually, yes.

"I'm aware you all have to follow protocol about naming a person as a suspect," I said humbly, "but have you considered

Penny Vaughan or Dr. Smythe?"

He snorted. "I already told you, I knew about Ginger's threat to burn down the dentist's office long before she was killed."

"I know." I kept my tone level. "But Penny told me recently that the real reason Ginger was so upset that day was because, well..." Now that I was saying this out loud, it sounded super petty and soap opera-ish. "Never mind."

"Miz Erickson, if you have something to say, then spit it out."

Right. "Apparently Penny and Dr. Smythe are, shall we say, romantically involved."

The sheriff rolled his eyes.

"No, seriously." I fiddled with the stack of napkins. "And Penny said Ginger also had feelings for Dr. Smythe, but Dr. Smythe apparently snubbed Ginger's invitation to the Canoodle Doodle because he was already planning to attend with Penny. And also—" I weighed out whether or not I should tell him what Mona said about Penny. "And Penny lives on Rob and Mona's street, you know, and Rob says Penny drives around all the time in the middle of the night."

"Lord have mercy." He smacked his forehead. "It's not against the law for adults to date each other or to drive around at night, Miz Erickson."

"I know that. But I'm suggesting—"

"I'll check them out again. Not like I have anything else to do all day than interrogate folks about their love life." He turned and headed toward the door.

"I could help." Oops, how had that slipped out?

He stopped with his back to me and rested his hand on his holstered gun. "Miz Erickson. You have 'helped' enough. Please, please don't help anymore."

How could I promise not to do anything? This was my life we were talking about, not his.

My landline rang, sparing me from answering him. "C. Willikers. This is Callie. How may I help you?"

By the time I had taken an order for a get-well floral arrangement, the sheriff was gone. I blew out my breath.

"Dodged that one, boss." Sharlene reappeared from the back room and grinned at me. "You're gonna solve this one before him, aren't you?"

"Not if Todd has anything to do with it." I filled the tea kettle with water from the utility sink. "I was trying to stay out of it. Honest. But then Wormy told me all that stuff this morning, and now Wayne comes in and stirs it all up again. Plus, I remembered Houston saying he saw someone the morning my roses were stolen. I need to remember to ask him about it when I see him."

"Mona texted a sec ago to say they'll be here in a minute. Something about the crock pot dripping or something."

"Ah." Mona must have made her famous baked beans. At least that was something to be happy about. Mona's beans were known far and wide for their sweet, bacon-y goodness. I glanced out the window. "Lonnie and Rick are here."

"Probably a good thing Wayne left before they got here."

"For sure." Everyone in town knew that Wayne and Rick, the mayor of Short Creek, had a love-hate relationship. "Especially because I know Rick would take my side."

"I would hope so." Sharlene was one of my biggest encouragers. I could always count on her to look on the bright side of things.

Lonnie and Rick trooped into the store carrying an enormous birthday cake. I was sure Lonnie had made it from scratch and decorated it herself. Harry followed them in, handling Aunt Dot's wheelchair like he'd done it all his life.

"Hi, hi, hi! Hi, everyone!" Aunt Dot, dressed to the nines in an elegant mint-green linen sheath with matching shoes and purse, was clearly tickled to be at the party.

Lonnie handed Sharlene the birthday cake and pulled me into a side hug while the men shook hands. "How are you, friend?"

I made a face. "I'll tell you later."

"Where's the birthday boy?" Harry boomed as I bent to hug my aunt. "Late to his own party?"

"He had to help Mona with the crock pot." Sharlene moved a veggie tray to make room on the counter for the cake,

Houston's favorite Red Velvet with cream cheese frosting. At least that's what I hoped it was.

"Is Todd coming?" Rick asked. "I was hoping to run something by him."

"He is if he can get off for a few minutes. Sounded like it was a pretty crazy day so far."

"How are the wedding plans coming, Dorrie?" Lonnie called my aunt by her other nickname.

"Real fine, from what Callie tells me." Aunt Dot reached out to squeeze my hand, but continued to speak to Lonnie. "But Harry and I asked her to consider waiting until this Ginger Slayton hubbub calms down."

The room fell silent.

Rick cleared his throat.

"You mean postpone the wedding?" Lonnie finally said.

"Yes, if need be. We've been talking about it, and we don't want it to put an undue pressure on Callie while she's dealing with these accusations."

I wanted to stomp my foot like a four-year-old. "I don't want to change the date of the wedding. That's not right." To my chagrin, I felt hot tears well up.

"We all know this lovely young lady is innocent, of course." Harry draped an arm around my shoulder. "Only a matter of time until everything is cleared up."

Rick ran a hand down his jaw. "That's the rub, though, because Wayne—"

"Happy Birthday!" Everyone hollered as Houston ambled into the store.

I swiped at my eyes and slipped into the bathroom while everyone gathered around Houston. I needed all this stupid stuff to end, so we could get on with the wedding and our lives.

Aren't you supposed to be leaving it in My hands, child?

I sighed, frowning at myself in the mirror. Yes, but—

Either you are or you aren't, dear heart.

I gulped. I get it, Lord. I'm sorry I took it back from You. I do trust You. Please help me to leave it with You this time.

I re-braided my hair and blew my nose before rejoining the party.

Todd had arrived while I was in the bathroom.

"Hey, beautiful." He slipped past our knot of friends to give me a quick hug. "Everything okay?"

I rested my head against his chest for a moment before pulling back to smile up into his gorgeous blue eyes, remembering our lovely time together last evening before he left to pick up Chad. "I hope so."

He raised his eyebrows.

"I was trying to let things go after we talked last night." The dumb tears welled again. I wasn't usually much of a crier. "But then Wayne came in a little while ago and got me all worked up again."

Todd muttered something under his breath. "People are afraid, Callie. No one wants to think there's a murderer on the loose in Short Creek, so they're calling the station and posting all kinds of crazy stuff on social media. It's a lot for Wayne to try to deal with, even with the help from the Temple PD. He's not used to having the spotlight on him and his department."

"I know. That's why I offered to help him."

He choked. "What?"

"I offered to help find out more information about Penny and Dr. Smythe."

Todd shook his head. "Absolutely not. We had a couple more leads come in today and the detectives are working on this case almost round the clock. We'll get a break soon."

CHAPTER ELEVEN

"I hope so." I picked a dog hair off my jeans. "I keep trying to stay out of it, but it's hard to shut my brain off once I start thinking about everything."

"I know. You'd make a good detective."

"You think so?" I never expected him to admit such a thing.

"Unfortunately, yes." He growled and pulled me toward him again, his intense gaze half- frustrated, half-inviting. "But don't get any crazy ideas. I don't want a colleague. I want a wi—"

"Hey, you two!" Harry appeared at Todd's elbow, balancing two jelly donuts on a napkin. "Come join the party!"

Nice timing.

I sighed. Maybe one of these days Todd and I would have some uninterrupted time to dedicate to our relationship.

"We're coming," I said to Harry, threading my fingers through Todd's and tugging him toward our friends. "I need to at least talk to Houston about what he saw the morning the roses disappeared," I murmured.

Todd stopped. "Callie. I'm serious. It is not your job to solve this case. Can you at least let it go for now and enjoy the party?"

One peek at his face showed me how adamant he was.

"Sure." I would try.

And I did. I truly did. But somewhere between sampling Mona's beans, joking with Harry, and kissing Todd goodbye, I decided I needed to have a little chat with Boranda Stiegler about the roses she brought to the crime scene. And then I'd call Houston.

As it turned out, I didn't need to call Houston. He hung around after the party as if sensing I needed to talk to him. "I hope you had a great birthday, Houston." I smiled at him as I pitched the last of the baked beans into the trash.

"It was a memorable time. I was hoping Nicole would have

been able to make it."

"Me too. But she'll be around a lot more now that she'll be working at Hope House."

He nodded. "Can I show you something?"

I stopped wiping the counter and truly looked at him. He had a glint in his eye that I'd never seen before. Hmm. I bet I could guess what he was going to show me, but I didn't want to steal his thunder. I grinned at him. "Of course."

He pulled a ring box out of his pocket and opened it with a trembling hand. "I'm going to do it, Callie. I'm going to ask her to marry me."

I swallowed against the sudden tightening of my throat. Nicole was going to be one happy girl. "I'm thrilled for you. It's been a long road."

"Longer than I ever thought." He snapped the box closed. "But God has worked so much healing in her—in us. Thank you for your prayers. You'll never know how much it meant to me to know you and your prayer group were holding us up in prayer for all this time."

"My pleasure. And we will continue." I squeezed his forearm. "When are you going to pop the question?"

He shrugged and smiled. "Soon."

"Come on. I wouldn't spill the beans."

He pressed his lips together and shook his head. "My lips are sealed."

"Oh, all right." I heaved an exaggerated sigh. "I guess I'll find out on social media."

"Nope. That's tacky."

"Agreed. And hey, since we have a minute, can you tell me again what you saw the day my rose bushes were stolen?"

He wrinkled his forehead. "Not much, except for the branch falling on my head."

"Yes, but you said something like 'I almost saw who did it.'"

"I did?" He pursed his lips. "Maybe I was more dazed than I thought."

Argh. I was hoping he'd be able to give me at least a little information about that morning.

He stood silent for a long minute, staring out the window at the pecan tree, then shook his head. "I'm sorry, Callie. I can't remember anything other than what I already told you."

Rats. Another dead end. "It's okay. If you can't, you can't. We'll get it figured out." Somehow. Maybe Boranda had something to tell me. I sighed.

After the first and only time Boranda cut my hair, many moons ago, I had vowed never to let her touch my head again. Not that I was a fashion model, but I liked my hair the way I liked it—straight and brown. She had somehow convinced me to add layers and bangs. Bangs! I hadn't had bangs since seventh grade, and they hadn't looked any better on me at thirty-three years old than they had at thirteen.

But I had to have a reason for visiting her salon, or she might become suspicious when I started asking her questions.

Hmm. Eyebrows?

Nope, too visible. What if she tried something new, and I ended up with weird eyebrows for a couple of months?

Nails? I might be able to deal with her doing my nails. Maybe a pedicure. Then if she messed it up, I could wear socks for a month. I often had cold feet anyway, especially when it came to Boranda's dubious salon services.

Ha ha. I chuckled at my own weak joke as I dialed her number.

But I wasn't laughing when I walked into her salon the next day and saw her face. Her heavily lined eyes were puffy, and a huge purple bruise marred her left cheek. I had never seen her look so terrible. Even her normally sleek, blonde updo was disheveled.

"Bo. What happened?"

"Oh, hi, Callie." She laughed and patted her face. "Doesn't it look awful? I tripped over the dog yesterday and did a face-plant into the edge of the counter."

"Wow. It looks painful."

She shrugged. "It looks worse than it feels."

"I hope so. Are you sure you're up to having customers today?" I wasn't the most observant person in the world, but even I noticed her hands shaking.

"Of course. I have to keep my business going, even if I look like a freak." Here she attempted another little laugh. "I'm fine."

I wasn't convinced, but obeyed as she waved me to the pedicure chair. I stepped out of my flip-flops. "Really. I can reschedule—"

"No!"

I jumped.

"I mean, no, you're fine." She bent to turn the water on, but not before I caught the glint of tears in her eyes. "I can't afford to take the day off."

Ah. I see.

I slipped both feet into the warm, fragrant water and settled into the chair, deciding not to press anymore. I had come looking for clues about the murder, but perhaps God had other plans for today. Clearly, Bo's pain went much deeper than the bruise on her face.

Holy Spirit, please guide me. Is there something You'd like me to do? Do you have something You would have me say to Bo?

I closed my eyes as the water swirled around my calves.

Tell her I love her.

I squirmed as Bo ran a pumice stone over the bottom of my foot.

She already knows that, Lord. I know she goes to Houston's church sometimes. I think she even sings in the choir and—

Tell her I love her and I am pleased with her.

That's it? I was thinking God was going to give me a profound message or special insight into her life.

I opened my eyes. "Bo, I was praying for you while I was sitting here, and God told me to tell you He loves you and is pleased with you."

Her hands stilled, and she slowly lifted her head to look me in the eye. "He did?"

I nodded, watching as her face crumpled.

"Thank you, Jesus. Thank you, Jesus." She turned away, snatching a tissue from the box in her workstation. She dabbed at her eyes and blew her nose before turning back to me. "You don't know how much that means to me. I've been so desperate. This thing is the hardest thing I've ever been through, and some days I don't think I can make it."

I had no idea what she was talking about, but I made comforting noises as I nodded my head.

"This morning I was praying—" Here fresh tears welled and she paused. "I was feeling so alone and discouraged. I begged God to show me He cared by having someone tell me they were praying for me. Or that they love me."

"He heard your prayer, then, didn't He?"

She nodded and blew her nose again. "I'm sorry. I didn't mean to get so emotional. Here you're paying for a pedicure and I'm letting my personal issues interfere."

"Please don't worry about that." I hesitated, not wanting to pry, but she had talked like she thought I already knew what she was referring to. "I don't know what's going on in your life at all, but I'm glad God does. I'll keep praying for you."

She picked up a bottle of green goop and squeezed out a generous amount on my left shin. "Jake and I are getting divorced."

I was shocked. They had only been married, what, two or three years? They seemed like a perfect couple whenever I saw them around town. "I'm sorry to hear that."

She shrugged. "I thought you knew. It's not like it's a secret anymore."

"I'm so sorry," I repeated.

"I am too." She scrubbed my calf with the gritty green goo until I thought my skin was going to peel off. "And I owe you an apology." She looked up at me.

"Me? Why?" I couldn't imagine anything Boranda had ever done to me that would require an apology, except The Haircut.

She sat back and dried her hands. "You know that day right after Ginger died? When I saw you and Mona in Sherm's yard?"

I held my breath and nodded. Boy, did I ever.

"I didn't know her very well, but I guess my own suffering has made me more tuned in to other people's, you know?"

Actually, I did know. I nodded.

"I wanted to do something to express my sadness over her

death, and I guess I feel kind of silly admitting this now, but those roses I brought?"

I sucked in my breath.

"Jake had given them to me after one of his apologies. I don't have a lot of extra money to buy things like flowers, and they were so beautiful I hated to throw them out, even though I was still furious with Jake." She glanced away, then met my gaze again. "I didn't know then where he got them. I guess I assumed he bought them somewhere, but Mona was in the other day for her highlights and told me the whole story of your rosebushes. I should have talked to you about it before now, but I was so embarrassed that I had given second-hand roses to begin with, and then to think that maybe Jake stole them from you...I'm hoping they were ones that looked like yours and that he didn't have anything to do with stealing your bushes. I'm so sorry."

No, I was the one who was sorry. I shook my head. How had I ever suspected Bo of murder? True, she had seemed kind of catty that day, but now I realized she was probably having a hard time dealing with her own issues.

"No worries. It's not your fault."

I was a hypocrite. I was so concerned about clearing my own name and dealing with the inconveniences of being involved in an investigation that I had let my imagination run away with me and thought up terrible things about people who were my neighbors and friends. Worse, I hadn't taken the time to ask God what He thought about all of this. I simply pushed my way ahead like a stubborn...a stubborn fool.

"Be more anxious to learn the lesson than to get rid of the problem," I murmured.

"What?"

I shook my head. "Something I read in my devotional the other day. Here, I'll look it up online." I pulled out my phone. "It's from *Streams in the Desert*. It says, '...let us be more careful to learn all the lessons in the school of sorrow than we are anxious for the hour of deliverance."

"Wow, that's good." She reached down into the water to pull the plug. "Is that how you're making it through the Slayton situation?"

What? I frowned.

She pushed her hair back. "I mean, I've heard people saying you had something to do with it. I've been praying the real murderer will be found."

I was a worm. Beyond humbled. I had come into Bo's salon to pump her for information, and she'd been praying for me.

"Thank you so much. It's been a little rough." But based on her bruised cheek, not as rough as dealing with a violent almost-ex-husband, I was sure. "I guess we should keep praying for each other. God will see us both through one day at a time."

"It's a deal, friend." She flashed me a true smile then, right before she pulled out the bottle of neon purple nail polish. With glitter.

CHAPTER TWELVE

I know I could have voiced an opinion over the nail polish color, but at that point, if Bo had wanted to paint my nails orange with blue spots, I would have let her. As I climbed into my van, I glanced down at my toes again and giggled. Mona would have a fit when she saw them. Speaking of Mona, I wondered what else and who else she had talked to about Ginger's case. She was my best friend, but sometimes she didn't use a whole lot of wisdom when it came to things like that.

I dug in my purse for my phone and found it right as it rang. I didn't recognize the number, but answered it anyway, hoping it wasn't a nosy reporter.

"This is Callie."

"Hello, Ms. Erickson. This is Amity Shoenwell with Heart of Africa Missions. I'm calling concerning your parents, Jerry and Bettina Williamson. Have you been in contact with them in the last day or two, by any chance?"

My chest constricted. Why would my parents' missionary organization be calling me to check up on them?

"No, I haven't. Is everything okay?"

"We hope so. You were aware that they were planning to travel back to the States shortly?"

"Yes, but I—"

"Their colleagues in Zambia alerted us this morning that they did not show up for their last staff meeting and have not been in contact with anyone for the last two days."

I stared out my windshield at the brown lawn of Bo's salon. "What could have happened? Has anyone checked their flat?"

"We're looking into it right now, but have been unable to confirm anything yet. I'm very sorry. As you know, communication can be pretty sketchy in third-world countries." She cleared her throat. "At this point, we are concerned, but not alarmed. It is not uncommon for our workers to sometimes be in a...situation...where they are unable to communicate for a few days."

Still. My parents always assured me that they felt quite safe in their area of rural Zambia.

Jesus? I need You.

I cleared my throat. "Will you keep me informed?"

"Of course. And please know all of us here in the Des Moines office are praying for you and your family."

"Thank you." I laid the phone on my lap, heaving out a sigh, then snatched it up again. Maybe it was all a mistake. My parents were busy people, and as the woman said, communication to and from Zambia was not always reliable.

Or maybe my mom dropped her phone and broke it. Or let the battery run out. I snorted. Knowing my mother, the likelihood of either of those things happening was next to nothing. But I could at least try.

Oh, Mom. She had tried to call me—what? A few days ago? And I had never bothered to call her back. *Please don't let it be too late.* I touched my mother's number and held my breath while it rang. And rang. *Come on, Lord. Please let her answer.* Nothing. Not even a voicemail message. I blew out my breath and dashed off a text to first her phone, then my dad's.

Are you two okay? Please call me. I love you.

My parents were missing. In Africa.

The enormity of the situation struck me, and I squeezed my hands together. It was one thing to be missing in America, where we had police and real-time communication, and the latest technology. It was another thing to be missing in Africa. I hadn't felt this helpless since the day my brother Jason had been sentenced to prison.

Should I fly to Zambia and try to find them myself? I didn't even know what I would need to travel to Zambia. At the very least I would need a passport, I supposed. I had let mine expire a couple of months ago, so chances are it would take weeks or even months for me to obtain a new one.

What had happened to my parents?

Probably nothing.

True, missing a staff meeting would be out of character for them, but I knew they often traveled to the outlying areas in their ancient Jeep. If the vehicle broke down somewhere out in the bush, there wouldn't be a way for them to contact anyone. Which didn't necessarily mean they were in dire straits. By all accounts, my parents were well-loved by the people in the area.

But still. I scrolled through my texts again, knowing what I would find. Nothing. I hadn't had a call or text from either of them in the last five days. And the voicemail my mom had left then, I had ignored, planning to get back with her when I wasn't so busy. But I hadn't, and now…

God, please forgive me. What if something terrible had happened to them? What if I never saw them again?

I called Todd, but he didn't answer. I needed to discuss this with someone. Now.

I headed toward Willowbough, hoping Aunt Dot wasn't tied up with her Bible study group. Or was today her pottery class?

Five minutes later, I pushed through the double doors into the familiar bright entryway. I waved at the receptionist, groaning as I saw the unhappy employee who had loudly accused me of Ginger's murder the last time I was here. Not what I needed right now. Maybe if I kept walking—

"Hey, Callie!" She smiled at me across her cart of food trays. "Coming to visit Dot?"

I raised my eyebrows. Was this the same woman who had practically accosted me last time? Maybe she was being extra nice so she wouldn't lose her job. "Hey, there." What was her name? Vivian? Valerie? I tried for a smile as I skirted her cart. "Yep. I try to see her as often as I can."

"She's a real sweet lady." She dug around in the pocket of her purple scrubs and held up a battered photo. "I don't have much family, but these are my kids."

I glanced at the picture of the two teenagers, a boy and a girl, posing in front of a house. A golden Lab lay on the lawn in front of the kids. "Lovely family." I backed away.

"Have a good visit," she called down the hall to me. "You're lucky to have your aunt."

I sighed. Apparently, the woman wanted to be my friend

now.

Be nice, Callie. She's probably lonely. I turned and waved at her. "See you later."

She waved back and disappeared around the corner.

Yes, I was blessed to have Aunt Dot in my life, I reflected as I knocked lightly on her door. "It's me, Auntie," I called as I pushed it open.

"Well, you're a sight for sore eyes." Aunt Dot grinned at me from her wheelchair. "I didn't expect I'd get to see you today. You look a little less stressed than the last time I saw you."

I do? I grasped her extended hand and bent to kiss her on her rose-petal cheek. Maybe I shouldn't tell her about my parents' situation. I didn't want to worry her unduly, especially since I didn't know yet whether or not anything was truly amiss. "I had a pedicure at Bo's this morning."

"Really." She peered at me, then my feet, over her reading glasses as she picked up her crochet hook. "Quite a flashy color. I didn't know you enjoyed pedicures."

"I've had a few before. They are pretty relaxing." I flushed. I might as well tell the truth, because she'd pry it out of me, anyway. "Truthfully, I only scheduled a pedicure with Bo because I wanted to ask her about the roses."

She nodded. "And what did you find out?"

That I'm a prideful fool.

I picked a skein of merino wool out of Aunt Dot's basket and inspected it. "Bo and Jake are getting a divorce."

"Oh, my. I'm sorry to hear that."

"Me too. She had a huge bruise on the side of her face. She said she tripped over the dog and hit her cheek on the counter, but..."

Aunt Dot sucked in her breath. "Oh, I'd hate to think it."

"I know." I fiddled with the yarn skein. "She said Jake had given her those roses and she didn't know where they came from."

"Do you believe that?"

"I don't know. I believe her, but if Jake is such a snake, then who knows if he was telling the truth or not?"

"Well, I never did suspect Boranda of having anything to

do with Ginger's death. Bo's a little flaky sometimes, but she's as genuine as they come. Now, that Jake, I'm not so sure about. I've heard he's been in on some questionable business deals. He's in financing, isn't he?"

I shrugged. "I don't know what he does." Other than steal rosebushes in the middle of the night. I couldn't prove it was Jake, but I still couldn't get over the thought. I mean, who does that? If he would hit his wife, why couldn't he be a thief too?

"Well, I'll certainly put both of them on my prayer list. It's a shame the way marriage is taken so lightly these days." Aunt Dot sighed and held up the rainbow-colored baby afghan she was working on. "Isn't this a fun pattern?"

"Very pretty." I glanced surreptitiously at my phone, hoping Mom had texted. Nothing. Except a text from Mona with a picture of the wedding dress. I turned my screen off and refocused on Aunt Dot. "Who's having a baby? Anyone I know?"

"No. But the local pregnancy center always loves to have folks donate handmade items. They give them to the new mammas who need them."

"Nice." I cleared my throat. "I have something else we need to pray about."

She straightened up, her handwork forgotten. "I sensed you had something on your mind."

"Yeah. A woman from Mom and Dad's organization called a little while ago to check if I had heard anything from them in the last few days."

"Oh? And had you?"

"No. She said one of their colleagues alerted them this morning that no one has seen them or heard from them in the last two days."

Her hand flew to her throat. "Is she saying they're missing?"

"No, not exactly. In fact, she didn't seem super alarmed. Just wanted me to try to get ahold of them." I held up my phone. "I've texted them both and tried to call them both, but no response yet."

"Hmm. Not too surprising, given what time it is there." She

squared her shoulders, a familiar gleam lighting her eyes. "Our God knows exactly where they are. Did you let everyone at prayer group know about this yet? We need to get on this."

I smiled in spite of the fear in my heart. "I want to be like you when I grow up."

She shook her head. "I've told you this before, darlin'. You can't give up before the fight begins. A long time ago, I asked Father God to give me a love for the battle."

"Back to the 'life is an adventure' theme, huh?"

She grinned at me. "Never a dull moment. Now, hand me my phone so I can text Harry. That man is a praying machine."

I could testify to that. I watched as she texted Harry. They were so cute together.

Speaking of which... "My bridesmaid dress finally fits. I was beginning to wonder if the seamstress would have it done in time for the wedding."

"You're looking a little thin. Are you eating enough?"

Good. She didn't fuss at me again about changing the wedding date. "I am eating. I even had Mona over for lunch the other day. And Todd and I are going out for dinner tonight, hopefully. We're going to try the new Mexican restaurant."

"I'm glad to hear that. Give him a squeeze for me." She pinned me with her gaze. "Now. We have some serious warfare to do, young lady. Are you ready?"

CHAPTER THIRTEEN

"Whew." An hour later, I stood and stretched. "That was powerful prayer." And not quiet, either. Thankfully, the elderly woman in the apartment next to Aunt Dot's was quite deaf, otherwise we might have had Vicious Valerie or Veronica or whatever her name was, giving us a lecture.

Aunt Dot steepled her hands under her chin and sat unmoving for a long moment, as if she needed time to switch back to normal conversation. Her face betrayed her weariness, but her voice was strong. "Yes. I know your parents will be all right, but remember that we walk by faith, not by sight. Even if things get crazier, keep your focus on Him."

I bent over to hug her. "I will."

But some things are easier said than done. As the hours wore on and I still hadn't had any communication from my parents, I found myself pacing around my shop, Annie trailing behind me step for step.

Finally, Mona bustled through the door, Todd on her heels. "Any news?"

Todd took one look at my face. "I'm sorry, honey. I've been praying."

"Me too. It's frustrating to be thousands of miles away."

"We have to remember that none of this took God by surprise. He is still in control."

"I know. But it's still difficult."

"I know. I'm sorry." He pulled me into a brief hug. "I can't stay long. Why don't you call your contact at the mission agency for an update? I'd like to hear what's happening before I have to head back to the city offices."

"Oh, I thought you were off for the rest of the day." I reached for my phone, my stomach suddenly one big knot. At this point, no news was probably still good news. I drew a deep breath. "I'll call her now."

She answered on the fifth ring. "Amity Shoenwell. May I

help you?" Her professional tone dissolved as soon as I gave her my name. "Oh, Miss Erickson. I'm so sorry. We still have no concrete information about your parents."

I grimaced and shook my head at Todd and Mona before continuing the conversation.

"What about their fellow missionaries? No one has seen them at all?"

"Ask what their agency is doing to find them," Todd whispered to me.

"Yes, I see. That's understandable. And, uh, what is your agency doing to help find them?" I grabbed a pen and paper, scribbling down a couple of names and phone numbers. "I see. Should I call them today? Okay. I'll be in touch."

I laid the phone down on the counter, wishing I had better news—any news—to relay. I plucked a skein of pink angora yarn out of the basket on the counter and stroked the fuzzy softness. "She says it's good that there's been no demand for ransom."

Mona snorted. "That's the good news? What kind of wacka-doodle organization is this?"

"Mona—" Todd had his police officer face on. "What else did she say?"

"Not much. Um, and if it is something like a kidnapping, the ransom note is usually sent within the first twenty-four to forty-eight hours. So, if there hasn't been one yet..."

Todd growled. "That's less than helpful. No sightings of them? No communication? Has anyone contacted the embassy?"

"Apparently a couple of their fellow missionaries are out searching for them in the outlying areas. And the mission agency has been in touch with the American embassy, but not until this morning."

"Why not?" Mona planted her hands on her ample hips. "We need to start bombarding these people with phone calls and emails until they do something, Callie. Are you going to fly over there? We could all pitch in and help you. I bet plane tickets to Zimbabwe are super expensive."

"Zambia." I was touched that my friends cared so much,

but I sensed that I needed to proceed with utmost caution. "Let's just say that the mission agency is encouraging me strongly not to try to go over there. And as much as I wish I could, I can't force something to happen. God knows where my parents are."

"How can you be so calm?" Mona's gold hoop earrings quivered, matching her voice. "These are your parents. If my parents were lost in the jungle somewhere, I'd be on the first plane over there. Who cares what the head honcho mission lady says?"

Mona's question stabbed me in the heart. Why was I so calm? Was it because I didn't love them enough?

I couldn't count how many times I had wrestled with self-recrimination for my tendency toward holding myself aloof in relationships, especially after my husband Kevin's car accident. We hadn't had a great marriage to begin with, and I had mourned for years that I hadn't loved him as well or as deeply as I should have. "I—"

But no. God had freed me from that. I wasn't going to go there anymore. And if I had learned anything during all the craziness last year with Houston and the sex trafficking ring and that whole big mess, it was that I could trust in God's unfailing love and mercy. He could and would grant me peace in the midst of the storm.

"I know they're alive, Mona. And I know God was not surprised by any of this, as Todd reminded me." I shrugged. "I have to rest in that."

Todd wrapped his arm around my shoulder. "I agree. At this point, it will be more helpful for everyone involved for Callie to stay put and do what she can stateside. We don't need her to be in danger too."

Todd was headed over to pick me up for dinner, but I wasn't sure I'd be able to enjoy myself, even though we were going to try the new Mexican restaurant in Belton. I glanced at my sparkly purple toenails and headed into the house to change into close-toed shoes. I was used to my flashy toes by now, but

Todd hadn't seen them yet and if he did, he'd never let me live them down. Not that he minded what color I painted my toenails, but purple sparkles were so out of character for me—the original Plain Jane—that he wouldn't be able to resist teasing me.

He still hadn't arrived, so I wandered out into the back yard, Annie trotting after me. Two Inca doves, smaller and with more ruffly feathers than common white-winged doves, perched on the edge of the birdbath, fluttering away as I approached with the hose. I tipped the concrete basin to drain the old water, then refilled it with an inch or two of clean water before hosing off the bird seed shells that littered the stone pavers beneath the bird feeder.

Wait. What was that? I lay the hose down and bent to pick up what looked like a dime lying on the paver.

"Eew!" I dropped it and wiped my fingers on my jeans. I wasn't sure what it was, but it wasn't a dime. I thought maybe it was the round, silver part from a fishing lure—complete with dried worm still stuck to it. How had that gotten into my yard?

Annie sniffed at it, then yipped and ran to greet Todd as he appeared at my side gate. "There you two are."

He leaned down to Annie, and I listened to him sweet-talk her while she danced around his legs.

"Hey, there." I skirted the dog and smiled up at him. His ever-present A & M ballcap, deep blue eyes, and familiar grin never failed to cause my heart to skip a beat.

He ran a hand down my cheek, his warm gaze searching my face. "How are you? Any news?"

"No." I stepped into his embrace. "Nothing."

"Aww, I'm sorry, honey." He held me against his chest. "I hope you hear something soon."

"Me too." I pulled away to look up at him and slipped my hand into his. We headed toward the truck in silence, until I voiced what I hadn't wanted to suggest to Aunt Dot—or Mona. "What if they've been kidnapped by some crazy terrorist group?"

Todd stroked Annie's back, staring out across the lawn,

and I watched as he switched from boyfriend mode to cop mode. "I don't think you should jump to any conclusions yet. Maybe they had to travel somewhere where there is no communication infrastructure." He turned to look at me. "What do you know about their travel plans?"

I leaned against the side of his pickup. The hot metal warmed my back, but did nothing to lessen the chill of fear in my heart. "Unless something changed, I know they were planning to leave Zambia early next week. They were scheduled to fly into Des Moines because they're required to spend a few days there debriefing before they can come down here."

"But this morning was the first time you knew about this, right?"

"Yes." I wound a strand of my hair around my finger. "I tried to call my mom right when I got off the phone with the woman from the agency, but there was no answer. I also texted, but texts don't always go through immediately, so she might not have even received it yet."

"What about your dad? Just in case they're not together."

I winced at the idea. "I've sent them both, like, a hundred texts."

"It won't hurt to keep trying." Todd's eyes narrowed, and he leaned his shoulder against the side of the truck cab, his arms crossed. "Did you verify that the woman who spoke to you was legit?"

I raised my eyebrows. The thought had never crossed my mind. "You were there when I talked to her on the phone earlier. Why would someone call me and pretend to be from my parents' missionary agency? That seems pretty far-fetched."

He shrugged. "Maybe to distract you?"

"Distract me from what?" I squinted at him. Surely, he wasn't suggesting this whole thing was connected to the Ginger Slayton accusations. I felt the blood drain from my face. "Are you saying someone is trying to make me worried about my parents so I stop thinking about Ginger's murder?"

"Someone killed her, sweetheart. And if that someone is

still in town..." He shook his head. "You have been doing a fair amount of snooping around despite me asking you to stay out of it. I might as well have saved my breath on that one."

I grimaced. "I'm trying, but stuff keeps coming up and I get sucked into thinking about it again. But seriously. The thought that maybe I've made the real killer nervous is creepy. And who could it be?" I pushed my glasses up higher on my nose. "I've thought of a bunch of different people, but I truly can't see any of them actually doing it."

He pulled his cap off and resettled it. "Too much speculation on an empty stomach. Let's go eat and try to get our minds off of things for a little while. You need a break."

Dinner sounded like a great idea until we walked into the restaurant. It looked like everyone and his brother were trying the new place in town.

"Todd." I clutched his arm. "Don't look now, but Dr. Smythe is sitting over there with Jake. At the corner table by the bar."

"Two, please." Todd smiled at the hostess, then darted a quick glance in the direction I had indicated as we sat down in the crowded waiting area. "Jake who?"

"Boranda's husband. Jake Haskell." I had already filled Todd in about what Boranda told me about her soon-to-be ex-husband. "What if Dr. Smythe and Jake are working together secretly?"

Could the two men have teamed up to kill Ginger? And if so, why?

"Callie." Todd waited until I looked at him. He squeezed my hand. "Please let it go for the evening, honey. We were supposed to be relaxing together, remember?"

He was right. I needed to stop suspecting everyone. But how did Dr. Smythe and Jake know each other?

"Aunt Dot said she thought Jake worked for some kind of financial planning company or something," I murmured.

Todd growled.

"Okay. I'm done talking about it. I promise." I grabbed a

menu and, with effort, kept my gaze from the corner table. "I'm going to try the chiles rellenos. I hope they're the kind with crispy batter. The eggy-battered ones kind of gross me out."

Between glancing at my phone every five minutes to make sure I hadn't missed a text from my parents and keeping tabs on the two men at the corner table, I'm sure I wasn't a very attentive dinner partner. But the food was good.

"How are your chicken enchiladas?" I dabbed at my mouth with my napkin.

"Not as good as yours, but for restaurant food, they're pretty decent."

"I'll have to make them for you again sometime." I scraped my leftovers into a to-go box, then turned, feeling the weight of someone's gaze on my back. Dr. Smythe smiled and winked at me across the noisy room before turning his attention to Jake again. I gulped. "The man is a weirdo even if he didn't kill anyone."

Todd laughed, his usual good humor restored now that he had eaten. "He is kind of an odd bird. But he must have some redeeming qualities since Penny is so smitten with him."

"Yeah, I guess." I thought of something I'd been meaning to tell Todd. "Did I tell you that a reporter for the *CenTex Courier* interviewed me for the magazine a few days ago?"

His eyebrows shot up. "About the Ginger Slayton case? Callie, you know you shouldn't talk to anyone from the press about this right now. Please tell me you didn't."

"No, not about Ginger. This gal is doing a story on some of the local businesses in Short Creek. She interviewed Wormy, too. That's where I met her. Her name was Carly something or other."

He looked relieved. "Good for you. Sounds like great publicity for your business. Is she featuring other businesses besides C. Willikers and the Donut Hut?"

"I don't know. I thought she said something about the new dentist office, too, but I might have made that up." My gaze strayed to the back booth again.

"I'm proud of you, honey. Callie Erickson, business owner

extraordinaire. I'll hang a copy of the article on the wall in my office." Todd grinned at me and pushed his chair away from the table. "Are you ready to go?"

We stood just as Mr. Creepy Dentist and Jake the Snake swaggered up to us. "Deputy Whitney. Callie. Out on a hot date?" Dr. Smythe flashed his toothy smile.

"No, only mild for me." I gestured to my take-out box, proud of my witty comeback.

Jake snorted. "You stepped into that one, Smythe." He held his hand out to me. "Jake Haskell. I'm not sure we've ever formally met."

"I don't think so. But I've seen you around town, of course."

With your wife, Bo.

I managed a small smile as I took his hand briefly. Was this the hand that dug up my rosebushes? "Have you met Todd?"

While the men shook hands, I turned to Dr. Smythe. "Left Penny at home tonight?"

He started, then covered with a cough. "She never was at *my* home, if you know what I mean."

No, not really. Why don't you explain it, Dr. Smythe?

I squinted at him. "Oh, really? She made it sound like y'all were an item, if you know what I mean."

His face reddened as Jake guffawed and slapped him on the back. "Me and the doc here have sworn off women, haven't we, Griff?"

"Wow, that's pretty drastic." I smiled sweetly at both of the men, ignoring Todd's warning grip on my arm. "How do you two know one another? Oh, I bet from the gardening club."

I doubted either of them cared a fig about gardening, but maybe they cared about covering for themselves if they were the murderers.

Dr. Smythe grimaced. "I've heard all I've ever wanted to know about gardening clubs since Ginger Slayton kicked the bucket, but Jake might be able to tell you a thing or two. He does landscaping in his spare time."

Aha.

"Really." I swung around to face Jake. "I saw the gorgeous roses you gave Bo. Amazing. Where did you find such unique roses? And so many of them? Because I'm a florist, you know. I like to know who my competitors are."

I was on a roll. Mona would be proud. Todd, on the other hand, was glaring at me.

"Sorry. I don't remember." Jake pushed past Todd and me, his arm brushing mine none too gently. "Let's hit the road, Griff. I'm tired of twenty questions."

Dr. Smythe leaned in close enough for me to smell the garlic on his breath. "I'd be careful if I were you, Miss Erickson. I've learned that some folks around Short Creek don't take kindly to Nosy Nellies. And in case you're asking, I happen to know exactly where Jake was the night Ginger was killed. But it seems everyone is not so sure where *you* were that night, hmm?"

Todd stiffened. "I'm not liking your tone, Doctor."

"Merely a friendly observation, Deputy." The older man flashed his slimy smile. "Let's just say my friend Jake has a short fuse. It's best if everyone knows that at the get-go."

CHAPTER fOURTEEN

At the get-go of what?

"Wow." I backed into Todd's chest as Dr. Smythe strolled out of the restaurant. "Only a tiny bit suspicious."

Todd flexed his jaw. "I don't know what I'm going to do with you, Callie. Were you purposely trying to irritate them?"

"No, of course not. You know me better than that." I dug around in my purse for my phone. "I simply wanted to know how they knew each other."

"And you had to throw in the roses."

"You said I was a good detective." I patted his cheek.

He groaned. "I knew that would come back to bite me."

I gave him my best flirty smile and looped my arm through his. "Want to go get ice cream and talk strategy?"

"You, my dear, are incorrigible." He shook his head before bending to kiss me. "I'm sure I'll regret this at some point," he murmured. "But I'm no fool. If you can't beat 'em, join 'em."

Yesss. Now we're talkin'.

It was while we still sat at Temple Two-Scoops, sharing a chocolate-raspberry double-fudge brownie ice cream cone that I got the text from my dad.

"My dad says they're fine." I blew out a long breath, feeling a huge weight lift off my heart. "Thank you, Jesus. Thank you, Father God."

"What happened? Why were they out of contact so long?"

I scanned the short text again. "He says he'll call and explain later, but their truck broke down somewhere out in the bush, and they had, in his words, 'quite an adventure' getting back to civilization." I took a sip of ice water. "He says they are fine but exhausted and are sorry everyone was so worried. He wants me to tell Aunt Dot. But I wonder why my mom didn't text me? Dad usually lets her handle the communication. That's a little unusual."

Oh, well. Maybe Mom's phone wasn't charged. I dialed

Aunt Dot's number, mindlessly watching Todd finish the rest of the waffle cone while I delivered the great news to my aunt.

"Aunt Dot is so excited. Thank God. I never want to have to go through something like that again."

Todd nodded. "It's crazy how your perspective on relationships change when you're in a crisis. Thankfully, yours ended well. Some don't."

"Yes, I know." I thought of Ginger Slayton's family, if she had one, working through the unexpected death of their loved one. I sighed. "Do you think Jake could be involved?"

"With the Slayton case?" He rubbed his hand down his cheek. "I don't think we can rule anyone out at this moment."

"Does that mean yes?"

He shrugged. "I don't know. But it's worth keeping in mind. He's not lived in Short Creek very long. Didn't he move from back East somewhere before he and Bo got married?

"I don't remember. But I could find out," I said teasingly.

"No, ma'am. I didn't like how he reacted to your questioning." He tapped his fingers on the tabletop. "How about if you leave Jake to me? I can easily run a background check on him."

"Good idea. I'll keep working the other angles. I think I need to talk to Penny again." I stood, feeling lighter. God had protected my parents, and He would help me in this situation too. "And now I know my parents are safe, I hopefully can concentrate on finishing up the wedding details. Dad says they're still flying in next week as planned. Can you believe the wedding is next weekend?"

"I'm sure it's felt like forever to Harry. He wanted the wedding to be the same day he proposed." Todd chuckled.

I raised an eyebrow. "Is that a guy thing?"

He choked on his iced tea, and I pretended to pout. "A wedding is one of the most important days of a woman's life. These things take time to plan, you know."

"I know." He pulled me down into his lap and whispered into my ear. "Our time is coming, Callie. I promise."

Todd's words popped into my thoughts at the most random times over the next few days. We had talked about marriage more than once, but were both committed to taking it slow. However, there was a marked difference in "slow" and "barely moving," as I commented to Sharlene one morning at C. Willikers.

"I thought for sure he'd propose on Valentine's Day." I poked a stem of yellow gladiola into the funeral arrangement I was working on, then stood back to look at it. "But here it is almost Memorial Day and no ring."

Sharlene snickered. "I hear Mona found you a dress."

"So I've heard." I rolled my eyes.

"Don't you even want to go see it?"

Yes, of course I wanted to go see it. In fact, I had gone and seen it. Twice, to be exact. It was a lovely champagne-colored ball gown with a fitted waist and lot of lace. I had fallen in love with it immediately. But that was no one else's business.

Sharlene emptied the dustpan into the trash and grinned at me. "Maybe Todd's taking his time because he's planning something, like, super cool."

"Like what?" I dried my hands on my apron. "I'm not exactly the type to jump out of an airplane or go scuba diving. Just a plain ol' proposal would be fine. What is he waiting for?"

She shook her head. "You're boring, Callie. If I had a boyfriend and I knew he was going to ask me to marry him, I'd do whatever the man wanted."

Right. Okay, Lord. Once again, the focus was on me. I sighed. "I know you're praying for a husband. God will bring you the perfect guy when it's the right time for both of you."

Now it was her turn to sigh. "I hope so. And not someone else's husband, either. Do you know Jake Haskell? Bo's husband?" She made a face. "Their divorce isn't even final yet. He tried to hit on me the other day while I rang him up."

What?

"Jake Haskell was here in the store?"

"Yep." She pushed her thin blonde hair over her shoulder.

"Tromped around looking at everything for the longest time, then bought a book or something. I can't remember."

"Really." I slumped onto the stool in front of the counter. "You know Dr. Smythe? Todd and I saw him and Jake together at the Mexican restaurant the other night. I don't think I'd like to get on Jake's bad side."

She shivered. "Me, neither. He's pretty easy on the eyes, but I've dated a couple of guys like him before. They act, like, all nice and everything to get you to do what they want, but they're really mean people inside."

I had a hunch that Jake was more than "mean." Even in the short time I had interacted with him at the restaurant, I had sensed an edge of cruelty under his suave demeanor. "I'm glad you didn't encourage him. Did he mention anything about me?"

"Nope. Just talked about how he had a bunch of landscaping jobs to do, and he wanted to see if you had any bedding plants since he'd never been in here before. Here, I think I saved his card." She dug through a pile of paperwork under the counter and emerged with the business card.

I scanned the card. *TemBel Garden Design and Landscaping. Owner, Jim Slayton.* I gasped. "Sharlene, this is Ginger Slayton's ex-husband's business. Jake works for Ginger's ex?"

We stared at each other.

"I was already suspicious of Jake. But now..." I blew out my breath. "Wait a minute. If he is a financial guy, why is he doing landscaping?"

"Maybe he needs extra cash?"

Hmm. "Or maybe he likes digging holes. Maybe he dug out my rosebushes planning to bury Ginger there."

Sharlene rolled her eyes. "Dr. Smythe kills them and Jake buries them? That seems a little too weird, Callie."

"You're right. My imagination is running away with me." I stuck Jake's card in my pocket then wiped down the counter. "But still. I need to at least alert Todd to Jake's connection with Ginger. Hopefully he won't make me tell the sheriff."

"It does seem kinda strange—"

The front door opened, and I glanced up. "Welcome to C.

Willikers. How may I help you?"

J.T. Culpepper, wearing his flip-flops, stopped right inside the door.

I gulped, remembering the last time I had seen those white, hairy legs in Ginger Slayton's garage.

J. T. lifted his unshaven chin in acknowledgment of my greeting. "Came to see if y'all carry birdseed in here."

Birdseed?

Well, that was a first. I had pretty much concluded that day in Ginger's garage that J.T. wasn't the murderer, anyway, so I felt safe to walk out from behind the counter. "No, I'm sorry. I occasionally have a few decorative bird houses, but I don't carry seed at all."

He shuffled his feet. "I figured. Hopin' I'd save myself a trip into town. Don't guess it matters as much now that Ms. Slayton is gone. She hated my birds."

Wait, what?

I stepped closer to him, trying not to stare at the tattoos that traced down all of his fingers. "Why did Ginger hate your birds?"

He shrugged, his hand on the door knob. "Said they made too much racket. And she didn't like the mess. Fussed at me all the time about them. Thanks anyway."

I clutched my hair up into my fist as he left. "Now what?"

Sharlene laughed. "Too many suspects?"

"Yes." I released my hair. "I'm all hot about Jake and Dr. Smythe, then all of a sudden J.T. drops a bombshell. Maybe he killed Ginger over the bird situation."

"Probably not." Sharlene's matter-of-fact tone brought me back to earth.

"You're right." I needed to calm down. "But somebody killed her. And it's been two weeks now, and I'm apparently still the main suspect. What if the real murderer is getting ready to kill someone else for some unknown reason?"

CHAPTER FIFTEEN

Fortunately for Sharlene, we experienced a small rush of customers, which deflected my attention from wild speculation about murder suspects to the gentler and kinder world of yarn and floral arrangements. After the last woman had paid for her new circular needles and left, I plugged in my electric tea kettle.

"Well, I guess at least not everyone thinks I should be in jail," I remarked to Sharlene.

"Or they care more about their knitting projects than what's happening in the news." She winked at me. "Anyway, I don't think anyone would be rude enough to accuse you to your face."

No one except the housekeeper woman at Willowbough. I still couldn't get over that. I mean, who says stuff like that?

"Do you want tea?" I grabbed two mugs from underneath the counter, then added a third. Mona should be dropping by soon. "I need to let it go. Todd assures me they are still working on the case."

"No tea, thanks." Sharlene pulled a water bottle from the mini-fridge and twisted it open. "I still didn't hear the whole story about your parents. I was so excited to hear they were safe."

"Me too." I poured boiling water over my tea bag. "I'll feel better when they're safe and sound here in the States again. I think they tried to minimize the situation when they finally called me, but it sounds like they were really rattled. My mom still sounded kind of befuddled, which is unusual for her."

"They had car trouble?"

"Yes, but it was more than that. They had received some threats for a few days preceding their trip."

"Oh, no. Why? So someone messed with their car on purpose?"

"No, I don't think so. But they were unnerved by the threats to begin with, then the car trouble happened, and they had to stay in one of the villages a couple of days. They were fine but knew how much everyone would worry."

"Nothing came of the threats?"

"Not that I know of. I guess sometimes people in the villages get upset about things and blame the missionaries because they are the outsiders. At least that's what I gather happened. Dad was a little vague."

"Hmm."

I dribbled half and half into my mug. "They're leaving Zambia tomorrow, but they have to debrief at their organization's headquarters in Des Moines for a few days before they head down here. It will be good to see them again." I hope.

She nodded. "It must be so cool to have parents."

My heart ached long after Sharlene had left for the day. Once again, I had been thinking only of myself and how awkward our first meeting might be, rather than praising God for the blessing of having loving parents. Or thinking about how my friend must feel, having never known the love of a parent.

And speaking of Sharlene, I need to make a point to ask her about her neighbor, the one we'd been praying for. I sighed. I'd been so consumed with all the craziness lately I'd forgotten to ask if she'd made any headway. I hadn't prayed about it very much, either, though I had promised I would.

"Lord, please forgive me," I murmured. "I pray right now for Sharlene, that You would give her an opportunity to talk with her neighbor lady. I pray for the neighbor, that You would begin to draw her by Your Holy Spirit. Give her a desire to know You. Make her weary of her sin and convict her heart—"

The bell above the door rang.

"Hi, Mona," I called, expecting to see my friend.

"It's Veronica." The weary-looking woman slipped through the door, still in her scrubs and clutching her car keys in her hand. "I've heard so much about your store. I thought I'd stop by after work today."

"Cool," I said cautiously. Veronica had been nothing but sugary-sweetness since the day she accused me about Ginger.

Maybe she was still trying to make amends. "Do you knit?"

"No. I..." she twisted her hands together and dropped her keys.

We both bent to pick them up from the floor, but I reached them first. I grabbed them up and handed them back to her, wondering why a grown woman would have so many things hanging from her key chain besides keys. One of those fluffy balls that all the teenage girls at youth group had. A long string of multicolored beads. Some kind of house-shaped keychain thingy. A miniature can of pepper spray. A small—

"Thanks." She shoved the whole jangling mess into her pocket. "I want to make your aunt something for her wedding. A gift, I mean. Like maybe flowers in a basket or something."

"Aww, that's sweet of you." Maybe Aunt Dot's prayers for this woman were being answered. "Did you want to order an arrangement? Or you want to make it yourself?"

Her face reddened. "I don't have much money, so..." She straightened her shoulders. "I thought you might have ideas for something she would like. Something small."

"How about a potted plant rather than cut flowers?" I placed a goldfish plant on the counter. "It would last longer and you could, like, decorate it with ribbon or something."

Veronica's eyes lit up at the sight of the plant with its glossy green leaves and perky little orange blossoms. "Sure. Then she could take it to their new apartment with her after the wedding."

"But the wedding isn't until next weekend. Do you want to care for the plant until then? Or come back and pick one out closer to the wedding?" I plucked a dead blossom off the plant. "These are pretty easy to care for, and I usually keep a few of them in stock."

"No. I don't know nothing about plants." She brushed her long braid over her shoulder. "I'll come back next week."

I smiled at her. "No problem. I'll make sure to have one or two on hand. I'm sure Aunt Dot will be thrilled with whatever you choose."

"Okay. And—" She jammed her hands into the pockets of her scrubs. "I wanted to apologize again for being so rude. You know, about the lady who was killed."

"It's fine. I know it's scary for everyone to think there could be a crazy person running around. Did you know Ginger?"

She shrugged again. "Not really. I worked at the school one of the years she was the principal."

Ah. I remembered hearing somewhere that Ginger had been the principal of the middle school for a few years. That would have been well before I moved to Short Creek. I glanced up as another customer entered the store. "Sure thing, Veronica. I'll save a goldfish plant for you. Thanks for coming in today."

"Thanks. And, uh..." She pulled some items from her purse and laid them on the counter. "I was wondering if...I mean, if you'd like to carry my stuff in your store."

I raised my eyebrows at the homemade soaps, each one with what looked like a hand-lettered little tag. Was this the real reason Veronica came in today? To try to sell me something? "You make these?"

She nodded, picking at her thumbnail. "And other stuff too, like lotion and lip balm. I use all-natural ingredients like coconut oil and stuff. And essential oils."

"They're very pretty." I picked up a mint-green colored bar and sniffed it. Somehow, Veronica didn't seem the crafty type, but I guess if she needed extra money... "I don't usually carry stuff on consignment, if that's what you had in mind."

"I thought I'd ask." She shrugged and gathered up the bars.

I felt like a heel. "Do you have a card? I'll give it some thought."

"No, but I'm at Willowbough all the time. Thanks for thinking about it." She headed toward the door, then paused and turned to me. "I want you to know I truly am sorry."

Wow, it wasn't that big of a deal. She had already apologized several times now. "It's okay, Veronica, really. I forgive you."

She nodded and slipped out the door as my phone rang.

"Whew." I slouched down onto my couch next to Todd later that evening. "Super busy day at the store today."

"That's awesome." He threaded his fingers through mine. "Have you been able to have any peace now you know your parents are safe?"

I nodded. "Yes, about them, at least."

"I don't have any new information to report, if that's what you're hoping." He grinned at me.

Was it that obvious? "Do things usually take this long?"

"Yep. And longer."

I heaved a sigh. Looked like if this thing was going to end anytime soon, I'd have to keep working on it. I sat up straight. It was time to get this mess figured out once and for all. "Okay. So, we have J.T."

"J.T. Culpepper? I don't think he's even on Wayne's radar."

"I know." I pushed my glasses up. "I had pretty much decided that, except when he made a remark the other day about Ginger hating his birds, I put him back on my list."

Todd shook his head. "Seems pretty far-fetched to me."

"Depends on how important his birds are and how much Ginger fussed about them, I suppose."

"Did he mean pet birds?"

I frowned. "I assumed he was talking about wild birds. You know, like he attracted lots of them because he put seed out. He has, like, a bazillion feeders in his yard."

"Even more than you?" He tugged a lock of my hair. "Either way, it doesn't seem like much motive."

"You're right. I really don't think he did it, but he's on the list for now. Then there's Penny. She's been Jonesing to be president of the garden club for years, from what I hear. And she seemed to recognize the charm I found in Ginger's garage. And—" I held up my index finger. "Let's not forget she was still apparently simmering over the fact that Ginger won the lawn and garden show prize three years in a row."

"Right. But all those things seem so petty."

"To us." I shrugged. "Some people get really worked up

about such things."

"True. And I've seen people commit crazy crimes for lesser reasons."

"Plus, if she was romantically involved with Dr. Smythe, even in her imagination, she would have seen Ginger as a major threat."

"I suppose. To me, Smythe seems like he'd have greater motive, since Ginger actually threatened to burn down his dental office."

"I don't know. You know how Ginger ranted about stuff." I stood up to pace. "And what about Jake? Boranda's husband? I need to find out more about him."

"His background check came in pretty clean. A couple of speeding tickets and a DUI from a year ago or so." Todd shrugged. "Looks like Bo got a restraining order against him a few months ago, but it seems he's complying with that since she hasn't reported anything."

"Darn. I was hoping it would show something more definitive."

"Like what?" He grinned at me. "He had already killed three other people?"

I sighed. "Yeah, I guess that would have been too easy. I don't know what motive he would have had, unless he had gotten into a fuss with Ginger over something we don't know about."

"Well, if he works for her husband, that's a definite possibility."

Hmm. I pursed my lips. "Maybe I'll pay a little visit to the TemBel Landscape Company. To discuss my garden, of course."

"I'll go with you."

I shook my head. "Everybody knows you're a cop. I don't want to make Jake or his boss suspicious."

"At least take Mona with you."

"I will. But what about Bo herself? I was a little suspicious about her over the deal with the roses, but now I can't picture her being a suspect at all." I sipped my tea. "The only possible motive I know of is that Ginger accidentally put a big ol' scratch on the side of Bo's truck one day."

"I guess we can't totally discount that as a motive, but I'd be hard-pressed to imagine Bo doing something so awful."

"What about Wormy?"

Todd raised his eyebrows. "Wormy? At the Donut Hut? Why would you suspect him?"

"Remember I told you that Ginger beat them out in a bid for the house a few years ago? And that Wormy's wife's relatives used to own it and she really wants it back in the family?"

"I forgot about that." He drummed his fingers on the table. "But Wormy has a nice home already. And he's on the city council and a local businessman. I can't see him doing something so foolish."

"Yeah, but Ginger also slandered him and made a big fuss when she was running against him in the city council election last year. I mean, I know he ended up winning the seat anyway, but it was pretty ugly."

Todd shook his head. "I've known Wormy for a lot of years. I'd be shocked if he was involved in anything that wasn't above board."

"I know, me too." I pictured the jolly donut-shop owner. "I don't think he has a mean bone in his tall, thin body."

"Nope." Todd stood and stretched. "I know the Temple PD is helping in the investigation, and they've got someone on it full-time, so hopefully we'll have a break soon. I'm praying we will."

"Me too. Someone has got to know something." I stared up at him. "I'm asking the Lord to show us who or what it is."

"Yes. But you know we can't rule out the possibility that it was a random act. Maybe Ginger was in the wrong place at the wrong time, and the murder was not premeditated. It could have been someone driving through the area."

I swallowed hard. "I know. But even then, why would someone kill her and leave her in Sherm's yard?"

"Why does anyone kill anyone else to begin with? All murder is evil and senseless, no matter the reason for it or who did it."

"You're right." I poked at the dirt in the philodendron. "If sin causes this much grief and heartache for humans, I can't imagine how much God hates it."

"I think about that every day. Surely every believer who is in law enforcement would have to reflect on it at some point. I guess it's part of what motivates me, in a way."

I nodded. "It should light a fire under every believer, shouldn't it?"

"Theoretically." He rubbed a hand down his jaw. "But sometimes the sheer amount of evil and the depth of depravity I see on a daily basis is overwhelming. I hate to admit it, but I find myself hardening to it some days."

Ah, my tender man of God. I loved him for his heart and his vulnerability in letting me see into it. I slipped my hand into his. "I can't imagine. I will pray for you specifically for that."

He wrapped his arms around me and rested his chin on the top of my head. We stood together, unmoving, for a long moment. Finally, he pulled away, cupping my cheek in his hand. "Thank you, sweetheart. It comforts me to know you are holding me up in prayer." He sighed and smoothed my hair back behind my right ear. "I'll be grateful when we get these next few busy weeks out of the way and can settle down again. There are some important things we need to discuss, Detective Erickson."

"Oh, really?" I tilted my head. "Like wedding plans?"

"Maybe." He laughed softly and bent to kiss me, and I didn't think about murder suspects anymore.

CHAPTER SIXTEEN

I didn't think about murder suspects anymore, until the next day, that is. After knocking for a minute, I turned the knob of the painted wooden door and let myself into the one-room office of TemBel Landscape and Design. Pretty fancy name for a dilapidated building in North Temple. At least the two large greenhouses behind it looked decent. I wondered if they were open to the public.

"Hello? Anyone home?" I called.

I heard water running from behind the closed door near the desk. Mr. Slayton must be in the restroom. Perfect. I'd slip out to the greenhouses and see what I could see before the man even knew I was here.

Closing the office door behind me, I sauntered past neat rows of potted crepe myrtle trees, an enormous pile of mulch, and a stack of wooden pallets before slipping inside the greenhouse, ignoring the "Employees Only" sign. I sucked in my breath.

Rows and rows of David Austin roses dazzled my senses. Their signature ruffled blossoms shone in every pastel shade of mauve, lavender, pink, pale yellow...and peach, of course. Peach roses, exactly like mine. Would Ginger's ex-husband have motive to steal my roses? Or worse...could he have taken her life? If so, why? And what connection could my roses possibly have to the two of them?

I wandered over to an exquisite climbing Joseph's Coat rose, remembering the lovely one I had left in my parents' garden in Ohio years ago when I moved down here to Texas. I bent to sniff it, its fragrance transporting me back to the pleasant days of my childhood. Never mind gathering clues. I could sit and bask in here, enjoying the heavenly—

"Quite lovely, aren't they?"

I jumped and turned to see a pleasant-looking man about Ginger's age standing just inside the doorway. "Breathtaking." I stepped toward him, my hand extended. "I'm Callie Erickson. I own C. Willikers Florist Shop in Short Creek, and I've heard about your roses."

He shook my hand, and I was struck by the kindness in his gaze and the pencil stuck behind his ear. "Ah, a fellow rose-lover. I'm not familiar with your business. Are you new in town?"

"Fairly. A few years old. I don't deal with nursery stock," I gestured to the roses, "but I am a full-service florist, among other things."

He nodded. "If you're who I'm thinking you are, my ex-wife spoke highly of you. Said you had a good-looking shop and had done wonders with that old property you bought."

She did? Maybe that was before she thought I was accusing her of stealing my rose bushes. "I didn't know her well, but I'm sorry for your loss. I'm sure it was a great shock."

A pained look crossed his face. "Still is. I know she could have a sharp tongue sometimes, but I—we were talking about getting back together." He looked down and cleared his throat before meeting my gaze again. "I still struggle with the fact that someone purposely took her life."

"I know. It's unbelievable. I'm sorry."

"Thanks." He straightened his shoulders and frowned slightly, as if suddenly realizing I was trespassing in his greenhouse. "Can I help you with something today?"

"I guess I should have gone to the office instead of coming out here to the greenhouse, but..." I let my words trail off and gave him my best smile, hoping he'd take me for a ditzy bumpkin from Short Creek.

"Yes, you should have." He bent to move a stack of plastic pots while I sent up a quick prayer for wisdom and direction.

Should I tell him about my stolen roses? And what about Jake? I was itching to see Jim's reaction to both topics, but I didn't want to make him angry. So far, he seemed like a very nice, reasonable man. Certainly not the type who would steal his competition's rose bushes or hire a murderer. At least not knowingly. In fact, I felt drawn to him somehow.

"I'm hunting for some Eden roses," I said to his back.

He straightened slowly, then let his gaze sweep me from head to toe and back again. "Edens."

I gulped at the look on his face. "Yep. I had some thriving bushes that I had grown from cuttings from my mother's bushes in Ohio and—"

"Are you a cop?"

What?

"No."

He took a step closer to me. "Because if you are, you can drop the act right now. I don't like games. Y'all know as well as I do that the killer placed an Eden rose in Ginger's hand. Obviously, someone is trying to frame me, and I have no idea who. Believe me, if I knew, I'd tell you." He breathed hard, his face red. "So stop sending people to try to pump more information from me."

Ah, so Wayne's people had already made this connection too, huh? I stood my ground, believing I saw grief, not malice, in his grey eyes. "I'm not a cop. I own C. Willikers and someone stole my rosebushes. I came here to see if you carried them so I could replace the ones I lost. That's all."

Not exactly all, all. But all for now.

He pinned me with his gaze, his eyes resting for a moment on the charm I still wore around my neck. "It seems strange that a beautiful young woman from Short Creek shows up in my greenhouse claiming to know my ex-wife and asking lots of questions after I already told the sheriff I wouldn't be talking to him again any time soon. So if you're not a cop, then what do you really want?"

Beautiful woman? Did he mean me? And why would Jim Slayton be so adamant about not talking to Sheriff Wayne again? Hmm. And double-hmm.

I held both my hands up. "I'm sorry we've gotten off on the wrong foot, Mr. Slayton. I really am who I say I am. If you care to look, you can see my delivery van parked out there in front of your office."

He ran a hand over his eyes, but not before I glimpsed the moisture in them. "No, I'm the one who's sorry. I believe you. This whole thing has been a nightmare, and I am constantly on edge. Will be, until we can get some closure."

I nodded, still feeling an undercurrent of...what?

Connection? Attraction? No, not really. Only a fleeting feeling that this meeting was more than chance. A God-moment, somehow.

"I understand. I'll come back another day." Although I longed to get a peek inside the second greenhouse, I would bide my time. However, I couldn't resist one more question. "Or maybe I'll ask Jake to help me. He still works for you, doesn't he?"

"Jake Haskell? You know Jake? Yeah, he works for me sometimes." He motioned for me to precede him to the door. "He's sure been a godsend during these last few crazy weeks."

A godsend? Were we talking about the same guy? "That's nice," I murmured. "Thanks for showing me around."

He escorted me to my van. "I hope you come again sometime when it's a better day, Miss Erickson."

"I will." I pulled the driver's side door open, then on impulse, I turned back to him. "God bless you today."

"And you too," he said. His serious gaze captured mine. "I can see He has His hand on you."

Really? I gave him a small smile. "Why do you say that?"

He braced his arm above the open van door. "I can sense when I've met a fellow believer. And I finally remembered where I knew your name from. Not from your store. You're connected with Hope House, aren't you?"

"Yes."

"I thought so. It took me awhile to put the pieces together. I attend Houston's church so I know all about Hope House. Y'all are going to open pretty soon, I hear."

"Yes, the first girls should move in shortly. We're excited to be up and running soon."

He reached into his pocket and produced a business card. "I've actually stopped by your store a couple of times recently, but I guess I picked the wrong times to do so since I've never caught you there. I'd like to make a donation to Hope House." He scribbled a phone number on the back. "I've been meaning to do it, but with all that's been happening with Ginger's untimely death, I haven't done it. Will you please email or call me and we'll set up a time to meet? That's my personal cell phone number."

"Uh, sure. I'd love to." I tucked the card into my wallet. "Thank you so much."

He backed away, seeming suddenly embarrassed. "My pleasure. I'll look forward to hearing from you."

I sat in the stifling heat of my van, staring after Jim as he disappeared into his office. My heart ached for the grief I read in his every movement as I remembered what it was like in those early days after I lost my husband, Kevin. I sighed and turned the ignition key.

Nothing.

I tried again. Not a click. Not a sound.

Argh. Was my battery dead? Everything seemed fine earlier.

I popped the hood latch and climbed out of the van. I don't know why I thought it would help for me to look under the hood, because I had absolutely no knowledge of what to look for, but it seemed like the thing to do when one's car wouldn't start. I wondered idly if Jim Slayton was watching me out his office window as I slung the van hood open.

I gasped. A fresh bouquet of peach-colored Eden roses lay on top of my engine.

CHAPTER SEVENTEEN

I backed away. Who had put them there?

I glanced over my shoulder at Jim's office. Was his niceness all a pretense? He could have put the roses in there while I was in the greenhouse. Maybe he had heard me in his office after all.

I raised my hand to slam the hood closed, then thought better of it and got my phone out instead. I took a bunch of pictures, then used a tissue to pick up the bouquet. I placed it on the floor behind the driver's seat and casually threw a blanket over it before I called roadside assistance.

Wowzers. Someone was sending me a message, loud and clear. First, my Eden rose bushes go missing. Then, Ginger is found dead with an Eden rose in her hand. Then Jake gives Bo, his estranged wife, a whole bouquet of them. Now I find five roses, freshly cut and neatly tied together with a white ribbon, on the engine of my disabled van.

I called Todd.

"Don't let the towing guys touch anything. I'm on my way. Is Mona with you?"

I wish. "No, I asked her to come but she had to pick the grandkids up from school today."

He growled something under his breath. "I'll be there in ten minutes. Don't try to start the van again."

"I won't." I wandered to the far side of my van where Jim couldn't see me from his window and leaned against the hot metal of the sliding door, my arms crossed. So Todd might disagree with me, but now I was thinking Ginger's murderer had to be someone local. And that someone was not happy I was talking to Jim Slayton. Or, maybe it didn't have anything to do with Jim. Maybe the killer was following me around and saw a convenient time to mess with my vehicle. Ugh.

I peeked under my van, having a sudden terrible thought of someone lurking under there, ready to reach out and grab me.

Nope, no one under the van. Thank God.

And why now? Why was I being threatened now and not days ago when Wayne first raised suspicions about me? Was it because the toxicology report was going to be released soon? Todd had told me about that this morning. Was the killer afraid his gig was going to be up once that information was sent to the media?

But what about Boranda? My breath caught. Was it a fluke that Jake gave her Eden roses? Or was Jake the killer and he was sending her a message too? I had to warn her. What if he was planning to murder her soon and that's why he gave her the roses? She wouldn't have known that when I found Ginger, she was clutching an Eden rose in her lifeless fingers. To my knowledge, no one knew that except me and the law enforcement folks, and obviously, Jim, since he was Ginger's ex-husband. So how would Boranda know the bouquet was meant as a death threat?

I pulled my phone out of my pocket, my hands shaking, and scrolled through my contacts. I pressed her name, praying she would answer.

"Shear Bliss, Bo speaking."

I blew out my breath. "Oh, thank God. Bo, are you all right?'

"Who is this?"

"Oh, sorry." Now I felt silly, but better safe than sorry, right? "It's Callie Erickson. I'm, uh, calling to check on you."

"That's so sweet of you. I'm fine." I pictured her holding her clunky landline phone to her ear with her shoulder like she always did while she was working. "Better than last time we talked. How are you?"

"Not great. I'm worried about Jake. Has he threatened you lately?"

"No, not at all, thankfully."

"Has he given you any more roses?"

She laughed. "No, I think we're past that point. He knows it's over, at least as far as I'm concerned."

I didn't want to scare her, but I was a little freaked out. "Please be super careful. If you hear from him or get any more flowers from anyone, will you please let me know?"

"Sure, Callie. Gotta run. Thanks for checking in with me."

I glanced at my watch, then scanned the area around me, hoping I wasn't looking like a huge pink target against the side of my silver van. I didn't know ten minutes could feel so long.

God, please send angels to watch over me. I plead the blood of Jesus over myself and over my vehicle. God, protect me from any plans of the evil one to harm me.

"Come on, Todd. Hurry, please," I whispered.

Why did someone have it in for me, anyway? I hadn't done anything to anyone. I'm minding my own business, hopefully doing what God put me on this earth to do, and suddenly I'm in the midst of craziness. What had I ever done that would make someone want me dead?

And worse, what if it wasn't only me. What if this crazy person tried to hurt my family or friends?

"So Todd shows up with one of the Temple PD detectives, and then Jim Slayton comes out of the office." I tucked my legs up underneath me on my Aunt Dot's couch and accepted the tea mug Harry held out to me. "Thank you. Then the car guys came and towed my van away to the police station or wherever they take them when there's an ongoing investigation."

"Oh, my, Callie." Aunt Dot's eyes were huge. "Jim is a precious man. I used to teach him in Sunday School when he was in junior high. I can't believe he'd be involved in something like this."

"I don't think anyone thinks he is. I wasn't going to tell you guys about any of it, because I didn't want you to worry about me, but—"

"I don't worry, darlin'. I pray. There's a big difference."

Yeah. And I seemed to constantly fluctuate between them. Why couldn't I learn to trust God more?

Harry paced around the small room. "We need a breakthrough. This has gone on long enough."

"Amen to that." I sipped my tea. Auntie always fixed it perfectly, with a touch of stevia and a whole lot more than a touch of half and half. "I'm concerned about you two. If this person is crazy enough to kill one person and then stay around town and threaten other people..." I shook my head. "And who knows why? That's what I can't figure out."

"Folks who are bent on doing evil don't think like the rest of us, darlin'." Aunt Dot smoothed the edge of her blouse. "But the Bible says we can be sure our sins will find us out. This person will be caught."

"What about my parents?"

Harry frowned. "What do you mean?"

I cupped my hands around my mug. "I'm concerned about them traveling here in the midst of this. What if someone threatens them too?"

Aunt Dot and Harry exchanged glances.

"I mean, if this person was bold enough to mess with my van in broad daylight..." I picked at the multi-colored afghan that lay on the armrest. I hated to bring this up, but— "And what about the wedding? I feel terrible to even think of postponing it, but I don't know what else to do. What if someone came in during the service and—"

"Let's not go there, sugar." Harry eased himself down on the coffee table in front of me and took both my hands in his big soft ones. "Our God is bigger than all of this, and He knows the beginning from the end. He's already there in your future."

I took a deep breath. "I know, but this is getting super scary. And what about the Hope House girls? They need to be in there now. I can't let some stupid threats keep that from happening."

"Hope House is God's work. He's not going to allow anything to hinder it—at least not forever." Aunt Dot scooched her chair closer to the two of us. "He is still on the throne, Callie. We walk by faith, not by sight, remember?

I drove up the gravel path to Hope House the next morning, admiring, as always, the decades-old live oaks that dotted the landscape, providing privacy from the highway and creating small oases of shade from the blistering Texas sun. The trees were easily seventy-five years old, direct descendants of the famous "Treaty Oak" under which legend holds that Stephen Austin and local Native Americans had signed the first boundary treaty back in the days of Texas' infancy. The elderly gentleman from whom we had purchased the land had told me the whole story of how, as a young, newly-married rancher in the 1950's, he had gathered the acorns from the historic tree, sprouted the acorns and planted a hundred of the little trees on his land.

The girls would love it here. The newly-finished log house was homey and welcoming, with a distinct "retreat" kind of feel, even though it was close to town. I parked in the circular drive, happy to see that someone had been out to mow since the last time I was here. Harry took care of all those details, thankfully.

"Come on, Annie." I opened the van door and she jumped out. She loved to roam around the spacious grounds. "No girls here, yet, but soon." My heart swelled at the thought. We were working closely with a local ministry who had contacts with both local and national law enforcement, and they were as thrilled as we were that our doors would soon be open to provide physical, spiritual, and emotional support to these young women.

Annie danced around my feet, her tail thumping against the side of the van.

"Let's go in." I headed up the wooden steps of the broad porch, pausing to check the hummingbird feeders that hung near the steps. I pictured the girls curled up in the large white rocking chairs, letting the peace and beauty of God's creation seep into their hurting hearts. How had God chosen me to be a part of this?

I turned the key in the lock and pushed the door open, breathing in the new-paint smell. Annie padded in behind me. The sun streamed in through the latticed picture window, highlighting the warm wood tones and comfy-casual design of the living room. I heard the air conditioner kick on and turned to close the front door behind me.

"Looks like everything is ready, girl." Annie and I wandered into the large, well-equipped kitchen. Soon, this room would be filled with laughter, hard work, and good food—all ingredients in the community we hoped to foster between the girls and the counselors. I ran my fingertips over the granite countertop donated by the women's group at Houston's church.

This place had truly been a collaborative effort between so many people in the community. But it wouldn't seem really real until the day our first girls walked through the—

Annie barked from somewhere near the back of the building.

I frowned. She didn't usually bark just to be barking.

She barked again, this time more insistently.

I hurried past the first bedroom and back to the sun room, my pulse rate doubling. What now?

Humid heat pushed against my face as I stopped in the doorway and stared. Broken glass covered the multi-colored rug. I groaned. "What in the world?"

Had the windows been blown in during that thunderstorm the other day?

Annie glanced at me over her shoulder and snuffled at the crack under the back door, whining.

"What is it, girl?" I picked my way across the hardwood floor toward where a bank of windows should have been, but only jagged remnants of glass stood between me and the great outdoors.

That's when I saw it.

A bouquet of Eden roses, tied with a white ribbon. Lying on the back porch.

"No!" I clenched my teeth, my blood burning into my cheeks. "This is ridiculous. I didn't do anything to anyone. How dare someone mess with Hope House?" I whopped my hand on the window frame. "This has got to stop."

CHAPTER EIGHTEEN

"I'm going to find whoever is doing this, if it's the last thing I do." An hour later, I glared at Todd across the counter at C. Willikers, too upset to think about the two old ladies in the back of the store looking at sock yarn.

"Easy now, sweetheart." Todd tried to grasp my hand, but I snatched it away and folded my arms.

"I know this is not your fault. But it's so aggravating." I worked my jaw, not caring who was watching. "Do you know I have people cancelling orders and events because of all the ridiculous rumors going around? Just yesterday, I lost the Perkins wedding. And now it's affecting Hope House, as well. Even without the vandalism, it doesn't look great to have the president of the board being accused of murder. And then there's Aunt Dot and Harry. It's not fair to them that their wedding plans are trashed because of some deranged idiot who—"

"Callie." Todd rose from his stool and came around to me where I stood, stiff and livid, behind my cash register. "This isn't helping, honey. I know you're upset and you haven't been sleeping well." He ran a knuckle down the side of my face. "My colleagues are working on this around the clock, and we have many, many people praying. It's going to be okay."

But what if it wasn't okay? Ever? I took a deep breath. *He will keep those in perfect peace whose minds are stayed on Him.* The fragment of scripture floated into my mind.

I'm trying, Lord. Jesus, please help me. I'm so weary.

I blew out my breath and wilted against Todd. "Please tell me this will be over soon."

He pulled me in tight.

I stood and listened to his heartbeat, then listened to His heartbeat. *Courage, dear heart. Courage. Peace.*

<hr>

"Courage. That's what I need, because I'm going to confront Jake," I told Mona that evening. "He's my top suspect." I gritted my teeth. "He is evil enough to do all of this."

She rolled her eyes. "How do you know? I mean, I know Bo told you a lot of stuff, but she could have been exaggerating."

"It's not only that. What about his connection to the roses? And to Jim Slayton?"

"Yeah, but what about J.T.?" She thrust her crochet hook through the scarf, her mouth contorting with the effort. "We never did find out why he was in Ginger's garage that day. And he was poking around in her flowerbeds."

"I know, but unless he has some kind of hidden motive, I don't think Ginger squabbling with him about a birdfeeder or two would be enough for him to murder her."

"I would hope not." She squinted up at me through her reading glasses. "But what about Dr. Smythe? I thought you thought he and Jake were working together."

"I know. I did think that for a while, but I can't figure out the connection. I haven't ruled it out. And I'm keeping Wormy on my list."

"What did poor Wormy ever do?"

"Nothing that I know of, but I don't know his wife, either. Supposedly she really wanted the house, but Ginger got it instead. Could she have talked Wormy into getting rid of Ginger so they could have the house?"

"Nah. He's too nice."

"I know. But that could be the perfect cover-up. Maybe he's been biding his time all these years, making everyone like him and then, bam! He does the deed and thinks no one would ever suspect him."

"No way. You've been reading too many mystery novels, friend. He and Rob are in that men's discipleship thingy together, and Rob says Wormy's the real deal." Mona grinned at me. "How's our hot-head sheriff been with all of this? You keepin' him all stirred up?"

I made a face. "I hope Wayne thinks I'm lying low. I've tried to stay out of his hair."

"How's that working for you?" she muttered, back to concentrating on the scarf. "I hope you're still not suspecting poor Bo."

"Not really. But I can't totally rule her out, because she's connected to Jake, and I think he has more going on than anyone knows. Maybe she was an unwilling participant in some of this. She didn't really seem like she wanted to talk to me when I called her the other day."

"Or maybe she was super busy. You know she doesn't have any help at the salon right now. She told me she had to let Miranda go too because she couldn't afford to pay her."

No, I hadn't realized that. I sighed. "Mostly I feel sorry for her. She's too nice of a person to have gotten mixed up with someone like Jake. I wonder why she was attracted to him to begin with?"

Mona snorted. "He's pretty easy on the eyes. And he's rich."

"He's rich?" If Jake was rich, why was he doing side jobs for Jim Slayton's landscaping business?

"Seems rich to me. Every time I see him, he has fancy clothes on. And he drives a super nice car."

I hadn't noticed Jake's car. I never noticed anyone's cars. "Hmm. Who knows?" I untangled Mona's green yarn from the arm of the chair. "Then there's Penny. I still think she could have had enough motive to take out Ginger."

"Maybe. But maybe it was someone who doesn't even live here. Maybe some desperate criminal on the run from the cops."

"I'm sure it's possible." At this point, anything was possible. I rubbed a hand over my eyes. "Which is why I need to talk to Jake."

"Not smart. And anyway, how are you going to find him? I don't think he lives here in Short Creek. Bo said something about him living in Temple."

"I'll find him. I'm sure Bo still has his phone number. Or I'll go sit at TemBel Landscaping until he shows up." Yes, that's what I would do. I'd go wait there and confront him again when he got to work in the morning. If he even showed up... Except that it hadn't gone well the first time I attempted to talk to him, and what if something else terrible happened before then? I needed to do something about this now.

"You should let Wayne take care of this."

I whirled around. "That's the problem. Wayne is not taking care of it, as far as I can tell."

"Okay, Nancy. Calm down. Do you want me to go with you?"

"Sure. But I'm not telling Todd until after I talk to Jake, because he will have a fit."

Mona pressed her lips together. "I hope you've prayed about this."

"Constantly. But there's a time for prayer and a time for action." I grabbed my purse and my keys, hoping I was right. "Let's go."

We pulled up to TemBel Landscaping half an hour later. A couple of cars were parked in front of the office. "Is one of those cars Jake's?"

"The black one looks like his." Mona pulled her sunglasses off. "Are you sure about this? What if he gets super mad? If he's really the murderer…" She glared at me and unbuckled her seatbelt, still mumbling.

I slid out of the van and slammed my door, ignoring Mona. "Jake, here I come. Hope you're ready." I marched up the walk and pounded on the door of the office, a woman on a mission. It was time to get this thing solved.

Jim Slayton pulled the door open, his eyes widening when he recognized me. "Ms. Erickson! Is something wrong?"

"Yes. There are a lot of things wrong. Is Jake here?"

Jim furrowed his brow. "Jake? Yeah, he's out in the first greenhouse. May I ask—"

I whirled around, almost knocking down Mona who had come up behind me. I needed to get this accomplished while my adrenaline was still rushing, or I'd never have the moxie to do it. "I need to speak with him," I yelled over my shoulder as I headed toward the greenhouse. Mona could deal with Jim.

I pushed open the greenhouse door, a blast of heat hitting me in the face. I closed the door behind me as Jake strode toward me, hose in hand.

"I'm sorry, ma'am. This greenhouse is for employees only." He wiped sweat off his forehead.

Oh, he was good. He was pretending like he didn't know who I was. I crossed my arms and planted my feet. "I don't care. Do you have a minute to talk?"

He looked at me more closely. "Ah, the nosy lady from the Mexican restaurant. Did your boyfriend, the cop, send you here to do his dirty work?"

"No. But I'm tired of being accused of something someone else did." I took a deep breath. "I think you killed Ginger Slayton."

He laughed, long and loud. "You're a real treat. Don't you think the cops have already talked to me? Maybe they should be talking to you. Or is your boyfriend pulling favors for you?"

I pinned him with my gaze. "You can insult me as much as you like, but you don't have an alibi for that night she was killed."

"Right." He drew himself up, amusement still dancing in his dark eyes. "And I have a whole lot of motive for killing my boss's ex-wife."

"Maybe you do."

"What are you, a junior detective or something? Get out of here before I get angry."

"No." I fought the urge to take a step backwards. "Where were you the night she was killed?"

Jake swore under his breath. "I was at the ER with my— with a friend, all right?" He hung his head for a minute. "I was still trying to patch things up with Bo then. I didn't want to hurt her any more than I already had by her finding out I was with someone else."

My mouth dropped open. Either Jake was a superb actor, or he was genuinely remorseful about his relationship with Boranda. I squinted at him. "Who's your girlfriend?"

"None of your business. Now get out of here. And stay away from Bo. She didn't do anything."

CHAPTER NINETEEN

"He said he was with his girlfriend." I glanced at Mona out of the corner of my eye while we sat at a red light.

"Do you believe him?"

"I don't know. But it seems like that would be easy enough to verify. If we knew his girlfriend's name." The light changed and I stepped on the gas pedal. "I don't want to bring it up to Bo, especially if she doesn't know he has been dating someone."

"I imagine she knows. In fact, I'm guessing that's the real reason she let the other hair stylist go." My friend's usually chirpy tone was sad. "I sort of read over the lines when Bo told me about it."

Between. Between the lines. "Hmm. That's sad. Do you know her?"

Mona was already pecking away busily on her phone screen. "No, only her first name, Allie-somebody-or-other. But a couple of my grans play soccer with her kid. I bet I can find her last name."

I sighed. Just what I didn't want to be doing today. Tracking down another person who didn't want to talk to me. When would this end?

But as it turned out, Allie the perky hair stylist was more than happy to talk about Jake when Mona and I popped into Cutie Cuts in Temple after lunch. We usually went to Shear Bliss in Short Creek, we told her, but we heard she wasn't working there anymore. And we heard she knew Jake Haskell?

"Oh. My. Gosh." She pressed her hands into the pockets of her purple smock as if to help keep her enthusiasm at bay. "Jake is amazing. How do y'all know him?" She gestured to her chair, and I obediently sat. At this point, information was more important than style.

Mona sidled up and sat in the empty stylist's chair next to mine. Out of the corner of my eye, I watched her lean forward, phone in hand. What was she up to?

"Oh, I've met Jake around town a few times lately," I said.

And apparently, he has a thing for bleached-blonde hair stylists.

Allie squirted my hair with more balsam-scented water than necessary. "He is a great guy. He saved my life a few weeks ago."

"Really." That's better than taking her life. I watched nervously as she parted my hair down the middle. Hopefully she wasn't too distracted talking about Jake while she cut my hair. I was paying a hefty price for information. "This better be worth it," I muttered.

"Huh?" Ally moved in front of me to comb my hair down flat and smooth on both sides of my face while I stared at the dainty silver crucifix she wore around her neck. I wondered briefly if she was a true follower of Christ or only wearing the bling. Of course, if she had an affair with Jake—

"Jake literally saved your life?"

"Yep." She grabbed my chin and tilted it upward. "A few weeks ago. We were hanging out at my apartment and I started having this terrible pain. Like cramps, except a billion times worse." She positioned my head again. "You need to hold still. I thought I was going to die. It was horrrrrible. But he drove me to the ER and stayed with me all night. I had a ruptured appendix."

"Ouch," I said, trying not to stare at her lip piercing. "You were there at the hospital all night?"

"All night. My neighbor came over and stayed with my son. Wasn't that a blessing?" She popped her gum. "And Jake never left my side the whole time. Did y'all both need a haircut? Or just you?" She stopped, scissors poised, and fingered the ends of my hair. "A good trim is all you need. Who's been cutting it lately?"

"I, uh, haven't had it cut in a while." And I wouldn't be having it cut now if I wasn't so desperate. I glanced at my watch. "But I really only want a trim. Nothing different. And definitely no bangs."

She shrugged. "No problem."

But apparently it was a problem. "How much more plainly could I say it than 'no bangs'?" I moaned to Mona as I drove my van to the Austin airport to pick my parents up the next day. "I'm done. I tried to solve this Ginger thing, and all I've gotten are 'wispy bangs' that will take from now until next year to grow out. You know that Barb confirmed Ally and Jake's account of being at the ER the night Ginger was killed." Barb was our nurse friend from church.

Mona nodded. "Yeah, you told me. The bangs do give you a different look. But I like it." She took a huge slurp of her soda. "At least Todd will be happier if you stop obsessing about the case. And you'll be able to concentrate on your parents if you're not worrying about it all the time. You are innocent, Callie. No one is going to be able to prove something that didn't happen, right?" She patted my leg. "Did you buy the dress yet?"

I glanced at her out of the side of my eye, then stared ahead at the traffic piling up in front of me.

"Ah ha. You did, didn't you?" She rubbed her hands together, cackling delightedly like Lonnie's hen when it laid an egg.

"I might have gone and seen it."

"Uh-huh. I knew you would love it."

I squirmed a little. Truth be told, I had put a down payment on the dress. In faith. But I wasn't quite ready to share that with anyone, even Mona. I would tell her when the time was right. Like when Todd actually proposed. I sighed.

Mona took pity on me and changed the subject. "Have you told your parents what's going on with the Ginger situation?"

"A little bit. I told them to be careful when they got to the airport. It seems pretty far-fetched that anyone would try anything. But still."

"Especially since not many people know they're coming, do they?"

I sped up to pass a semitruck. "People at church know. The mission team is planning a big dinner for them in a few weeks."

"That's fun."

I glanced at my friend. "You're quiet today."

"Just a little tired." She flashed me a grin. "Nothing you should be concerned about, friend. You have enough to deal with."

Hmm. I didn't like that answer. "I'm fine. Do you need to talk?"

"No. You need to pay attention to your driving. You're scaring me. We shoulda had Rob bring us."

I rolled my eyes and turned the radio up. "I'll get us there in one piece, Bess."

Minutes later, I spied my mother's suitcase at the far end of the baggage carousel. "There it is! The enormous black one with the purple bow on the handle."

Before I could grab it, Mona hefted it off the belt and thunked it down next to me. "Wow. What does she have in that thing?"

I laughed. The bag was almost as tall as my friend and more than half as wide. "My mother does not like to go anywhere unprepared. But Dad said he only had a duffel bag." I glanced at my phone. "I wonder what's taking them so long?"

"It's only been twenty minutes since their flight landed, Callie."

"I know. But I haven't seen them in three years." And I was more excited to see them than I thought I would be, which was a good thing. "I can't wait for them to meet you. I'm not sure they realize—"

A huge man pushed in front of me, stepping on my toes and blocking my view of the carousel. He held his phone to his ear, speaking rapidly in another language as he studied the luggage slipping by. Why was he wearing a sweat suit on a sticky May night? I could see the sweat glistening on his brown forehead. And smell it.

I backed away, and Mona clutched my forearm, pulling me further from the man's excited gesturing. "What a jerk," she muttered. "Must be either a really good or a really bad conversation."

"Yeah." And I'd hate to be on the receiving end of a bad conversation with that guy. He looked like some kind of professional athlete. I'm five-eight, and the dude towered over me, muscles bulging under his hoodie.

Mona glared at his back, her favorite Texas-shaped earrings quivering. "I don't like rude people. He didn't even care that he almost knocked you down."

Obviously. I turned to search the line of weary passengers coming down the escalator into baggage claim, expecting to see my parents any minute. "I hope they didn't get lost."

"Nah. Austin-Bergstrom is not that big of an airport. They probably stopped in the bathroom."

I pushed my glasses up on my nose and focused my attention on the baggage carousel again. A grey, military-style duffel bag caught my eye. My dad's. I would know that particular bag anywhere, especially since I could see the red stain from when I had spilled Kool-Aid on it about thirty years ago. "There's Dad's bag." I stepped around Mr. Rude to grab it.

Before I could reach the handle, the man snatched the bag and turned to leave, still talking on his phone.

"Hey! That's my friend's bag." Mona scooted in front of him.

Oh, dear. We didn't need an altercation in the airport. Maybe he had accidentally grabbed the wrong bag. I stepped toward him. "Excuse me, but I—"

"Callie Erickson. Callie Erickson. Will Miss Callie Erickson please report to the nearest information desk. Callie Erickson."

I froze, dread washing over me. Why was the airline paging me? *Had something happened to my parents?*

"Callie! He's leaving with your dad's bag!" Mona's frantic shout from the exit snapped me back to reality.

What in the world? I sprinted toward Mona as the man melded into a crowd, the sliding doors whooshing closed behind them.

"You chase him, Callie! I'm calling the police." The doors slid open again, and Mona herded me out into the humid darkness of the passenger pick-up area.

Chase him? The guy had disappeared. I scanned the vehicles idling at the curb, their drivers waiting to pick up the arriving passengers. Exhaust fumes hung heavy in the air.

Where did he go? Could he have jumped into a car in the fifteen seconds it took for us to follow him?

Mona pulled her phone away from her ear. "The police are telling me to report it to the airline, not to them." She dragged her hand through her spiky salt-and-pepper hair, frowning at me. "They better not try to wash this under the table."

Wash...What? If I wasn't so frazzled, I would have laughed at Mona's version of "sweep it under the rug." But—I sucked in a deep breath. *Maybe that bag wasn't even my dad's bag. Maybe his was still taking a slow ride around the carousel. But why was the airline paging me? Maybe—oh, no.* "I left Mom's suitcase in there." I whirled toward the door. I'd have to deal with Dad's bag later.

Mona bustled along behind me, continuing her tirade. "I hope no one snatched hers. What a bunch of baloney. He stole your dad's bag, right under our noses. And they're not going to do anything about it. I can't believe someone could do that and get away with it. What if there was some super important stuff in there?"

I ignored her, my pulse rate jumping as I spotted Mom's rolling suitcase right where I had left it beside the carousel. At least I hadn't lost both bags. "Thank you, God."

My relief was momentary. I had Mom's bag. But I didn't have her or Dad. I jerked the suitcase handle up and headed toward the escalator, wishing Todd was with us. Todd always knew what to do. And he was a cop. That came in handy more often than I'd like.

I yanked Mom's suitcase onto the first step of the escalator. "Come on, Mona. Let's find my parents.

"Uh, Callie?"

I turned to Mona as she crowded behind me.

"This just fell off your mom's suitcase." She handed me a single peach-colored Eden rose.

※

I stared at the woman behind the information desk, then down again at the piece of paper in my hand.

Callie, we had to take care of a problem. We will see you in a few days. We love you. Mom

What? Supposedly the message was from my mother, but it was not her handwriting. And if this was from my mom, why hadn't she simply texted or called me? The knot in my stomach tightened. "I'm not understanding. Who left me this message? Did my mother physically hand you this paper? Or did someone call in a message and a person here at the airport wrote it down for me? Or—?"

The woman stared over my shoulder at the line forming behind me. "I'm sorry, ma'am. I have no way of knowing that. And no one handed me anything personally. I've only been on my shift for fifteen minutes."

In other words, *go away.*

And do what? What had happened to my parents?

Mona pushed up to the counter and stood on tiptoe to lean closer to the unhelpful woman. "Can you at least verify they were on their flight? That they arrived here in Austin?" She tapped her long purple fingernails loudly on the counter in front of the monitor.

I held my breath while the woman stared at her screen for an eternity.

"Their flight originated in Des Moines, is that correct?" She didn't look at me.

"Yes, ma'am." I checked my phone for the twentieth time in the last five minutes. *Come on, Mom. Text me. This can't be happening.*

"It appears your parents did board their connecting flight in Kansas City."

I blew out my breath. "Which means they should be here in this airport somewhere." Maybe this was all a huge misunderstanding. Maybe the message was for a different person named Callie. Yeah. That had to be it. "Would you please page them? I think they're probably lost. They've never been to this airport before."

Mona threw her arm around my waist and squeezed tight. "I texted Todd for you," she murmured. "I think it's gonna be a long night."

CHAPTER TWENTY

Five hours later, Todd and I sat holding my Aunt Dot's hands in the surreal pre-dawn. Harry stood behind her wheelchair, his hands on her shoulders.

"What do you mean, they're 'missing'?" Aunt Dot searched my face. My mom was her beloved niece, so Aunt Dot was technically my great-aunt. "I talked to Bettina minutes before they boarded the plane in Kansas City yesterday afternoon."

"I know. I did too. They were so excited to see all of us." I sank back in my chair. The last few hours had been a nightmarish whirlwind of phone calls, reports and questions, but no answers. *Where were my parents?*

"I'm so sorry, darlin'." Aunt Dot squeezed my hand hard. "What could have happened? Did they somehow miss their flight in KC? But if they did, why didn't they text you?"

Todd's blue eyes sought mine, and I nodded. Aunt Dot and Harry needed to know the whole thing. Todd cleared his throat. "The airline has confirmed that Jerry and Bettina did board their plane in Kansas City. It was a direct flight to Austin. Their luggage arrived in Austin."

"What happened?" Harry squinted at Todd. "Are y'all suspecting foul play?"

Todd paused before answering, and I knew he was choosing his words carefully. He brushed his hand over the dark stubble on his jaw. "We have reason to believe that Callie's parents may have, um—" Todd cleared his throat again. "It appears Jerry and Bettina willfully disappeared after arriving in Austin."

"What?" Aunt Dot's hand flew to her throat. "Why would they do such a thing? They were so thrilled at the thought of spending this year with you, Callie. There must be a mistake."

I wish.

I laid my head back against the chair and closed my eyes, as if I could fend off the hurt and bewilderment in my aunt's voice. I didn't have any answers, either. My head was spinning like I had gotten off a merry-go-round after twirling around one too many times.

Harry growled. "I've never met Dot's niece and her husband but seems to me that folks who are servin' the Lord on the mission field wouldn't have any use for shenanigans like that."

I kept my eyes closed. *Jesus, please help me. I'm so afraid.* "None of it makes any sense."

"It's very early on in the investigation to say what happened for certain." Todd rested his hand on my knee. "Callie—"

"Have you checked with Jason to see if he's heard from them?" Aunt Dot fingered her phone.

"No, not yet. He's got enough to deal with." Everyday life was a struggle for my brother Jason right now.

"He can take it. He needs to know." Aunt Dot scowled. "I wish he could be down here with his family. He needs us."

I opened my eyes. "I agree. But the state of Ohio won't give him much of a leash yet. I think he said he would be allowed a short visit down here after like three or four months, if he stays sober and meets all of his probation requirements." And that was a topic for another day. Despite my struggle against it, a huge yawn overtook me.

Todd nudged me. "I know you're wiped out, but you need to tell them about the luggage."

I might as well get it over with. I pushed myself up to look into two anxious faces. "There was another rose. On my mom's suitcase."

"Oh, Callie," Aunt Dot breathed.

I shook my head wearily. I didn't have anything else to say about that. "So I got Mom's suitcase, but some guy grabbed Dad's bag off the carousel right in front of me and ran off with it. Mona and I tried to chase him down, but he disappeared."

"Oh, my. He stole it?" Aunt Dot exchanged a meaningful glance with Harry. "Maybe that's what the Lord has been showing me."

Harry steepled his fingers under his chin. "I believe so, sugar."

"What do you mean, Auntie?"

"As I've been praying for your parents lately, I've seen like a...a...it's hard to describe. Like the old-fashioned kind of knapsack that someone might have carried years ago."

Todd wrinkled his brow. "Like a little sack or bandanna or something tied to the end of a stick?"

"Yes, exactly." She beamed at him.

I pictured my dad dressed like Huckleberry Finn and carrying a knapsack. Of course, I was going on twenty-four hours with no sleep, but I couldn't see the significance. "What do you think it means?"

"That, darlin', is what we need to pray about." Aunt Dot sat up straighter, a gleam in her eye. "But I know this whole situation didn't take God by surprise."

"That's right. And we'll have people working on it twenty-four seven until your parents are located." Todd wrapped his arm around my shoulders. "And this girl needs to go home and get some sleep." He tugged me to my feet.

I got a head rush and plopped back down on the chair, putting my head between my knees until I could think straight again. "I can't sleep," I mumbled. "What if one of them tries to call me? Or what if you guys find out something?"

"I assure you that your aunt and I will be awake and praying, Calendula," Harry boomed.

I was so exhausted I barely noticed Harry use my given name, Calendula. He was the only one who called me that...except the angel. The angel in the hospital a few months ago called me Calendula. I could use a few more angels at this moment. *God, please send Your warrior angels to protect my parents. Release your ministering spirits to comfort and strengthen them...to sing songs of deliverance over them...shield them by Your power...*

Todd looped my hair over my ear, startling me. "If something important happens, I'll come over and wake you up."

I lifted my head, the vision of angels disappearing. "Promise?"

"Promise." He extended his hand, and I stood, slowly this time.

I woke three hours later with a start.

My parents were missing. This time for real.

Adrenaline rushed through my body, and I groaned. I wish I didn't know what this felt like, but in those first few days and weeks following my first husband's fatal car accident, it was the same pattern. Fall asleep. Wake a few hours later in the middle of the night, chest tight and heart racing.

Only this time, it wasn't night. I rolled over and grabbed my phone. It was ten in the morning, and still no text or call from either of my parents. Or from Todd, which probably meant nothing new had happened. Was that a good thing or a bad thing?

Breathe in. Breathe out. I lay flat on my back listening to the happy twittering of the birds at the feeder outside my window. Breathe in, breathe out. The pressure in my chest would subside soon, I hoped. *Jesus...*

I flung my arm over my eyes, blocking out the sunlight that pushed around the edges of the window blinds. What now? I had only been in my twenties when Kevin's death occurred, and in the six years since he had passed away, God had gradually brought me to a place of peace. Since then, I'd had my share of difficulties, but nothing like this. Even the Ginger Slayton deal didn't hold a candle to this. Except that maybe this whole thing was part of the Ginger Slayton case.

My thoughts wandered to the toxicology report. Todd had told me yesterday that they expected it to be released soon. I'd been so upset about my parents, I hadn't even given it another thought until now. And now it didn't seem to matter. Who cared what it said? I didn't kill Ginger, and Wayne could have a party investigating the whole thing on his own without me interfering.

Except for the rose.

I could almost latch onto the shred of hope that my parents might have done something out of character, like write a note and disappear, if it wasn't for the rose. The rose changed everything.

I sighed. My parents and I hadn't had the greatest relationship for the last fifteen or so years of my life, but I had been hoping maybe this time together would provide the chance for healing to take place.

Could they truly have decided to disappear without seeing me or telling me? Or what if the note was a total fake and not from my mother at all? What if they had been kidnapped? And if so, then why? Were they even still alive?

Sudden fear threatened to grip me.

Mom, Dad, where are you? I love you guys so much, even if I haven't shown it like I should.

I thrust myself off the bed, still wearing my shorts and t-shirt, and staggered into the spare bedroom that served as my home office, but more importantly, my prayer room. I sank down on my knees in front of the old chair. The tears started the moment I said His name, and in my mind's eye, I buried myself against His chest.

Jesus.

I am here, Beloved.

I'm so afraid.

I am here.

I clung to Him a little longer, then wiped my tears and settled back on the rug with a sigh. I knew I could not do this alone, but I had learned long ago where to run. I opened my Bible to the Psalms and read until the ache in my heart subsided.

Annie snuffled at the door, and I rose to let her in, limping on my foot that had fallen asleep.

"Hey, there, Miss Big Ears," I said, stroking the velvety fur on her head. She whined and licked my face to comfort me.

"You heard me crying, didn't you, girl?" I rubbed her ears and hugged her. "Where's those pugs? Still snoring?" Purl and Intarsia were not the most energetic little creatures in the world. Chances are, they were still in a furry knot in their cozy bed near the stove.

Annie headed toward the door, looking back over her shoulder to see if I was following.

"I'm coming." I made a detour into the bedroom to grab

my phone, then headed down the short hallway to the kitchen. Bright and sunshiny, it was one of my favorite rooms in the house. I put the kettle on for tea, then filled up my indoor watering can. I'd water the plants, then call Todd if he hadn't called me by then.

Surely Todd would have heard something by now. I knew he was working on getting permission to view the footage from the airport security cameras. And the police had made me give them Mom's suitcase. Maybe they would find something in her suitcase that would give us answers. Because the more I thought about it, the more I knew without a doubt my parents would never write a note like that and disappear. Something had to have happened. Were the threats made against them while they were still in Zambia connected to this disappearance?

I stepped back into my kitchen and pulled my phone out of my pocket right as it vibrated. "Hey, Houston."

"Callie. I hope I didn't wake you. Any news?"

My throat tightened. *No. No news.* My eyes filled, and I leaned against the sink, staring out the window until my voice would work. "No. I was getting ready to check in again with Todd when you called."

"I'll let you go then. I've been praying since you texted me last night." He cleared his throat, and I pictured his brow puckered in concern. "I hate to bring this up now, but I need to know what you want to do about the Hope House schedule. Should we plan to move the ribbon-cutting ceremony to a different time? Harry's got someone coming out to fix the windows this afternoon, but I know that's the least of your worries at the moment."

I groaned. After more than a year of planning and building, Hope House was supposed to become a reality in two weeks. The dedication and ribbon-cutting ceremony were planned for that Friday afternoon, with the first girls scheduled to move in on Saturday. "We can't move it. We're already behind schedule because of the roofing issue last month, and those girls need to be in there."

"I knew that's what you'd say, but—"

"No."

Annie jumped up at the tone of my voice and I straightened my shoulders. I could feel my spirit rising. "The enemy is not going to win. If he thinks he is going to use my parents' situation to derail what God has called us to do, then he has another think coming."

Houston chuckled. "I hear you, girl. Keep me posted, okay? You know Nicole and I are interceding constantly for you."

"Yes." I paced around the tiny kitchen, the pugs staring at me. The empowering presence of the Holy Spirit still pulsed through my body, buoying my expectancy of what He was going to do. "God has brought Nicole so far. She's going to be a mighty tool for Him with these girls." Over the last couple of years, Houston and I had watched God, little by little, deliver Nicole from the wreckage of being sex trafficked herself.

"I'm constantly in awe." Houston's voice cracked. He had loved my neighbor Nicole from afar since he met her years ago, before she had been trapped in addiction and slavery. "Who would have thought, even a year or two ago, that God could work so much healing in her life?"

My phone beeped, and I yanked it away from my ear to see a text from Todd, my heart skipping a beat. Had my parents been located?

I hope you got some rest, sweetheart. I'm in a meeting but will call you ASAP. No new news, but we're working on it. I love you.

I sighed. "Todd just texted and said there was no new news. I was hoping..." My throat closed again, and I pulled off my glasses and wiped them on my shirt.

"I know." Houston's voice slipped into his pastoral-counseling tone. "God is going to see you through this, Callie. Remember when you first found the P.I.'s body on the back doorstep of your shop a couple of years ago? It seemed like there were no answers. But then look what happened. In spite of that terrible event, God brought about justice and freedom for so many, especially Nicole."

He was right. I knew better than to give myself over to despair. And Nicole was a safe topic at the moment. "That girl is going to reach a lot of people." I was proud of Nicole for her commitment to walk through the pain of her memories, bringing them out into the light so God could heal them. I also knew that I knew that I knew that God had put this passion for these young women into my heart, and He had a plan for Hope House that would no doubt astonish even those of us who had been praying it into existence. I blew out a sigh. "God knows where my parents are, just like He knew where you were that time you were kidnapped, right before we found Nicole and the other girls. He showed me then where to find you, and He can do that again."

"Amen. I'll agree with you for that. But you don't think your parents' situation has anything to do with Hope House?"

What?

"I hadn't considered that." Actually, it was more likely it was connected to the Ginger Slayton case, if it was connected to anything. I stopped to stare out the window again, watching the chickadees hop around the feeder. "I haven't had much time to think since everything's been so crazy the last twenty-four hours, but..." I tapped my fingers on my lip, thinking. "I can't imagine how it could be overtly connected. They haven't been involved at all and don't know much about it, unless Aunt Dot has shared more than I have. But I don't doubt it could be a tactic of the enemy to hinder Hope House. I mean, think of the whole big deal with June Blackman last year."

"Right. But—oh, sorry, Callie. I have a call coming in from Harry. I'd better take it."

I pulled the phone from my ear and laid it on the counter, wishing it would ring with a call from one of my parents. It didn't, even after I stared at it for long moments.

Thank God that Houston and Harry were handling all the last-minute details for the Hope House event. I knew they would have everything under control there, at least. I should have reminded Houston to call the reporter from the *CenTex Courier*. What was her name? I couldn't remember, but she'd probably like to cover the ribbon-cutting. Maybe I'd remember to call him back later.

I sipped my lukewarm tea and typed yet another text to my mom, then one to my dad's phone for good measure. He didn't usually pay as much attention to his phone as my mother did, but at this point, it was worth a try. Did they still have their phones? Maybe they could see my texts but not respond for some reason.

I sighed, then read a text from Mona that I had ignored while I was talking to Houston.

Any news??? Can you talk now??? Rob and I have been praying and praying for you and your mama and daddy and we told Lonnie and Rick to pray and they said they would!! We love y'all. And Pastor Brian put y'all on the church prayer chain. Sad face emoji. Praying hands. Praying hands. *The grandkids are over and we're taking them to the pool to burn up some energy before they drive me crazier than I am, LOL but I'm bringing you lunch in a little while so don't eat nothing before I get there, ok???* Taco emoji, donut emoji, smiley face, smiley face.

I had to smile. I often reflected that Mona texted the way she lived—breathlessly and generously with everyone and everything. I wasn't sure I could eat any lunch, though, especially if it was tacos and donuts. Or even if it was Mona's famous extra-cheesy lasagna. Stress made me sick to my stomach. After Kev's death, I think I lived on apples and trail mix for two months.

I glanced at my watch, then texted Mona back.

Give me half an hour.

I needed to be outside in the fresh air, away from phones and tacos and stress. Even if it was almost 100 degrees out. I grabbed Annie's leash.

"Come on, girl. Want to take a walk?"

Usually we walked in the field near my house, but for some reason today, I headed down the street, feeling the perspiration run down my back by the end of the block. We walked and walked. I alternated between praying and worrying while trying to make myself relax, pulling Annie to a halt only when I realized how hard she was panting. Looking around, I realized we had walked all the way to the little park by Ginger Slayton's house. Annie gratefully lapped water from the small creek as I stared down the street.

Maybe we would stroll past Ginger's house on our way home. Just to see.

"Come on, girl." I didn't usually put Annie on a leash, but since we were walking in town instead of the field, I felt better having her on it. We sidled down the sidewalk on the opposite side of the street from Ginger's until we were a couple of houses away. I sucked in my breath.

Ginger's garage door was open.

And her Cadillac was no longer parked in the middle of the garage. In fact, it was backed up in the driveway, the trunk standing open. Neat piles of plastic tubs and cardboard boxes filled the entire left-hand section of the garage.

Hmm.

We stopped. I really, really wanted to see who was there, but it wouldn't be the smartest thing I'd ever done to have some kind of confrontation with someone at Ginger's house. I tugged on Annie's leash, and we slipped behind an overgrown oleander right as Jim Slayton pushed through the front screen door onto the porch, his arms full of cardboard boxes.

What was he doing at his ex-wife's house?

I watched him stack the boxes in the trunk, then disappear into the garage.

Maybe he truly had killed Ginger and he was trying to hide anything incriminating. Or maybe he still loved her and was gathering mementos of their life together. Or maybe he—

Stop it, Callie. The poor man is probably sorting through everything so he can sell the house. And obviously, if he was up to something underhanded, he wouldn't be walking around doing it in broad daylight.

I sighed. I had enough stuff to worry about without spying on Jim Slayton. But now I was stuck. I didn't want him to know I had been watching him, which meant I either needed to hang out behind this bush until he left or walk past him nonchalantly as if hiding behind bushes was my usual MO.

After a long ten minutes, Jim still hadn't come out of the

garage. Maybe he had gone inside for lunch or something.

Annie lay near my feet, gazing at me with a question in her keen brown eyes.

"Okay, we'll go now," I whispered. "Now's our ch—."

Jim strode out of the garage, talking into his headset.

I froze.

Was that my dad's duffel bag in his hand?

CHAPTER TWENTY-ONE

I shoved my sunglasses up on my head and parted a couple of big branches so I could see better. I sucked in my breath. It *was* my dad's duffel bag. The odd-shaped Kool-Aid stain was visible even from here.

Oh, man.

I quashed my impulse to run over there and grab the bag from Jim's hand. What was he doing with my dad's bag? And he had seemed so nice.

The old liar.

"I can't believe this," I murmured. I wished now I hadn't left my phone at home. Otherwise, I'd call the sheriff right now and have him catch Jim red-handed. It would serve him right, trying to trick me by all that talk about Hope House and giving a donation, blah, blah, blah. I watched him toss the duffel bag in the trunk on top of the boxes and slam the lid shut.

At least it was only my dad's bag he had thrown into the trunk, not my dad. I gulped.

Wait a minute.

If Jim Slayton had my dad's bag, wouldn't it be likely that he also had my dad? And my mom?

Jim headed back into the garage, and I tugged on Annie's leash.

"Let's go, girl!" I broke into a run back the way I came, Annie loping along next to me. I had to get Wayne or Todd or someone over here before Jim got away.

We made it to the park and slowed to a stop, panting. I glanced over my shoulder.

Good. Ginger's car was still parked in the driveway.

I sucked in a few deep breaths and headed home at a trot, ignoring the fire in my out-of-shape thighs. Flinging open the front door, I snatched my phone off the kitchen counter and called Wayne's personal cell phone number.

"Yello. Houle, here."

"Wayne, it's Callie Erickson. I was just over near Ginger Slayton's house and I—"

"Have a guilty conscience, Miz Erickson? I thought I'd have to drag the truth out of you."

What?

"Uh, I'm not sure what you're talking about, but—"

"I'm talkin' about I got a call from Jim Slayton no more'n an hour ago and he said someone's been in that house. Took some pictures off the wall or somethin'. You mean to tell me that wasn't you?"

"No." How dare he think... "What if Jim was making all of that up? Why would you believe him and not me?"

"I don't know who to b'lieve, but if I got somebody still messin' with Ginger's house, then I got a problem."

He had a problem? I gritted my teeth, then spoke more loudly than normal, enunciating every word so there would be no mistaking my meaning. "Sheriff, let me explain myself clearly. Point number one: Ginger Slayton is dead. I did not have anything to do with her murder, nor have I been in her house. Ever. Point number two: my parents are missing. Point number three: There seems to be some connection between the Slayton case and my parents' disappearance. I called to alert you that I saw Jim Slayton, less than fifteen minutes ago, throw my dad's missing duffel bag into the trunk of his car. The bag someone stole from the airport baggage claim. Point number four: I need you to do something about that. Now."

He mumbled something.

"What?" I snapped. "If you're incapable of taking care of this, I'll call the Temple PD and have them—"

"Ma'am. Please try to calm down." He coughed. "I've been tied up all morning with the pile-up on the highway. A fatality. I'm meeting Jim over at the house to take his report on the break-in, and I will make every effort to investigate your, ah, concern about the bag. In the meantime, will you please just stay out of my way?"

"I will as long as you're doing your job." I wasn't usually so difficult, but enough was enough.

He hung up on me.

I tossed my phone onto the kitchen table and stormed out the back door. Maybe I should sneak back over there to

Ginger's and watch to see if Wayne really was going to talk to Jim.

I paced around to the side yard, spooking a couple of female cardinals and a mockingbird. They flew into the pomegranate bush with a rush of wings. The old crow hopped along the top rail of the fence and cawed as if laughing at the smaller birds.

Or maybe I should just march over there and demand Jim give me my dad's bag. What if there was a clue in there? What if it was the last tangible link to my parents I would ever have?

Oh Dad, where are you?

I groaned, my brief rush of anger subsiding, drowned by the wave of fear and grief. What if I never saw my parents again? What if someone was hurting them right now? Or had already killed them?

I sank down onto the lawn chair by the back door and squeezed my eyes tight against the hot tears.

Breathe in, breathe out.

I opened my eyes and leaned back in the seat, forcing myself to relax. I had to get my mind off everything, if even for a couple of minutes. A blue jay screamed somewhere in the distance and I allowed my mind to imagine him flying free above the tree tops, up into the cloudless spring sky. If only I could fly free of these cares and concerns.

One day. One day I would be free. The day I finally reached Heaven and saw my Savior face to face, my loved ones surrounding me.

I sighed. But until then, I had to endure. Believe. Trust.

Purl waddled over to me and sat on my foot, and I smiled ruefully, thinking of the words from *The Practice of the Presence of God* I had memorized many years ago. "Let it be your business to keep your mind in the presence of the Lord: it sometimes wanders and withdraws itself from Him, do not much disquiet yourself for that. Trouble and disquiet serve rather to distract than to recall the mind; the will must bring it back in tranquility; if you persevere with your whole strength, God will have pity on you."

Forgive me, God. I do trust you. I will trust you. Please,

Father. Have mercy on me and my parents.

I rose and headed for the house, then stooped to pick up a tiny iridescent bead from the walkway. Where had it come from? I rolled it around in my fingers, then stuck it in my pocket. It had probably blown into the yard with all that wind we'd been having the last few days. "Springtime in Texas should be renamed 'constantly-blowing-wind time'," I muttered to the dogs.

Annie barked loudly and ran a circle around me before bolting toward the side gate.

"It wasn't that funny." I pushed the gate open and followed her, freezing as I strolled around the corner to the front of the house. Sheriff Wayne stood on my front porch, Annie already sniffing around his shoes.

"Hey, there," I called. I stayed where I was, right next to the boxwood hedge, my heart pounding. Had he come to arrest me after all? Or did he have information about my parents?

He turned toward me and held up my dad's bag. "This what you were fussin' about?"

I raised my eyebrows as we met halfway on the lawn. "You recovered it from Jim? Did you arrest him?"

"Nah." He handed me the bag. "I'm tellin' you, Jim didn't have nothin' to do with this whole deal."

I clutched the handle of the bag tightly, dying to look inside. But first I had to know what was going on with Jim. "Then why did he have my dad's bag? That seems super suspicious to me."

He shrugged. "He says he don't know how it got into the garage, but Ginger's sister'n him been cleaning out the house. The bag was piled with the rest of the stuff in the garage, so he thought it was in the donatin' pile, he said. Caught him right before he headed to Goodwill."

Hmm. That sounded plausible. Except for one thing. "So the bag belonging to my missing father just happens to turn up in Ginger Slayton's garage? Did you question him about my parents?"

He hooked his thumb in his belt loop. "Look, ma'am. You got the bag. Can you please be happy with that and let me do my job?"

I stared him down for a long minute, but he didn't budge, except to turn and spit on my grass before meeting my gaze with a glare of his own. What a frustrating man. Apparently, I wasn't going to get any more information from him at the moment. Maybe Todd could wrangle more details out of him later. "Thanks for getting the bag back for me."

Annie escorted Wayne to his car, then came and flumped down next to me on the porch. I stroked her velvety head. "At least we have the bag, even though we don't have Mom and Dad yet. Should we look in the bag?"

She whined and licked the tip of my nose, her chocolate brown eyes expressive.

"I know, it's been a crazy last few days, hasn't it?"

I texted Todd and asked him to call me when he could, then pulled the bag toward me.

"Toothbrush, Bible, socks...underwear, two ties and a crossword puzzle book," I said to Annie as I dug through my dad's bag. "Nothing unusual in here. But maybe whoever stole it already took out the important stuff." I sniffed, feeling a little closer to Dad just having his belongings in my hands. Soon, I would have both him and my mom in my arms. I simply had to believe that until—no, no 'until.' "I choose to hope," I said out loud.

I leaned over to poke the dirt in the potted pansies. Too dry. I'd have to water them when I got up, but right now, I needed to sit still for a few minutes and regroup. Thank God Sharlene was available to run C. Willikers for me this week. That took some pressure off, at least. And I didn't have any big jobs right now since I had lost the Perkins' wedding.

I rubbed my temples and replayed the events of the last few hours, starting from the time Mona and I arrived at the airport a few days ago. I stopped when I got to the incident at the luggage carousel. Everything had been so crazy since then, I hadn't had much time to think about the details. Now something bothered me about the guy who had grabbed my dad's duffel bag. For one thing, he seemed vaguely familiar. I'm not the most observant person in the world, but the guy was bigger than anyone else I'd ever met. Surely, I'd remember if I knew him from somewhere. And then there was Houston's question that kept replaying in my mind. Did my parents' disappearance have anything to do with Hope House? And if so, did the duffel bag thief have anything to do with it? And how was the duffel bag thief connected to Jim Slayton and/or Ginger Slayton?

I pushed myself up off the porch steps, deciding it would do me some good to go over to C. Willikers today after all, especially since I hadn't heard from Todd yet. I had a little bit of paperwork I had to finish before the weekend. Plus, I wasn't sure I wanted to be home by myself any more right now. Maybe it would be helpful to focus my mind on work for a few minutes. Sharlene would be happy for an update, anyway. Thank God she had been working for me long enough to know how to keep things afloat while I was gone.

Todd's white pick-up was parked outside my store when I pulled up. Was he waiting for me? I parked behind him and opened my door to step into his embrace. He held me tightly for a long time. I stood still, listening to his heart beat—feeling his warm breath on the top of my head. If only I could stay here in his arms, protected from the big scary world. However. I sighed and pulled away to look up at him. "What are you doing here? I thought you'd still be at work."

The grief in his eyes stole my breath away, and he crushed me into his chest, pressing me to him as if clinging to a life preserver.

What had happened?

"My parents?" I managed to croak.

I felt him shake his head, a low moan escaping him. "No."

Then what? Who? Had something terrible happened to Chad, Todd's son? God, please no.

I reached up to frame his face with both hands. "Look at me. I'm here. What is it?"

He groaned. "Carly. She was my partner. My friend."

What? I scrunched my forehead. "Who, Todd?"

"The car accident this morning. On Old 95. I got there first."

I hadn't known there was—oh, yeah. Now I remembered Wayne saying something about a bad car wreck this morning. The person who died was Todd's partner? Wasn't Jay his partner? But now wasn't the time for asking questions. I stroked his dark hair from his temple, then pulled him into a tight hug. "I'm so sorry, honey," I murmured against his chest.

He stroked his hand up and down my back, over and over for long moments.

I stood still, praying for this man whom I loved, a hundred questions running through my thoughts. The only other time I had seen him this distraught was when I almost got shot a couple of years ago.

His hand stilled on my back. "I knew I should have called her."

I made comforting noises, not knowing what else to do. "Do you want to talk about it?"

"No!" He thrust me away without warning and turned to slam his palm against the truck door. "God, why didn't I talk to her? I'm such a fool." His breath came in ragged gasps. "I call myself a Christian, and I couldn't even—oh, God. Please forgive me." He braced his arms against the truck, his head bowed down between them.

I stood frozen, stunned at the fierce display of raw emotion from this man who was my pillar of steadiness and predictability. What had he done?

"I'm going to go inside." I stepped toward him and laid my hand on his back for a moment. Clearly, he needed a few minutes to gather himself. "I love you."

He didn't respond, but I knew he heard me.

I paused with my hand on the front doorknob of C. Willikers, sensing a turning point in my relationship with Todd. Whatever was going on, it was real-life stuff. And he had been vulnerable enough to let me in.

The chimes on the door jingled as I entered my shop. "Hi, Sharlene."

Her pale, thin face brightened, and she held one finger up

while continuing to talk on the phone.

I glanced out the front picture window where Todd slumped against the side of the truck. My heart ached for his grief, but at the same time, I was tempted to feel a little alarmed about his relationship with the woman who had died.

I shook my head. No. I knew in my heart Todd was true to me. He had never given me occasion to question his character. I stowed my purse under the counter while Sharlene finished taking an order.

True, I didn't know everything about Todd's past. But he didn't know everything about mine, either. Just the things that mattered to both of us.

But wouldn't a female partner be someone he would have told me about? I sighed. Nope, I couldn't go there. I trusted Todd, and he would talk to me about her when he was ready. But what if—a new, terrible thought struck me. What if the "accident" wasn't an accident? If this woman was, or had been, Todd's partner, then she must be a law enforcement officer. Or maybe an investigator. What if she was somehow connected to my parents' case? I winced.

My parents were not a 'case'. They were my family. And I—

Stop it, Callie.

I took a deep breath. *God, please calm my spirit. I know You are in control and You know what is happening. Jesus, I trust you.*

"Jesus, I trust you." I whispered it out loud, needing to hear my own voice say it with my own ears. I fingered the fuzzy leaf of an African violet, letting my eyes—and my mind—rest on the pink, frilly blossoms for a moment as I cast my cares on the One who cared for me.

I turned around, hearing Sharlene finishing up her phone call. The store looked beautiful. Sharlene had an eye for decorating, and she was much more conscientious about dusting than I would ever be. I wandered over to the huge Christmas cactus on the stand by the front window, happy to see the tip of each leaf swelling with tiny, round pink buds. I pulled out my phone.

"I'll have to take a picture for Aunt Dot. The Christmas cactus is finally budding," I called to Sharlene. This particular plant had been handed down on Aunt Dot's side of the family for almost 100 years now. And when she moved into Willowbough a few years ago, she had bequeathed the flowering giant to me.

"I hadn't noticed." Sharlene came up beside me and laid her thin arm over my shoulders. "How are you, Boss? Any news?"

"Nothing on my parents, yet. Thank you for asking."

She squeezed my shoulders. "I'm sorry. I've been praying."

"Don't stop. Even though we don't see anything happening doesn't mean God isn't working."

"I'm learning that." She pushed her white-blonde hair behind her ear. "I read something, like, really, really cool in my devotional this morning. It was like, 'when there is a situation that needs prayer, pray until you defiantly believe God and can thank Him for the answer.' Isn't that awesome?"

Wow. Out of the mouths of babes. If I ever needed to defy fear and thank God in faith for a yet-unseen answer, it was today. I swallowed hard. "Thank you. I needed to hear that today."

She beamed. "That's so cool. Uh, what's wrong with Todd?"

CHAPTER TWENTY-TWO

I followed Sharlene's gaze out the large front window. Todd sat motionless in his truck; his head bowed onto the steering wheel.

"I think he's regrouping. Sometimes the stuff he has to deal with is hard to take." Should I tell Sharlene about the woman? I might as well, since it would probably be all over the news any minute now anyway if it wasn't already. "There was a really bad accident out on Old 95 this morning. A fatality. Apparently, it was a pretty grisly scene, and he was the first one to get there."

"Ewwww. What? Get out of here." Sharlene chewed on her thumbnail, staring at me wide-eyed. Then, "Was it anyone we know?"

"No, I don't think so." My stomach flipped over just thinking about it. It would be bad enough to have to deal with it, but then to realize it was a friend...

She looked out at Todd again. "That's so sad. I don't know how cops do stuff like that, ya know? All the blood and stuff." She shuddered.

I closed my eyes. "That's not helping."

"I'm sorry, Callie. I would be so freaked out if I were you."

I am freaked out. I'm holding it in, like I do with everything. I opened my eyes. "And the bad thing for Todd is it was someone he knew."

"Who?" She grasped my arm.

"I don't know. I didn't know her." Yes, I did. I gasped. I hadn't made the connection until now, but the face of the reporter who had recently interviewed me about an article for C. Willikers popped into my brain. Wasn't her name Carly? Yes, I was sure of it. I shuddered. "I think it was that reporter from the *CenTex Courier.*"

"Oh, man. She seemed so nice." She pushed her hands into the pockets of her hoodie. "This is so crazy. And at the same time your parents are missing. I'm so sorry, Callie. I'll keep praying."

I nodded. "Thank you. That helps a lot." I rubbed my temples. If I thought I had a headache before, I really had one now. "Why don't you head home for the day, Shar? I'll finish what I'm doing and lock up. Todd and I need to spend some time together this evening."

"Are you sure you're okay? You don't look so good." She pulled a tin of mints out of her pocket. "Want one? Might make you not feel like you're going to barf."

Did I look like I was going to? I knew I felt like it, but it was worse when someone else could tell. I filled the little electric tea kettle with water and switched it on. "I'll be fine. Mostly I need answers. And sleep." And preferably in that order.

I wandered outside with Sharlene. Maybe Todd was ready for company. I pulled open the passenger door of the truck and slid in close next to him, laying my head against his arm. He threaded my fingers through his, and we sat for long minutes, watching the cars go by on Main Street.

Finally, I lifted my head from his shoulder. The last few hours were catching up to me, and if I sat still much longer, I'd fall asleep. "Do you feel like talking?"

"I need to get back to the station. I needed a breather." He sighed deeply. "I know I owe you an explanation, but it's not what you think."

I smiled up at him. "What I think is that I trust you."

He squeezed my hand hard. "Thank you, sweetheart. You don't realize how much that means to me, especially after—"

"I know." One of the deepest hurts of Todd's previous marriage was his ex-wife's unfaithfulness and trust issues stemming from that. He and I had an ongoing discussion about what trust looks like in a marriage, and how we would build it and maintain it in our own relationship.

"Her name is—was—Carly." He choked. "Sorry."

I steeled myself, my head throbbing. "You can tell me about her later. It's okay."

"No. I need to tell you now, so you understand." He turned toward me in the faint light. "She was my partner for a couple of years, back when I was on the force in Dallas. We went through thick and thin together." He rubbed a hand over the back of his neck. "I know she saved my life more than once."

I waited.

"We were never involved romantically, but when you work with someone every day and trust that person with your life, you get pretty close."

"I imagine." Where was he going with this? And if she was a cop, why had she been posing as a reporter?

"She always had an ambition to be a Texas Ranger. Her dad was a Ranger who was killed in the line of duty. She wanted to honor him."

Oh, boy.

"She gave one-hundred percent to everything she did, and she was a dang good cop. It was her life." His voice roughened. "I attended her swearing-in the day she became a Ranger. I knew how hard she had worked and why she wanted it so badly."

Ah. Okay. I didn't know much about the Texas Rangers, except that they took on very serious cases that local law enforcement agencies couldn't handle. Like human trafficking rings. And serial murder cases.

I gulped. "Do you think she was here investigating my parents' situation?"

Nice, Callie. Todd's baring his heart and you're more concerned about your situation.

I laid my hand on his forearm. "Todd, I'm sorry. I know that's not what we're talking about here."

"It's all right." He rubbed his hand down his whiskery jaw. "I don't want to speculate, but it's possible. Anyway, after she became a Ranger, we kept in touch, but not much. I was going through the divorce, and she was super busy with her new job."

He offered me a piece of cinnamon gum, then folded one into his own mouth. "I heard things about her here and there over the last few years. Sounded like she was doing great." He sighed. "But for the last few weeks, I kept having this sense that I should call her."

Ah. "Just to reconnect?"

"No." He bounced his leg up and down for a full minute,

staring out the windshield at the gathering dusk. "I knew the Holy Spirit wanted me to talk to her about her soul." He turned to face me then, anguish washing over his features. "I meant to do it, Callie. In fact, one day I even had my phone in my hand to text her. But things got crazy and I was busy, and I just kept putting it off. And now—"

And now she's dead.

The unspoken thought hung in the air.

What could I say?

Todd groaned and buried his face in his hands. "She slipped out into eternity without knowing Christ. And I was supposed to tell her. Oh, God, how can You ever forgive me?"

"Todd, listen to me." I drew a deep breath, my heart breaking for him. And for Carly. "God is merciful. You don't know what the state of her soul was when she died. Maybe she had time to cry out to Him."

He raised his head. "Yeah, but He asked me to tell her about Him, and I didn't."

"Maybe He sent someone else who did."

"That doesn't change the fact that I should have put the importance of my friend's eternity in front of my own worthless stuff I thought was so urgent." He slammed his palm onto the dashboard.

I couldn't refute that. Shouldn't we all be living from a perspective of eternity all the time? But how often we failed, focusing only on the here and now. "Only God knows, Todd," I murmured. "I'm so sorry."

He leaned his head against the headrest. "Me, too. I will be sorry until the day I die. But that's not enough, is it?"

I pulled into the parking lot at Willowbough a couple of hours later. Todd had gone back to the scene, then home to catch a few minutes of rest. Mona had insisted on coming with me to catch Aunt Dot up on the latest details of the craziness. I turned the ignition off but didn't get out of my minivan. I glanced over at Mona. "Surely we should have had some news on my parents by now."

She shook her head, pulling her favorite purple reading glasses off the top of her head as she stared at her phone. "Listen to this headline. 'Police Suspect Foul Play in Missing Missionary Case'."

I groaned. "Great. I suppose I'll start getting calls from reporters now."

"Just send 'em to me. I'll give them an earful."

And then some, no doubt. I sighed. "Let's go in. I hope Harry's here."

We pushed through the familiar doors of Willowbough, the cool air welcome after the muggy heat outside. I fervently hoped I would not run into Veronica. I didn't have any emotional energy left to deal with her.

"Callie! Good to see you, Mona." Harry strode down the carpeted hall toward us. He held his arms out to me. "What's going on, darlin'? Any news?"

I stepped into his embrace for a moment, feeling his enormous western belt buckle bite into my ribs. Though we were not related by blood, Harry had become a rock for me in the last couple of years. I pulled away and sighed. "No. Nothing."

"Well, doggone it." Harry stuck his hands in his pockets and jingled his change, his expression grim. "I don't like it, Callie."

My stomach clenched. "What don't you like?"

"Something is fishy about the whole scenario."

"Fishy?" Mona snorted and crossed her plump arms across her chest. "It's more than fishy. First some wanna-be rap star steals Callie's dad's duffel bag. Then her parents disappear into thin air. Then Todd's ex-partner dies—"

"What?" Harry's eyes grew wide behind his glasses.

I closed my eyes. Surely, I would wake up any minute and realize all of this was a crazy dream. I opened my eyes and slumped down onto the yellow vinyl chair near the dining room. "She was the woman who died in the car wreck out on Old 95 this morning." I sighed and rubbed my temples. "Todd asked for you guys to pray. I'm assuming there's some suspicion it wasn't an accident. She was a Texas Ranger."

"Dear God." Harry's silver eyebrows drew together. "It happened this morning?"

"Yeah. Todd was the first one on the scene. He's taking it pretty hard." I somehow kept my voice even, but sudden hot panic clawed up my throat, threatening to cut off my breath. I shuddered, wrapping my arms around myself, picturing again the grief in Todd's eyes. How much more crisis could we take? *Jesus, please help me. I'm losing my grip...*

"Oh, Callie. I'm so sorry, darlin'." Harry's big hand, smelling of spicy aftershave, settled on the top of my head. "I speak peace to your spirit right now. Peace be still."

I pulled in a deep breath. Then another.

Mona looped her arm through mine. "Y'all are going to get through this. Thank God it wasn't anyone from church or anything."

I shuddered. That would have been worse. Maybe. I raised my head and caught Harry's eye, wanting to tell him more, but I would wait until Mona was out of earshot. She was my best friend, but she wasn't the greatest at keeping things quiet.

My phone rang and I jumped. I didn't recognize the number, but maybe it was someone calling to give me news of my parents. More likely, it was a nosy reporter. I sighed. I might as well answer it and get it over with. "Hello?"

No response.

"Hello?" Hmm. Hopefully just a pocket dial. But what if it was something more sinister? Someone trying to spook me?

Well, it was working. I hit the off button and gave my friends a shaky smile. "I need a few minutes in the sunshine."

I had to get a grip. I slipped out the front door and strode down the path toward the small courtyard behind the nursing-home section of the building. Good. No one else was out here, though I noticed one of the male employees heaving huge white trash bags into the dumpsters behind the facility. I paused for a moment, trying to remember where I had seen him before. Recently.

At the Mexican restaurant? No, I didn't think so. The grocery store? No. Oh, well. It would probably come to me later when I was driving. Or trying to sleep.

Shrugging, I slipped through the wrought-iron gate, pushing my growing anxiety down. No one had cleaned up since winter, it looked like. A few withered tomatoes, left over from autumn, still clung to the grey, brittle plants of the small vegetable garden, and a mockingbird perched on the edge of the concrete birdbath. I strolled around the path, stopping to examine the lobelia that still bloomed in the shaded pots under the Texas mountain laurel. I fingered the glossy leaves of the Texas mountain laurel tree, wishing it was in bloom. I sank down onto a concrete bench near the doorway, where a crepe myrtle tree lent a bit of dappled shade. The brilliant fuchsia blooms distracted me from my thoughts for a moment as I ran my hand down the smooth bark of the trunk.

I wondered briefly who was in charge of keeping the garden for the residents. If I lived here, I would want to see more birds, though. Maybe I could bring a couple of bird feeders and a bag of seed next time I came. I envisioned a hummingbird feeder tucked in between the two enormous oleander bushes, and maybe a seed feeder over there by the bench. I'm sure Aunt Dot would love it, especially since she had left all of her feeders for me when she moved to Willowbough a few years ago. And now that she and Harry would have their own place, they could do whatever they wanted to their little yard.

The sun was hot on my bare arms. I sat in the quiet, twisting around the charm that still hung from my neck. I don't know why I continued to wear the ugly thing. I guess I was holding out hope that it really was a clue to all of this. And maybe someone would notice it and say something incriminating.

I snorted. *Yeah, right, Callie.*

If it were that easy, we wouldn't be in the big mess we are now, would we? A painted lady fluttered past and lighted on the barely-pink hawthorn blooms. My throat tightened. My mom loved butterflies.

Where are you, Mom? Dad? Are you somewhere where you can see the sunshine? What if they were somewhere near, seeing the same clouds I was watching? Breathing the same air?

Hearing the same train whistle sounding?

I jumped up, retracing my steps around the small yard. Up until now, I couldn't bring myself to consider the possibility that my parents were willingly involved in something...out of the ordinary. But if the Texas Rangers were involved...What if my parents hadn't been kidnapped at all, but, as some of the law enforcement folks had hinted, had purposely left the airport? But if so, then why? And why hadn't they contacted me? Had they innocently become involved in something they thought was good, and then it turned out to be something they didn't expect? But, like what? I didn't even know what to imagine. Like, they trusted someone for a business deal, and it went bad? I frowned. That didn't make any sense. My parents were only going to be on furlough for a year, and then they would be heading back to Zambia. And what about the rose? Could that have been meant to throw me off the real case?

I absently plucked dead blossoms off a gangly geranium. Maybe my parents had inside information about...about what? A political thing in Zambia that had international implications? My thoughts were going in circles. Could my parents have truly concocted a scheme to disappear once they arrived in America? But why? Were they in danger from someone or something, and the only way to escape was to fake a disappearance?

"Callie."

I whirled but saw no one. Had I imagined hearing my name? Weird. My heart rate kicking up, I strolled around the small space again, listening intently but trying not to look like I was.

Nothing.

I stopped and turned 360 degrees on my heel. Not a soul around, and no place for anyone to hide, either. I shook my head, sudden weariness bearing down on me like a heavy blanket. "Now I'm hearing things. I need sleep."

I wandered back to Aunt Dot's, deciding not to tell everyone what I had imagined. Because that's all it was. Wishful imagining.

That's not enough, is it? Todd's words had followed me all afternoon. Followed me home from Willowbough. Followed me as I made a cup of tea, refilled the bird feeders, watered the pansies, and pretended not to see the yellow police tape still strung around Sherm's yard.

Not enough.

It wasn't enough to be sorry. I had to face the fact that though my heart ached over my parents' disappearance, I hurt as much or more at the prospect of never being able to ask their forgiveness for my self-centeredness these last few years. I recognized it now for what it was, and it wasn't pretty.

I leaned against my kitchen sink, staring out at the bird feeder in the side yard. A pair of cardinals hopped around underneath it, chirping happily, while a black-capped chickadee snatched a seed and flew to the safety of the oak tree. It must be so nice to be a bird, I thought for the hundredth time lately. No worries. No heartache.

My eyes filled, and I dried them with the dishtowel. What if I never saw my parents again on this earth? I couldn't bear the thought. "Someone has to know something. Or at least have seen them. Lord, please let us find them before it's too late."

Annie whined and nudged my leg with her nose.

"I'm sorry, girl. I haven't paid much attention to you today, have I?" I rubbed her ears, and she laid a large paw on my thigh. "Okay, we'll go outside. Where's your ball?"

She practically mowed the pugs over in her scramble to grab her tennis ball from the living room, then came skidding back into the kitchen with it in her mouth. I grabbed her ball thrower and headed out the front door. At least if we played in the front yard, we wouldn't have to be near the crime scene where the whole mind-boggling mess had started. And besides, I could see the sunset better from the front yard. It was one of those pink Texas sunsets that seemed to cast a magical glow on even the most mundane of scenery. It would be good to have a few minutes of normalcy in this crazy day.

"Give me your ball, Annie."

She dropped it at my feet, smiling up at me.

I fitted the ball into the plastic thrower and whipped it across the yard. Where were my parents? Maybe someone was holding them hostage.

Annie trotted toward me, her tail held high in victory. I lobbed the ball again, this time past the two tall pecan trees that stood between mine and Sherm's house.

But if they were being held hostage, why hadn't we received any kind of demand from the kidnapper? And why would someone hold my parents hostage to begin with? It's not like they had gobs of money or anything. And I sure didn't.

Surely this couldn't be connected to Hope House. I sighed, watching Annie throw herself, panting, onto the ground. I thought all the people who were involved in the sex trafficking ring we helped break up a couple of years ago were still behind bars. And even if they weren't, would they be foolish enough to go after me again? By messing with my parents?

It seemed ludicrous. But then again, I guess people who do things like that don't think the way I do. I set the ball thrower on the front porch swing, suddenly spent. I couldn't make sense of any of this, and my brain was too weary to try. "Come on, Annie. Let's go get your dinner."

The brilliant sunset had resolved into streaks of mauve and orange across a periwinkle sky as I detoured to the side yard to check the hummingbird feeder in the waning light. Full enough. I'd refill it tomorrow. The old crow, who had apparently become a full-time resident of my yard, shuffled around my feet.

"Good night to you too, Mr. Crow," I said. I supposed he was waiting for his nightly serving of dog food. I slipped into the garage, then flung a bowlful out on the walkway for him.

The exhaustion hit me as I set the dogs' bowls on the floor. It was only seven. I couldn't go to bed now. My parents were still missing. I should be doing—something, right? I should be making phone calls. Or praying fervently. Or...eating. I couldn't remember the last time I had eaten anything, though I had drunk enough cups of tea to set some kind of national tea-drinking record.

I opened the refrigerator, staring at the contents for a long minute, but my stomach rebelled at any of the choices. I finally grabbed a handful of purple grapes and staggered down the hallway to my bedroom, intending only to lie down for half an hour.

I knew nothing else until I jerked awake hours later in the pitch dark, acrid smoke burning my nostrils.

CHAPTER TWENTY-THREE

My house was on fire!

I jumped to my feet and crashed dizzily into the bedroom wall. I staggered over to switch on my lamp, my heart pounding, my thoughts jumbled. *I had to get out of here! Had someone set my house on fire?*

Annie raised her head to stare at me.

I grabbed my glasses from my nightstand. "Come on, Annie! We need to get out of here!"

She scrambled to her feet as I sprinted down the hallway, phone in hand. *Where was the fire?*

We bolted into the kitchen, and I flicked on the light. Nothing there.

I laid my palm on the wooden door leading into the garage. Thank God, no heat. I yanked the door open to peer into the black stuffiness. Nothing.

What in the world?

I sniffed the air, sure that I still smelled smoke. I should call 911, but...

Annie whined.

God?

I ran outside into the early-morning mist, straining to see beyond the circle of light from my front porch light. Nothing. Not a sound, not a spark.

I sniffed the air again. Still smoky, but only faintly. Maybe it wasn't my house at all. Maybe it was Sherm's. Or...maybe I had been dreaming.

An owl hooted in the thicket behind my house as I dropped onto the porch swing, Annie settling on top of my bare feet. My legs still trembled from the surge of adrenaline. Well, I was awake now, that was for sure. What a realistic dream.

Too bad my parents' situation wasn't all a bad dream. I stroked Annie's head, feeling a flood tide of tears rising. I hadn't allowed myself to cry yesterday. I had to be strong and keep my head about me while I dealt with the law enforcement people. I couldn't afford to be off in a corner somewhere crying when I needed to be providing information or making phone calls. But now, in the quiet darkness, the events of the previous two days poured over me in a torrent as if a dam had broken. I dropped my head and wept.

Annie whined and tried to lick my face, and I wrapped my arms around her furry neck. I wished Todd were here. Just the feel of his strong arms around me would help.

Help, but not fix. Only God could make right what was wrong. Only He could truly comfort me. I sucked in a shuddering breath, then blew it out, remembering a quote from Spurgeon I had read earlier in the week. *"I have learned to kiss the wave that throws me against the Rock of Ages."*

I couldn't say I had quite reached the point where I was ready to "kiss the wave," but I knew from long experience that God would somehow see me through this heartache. And I would know Him better and trust Him more for it.

I let loose of Annie and blew my nose heartily. Once I had some time to regroup, I would need to journal everything, so I remembered all the details. I tucked my feet underneath me and pulled out my phone, realizing I still wore my clothes from yesterday. Oh, well. Who really cared?

I scrolled through my text messages. What if God had done something amazing while I slept, and there was a text from one of my parents?

Nope. Nothing notable except a missed call from a Temple phone number. Was that the investigator's number? I squinted at it. I'd talked to so many people yesterday, I couldn't keep track of who was who. Well, whoever it was, I wasn't going to call him back at—I glanced at my phone again—three fifty-three in the morning. Probably it was a nosy news reporter, anyway.

The smell of smoke permeated my senses again.

Daughter.

I paused. I had been so frazzled the last couple of days, I hadn't taken much time to listen to His voice.

Smoke wafted past me again. Could there be a small fire just starting somewhere? Had I left my curling iron on? Or the oven? The dryer? The—*oh, no.*

My electric tea kettle at my shop.

I jumped up, then collapsed onto the swing again, my head rebelling at the sudden movement. I should know by now not to move from a sitting position so abruptly.

I hung my head between my legs for a moment, thinking. I had filled the kettle when Sharlene and I were talking, and I know I turned it on intending to make a cup of tea. But I never did make myself that cup because I went outside to talk to Todd. And I hadn't gone back in afterward; just locked the door and left. Could I have left the kettle on?

Groaning, I rose to my feet, slowly this time, picturing C. Willikers going up in flames. Surely the kettle had some sort of safety turn-off or something? Probably not, since it was an older model I had picked up from a garage sale. I sighed. I wouldn't be able to sleep anytime soon anyway, so I might as well head over there and check things out.

"Come on, Annie. You and I need to go on an adventure." I held the front door open for her, then followed her in to grab my purse. The pugs still snored in a knot in their bed by the stove, oblivious to everything.

I sniffed the air. No smoke.

Whatever.

I slipped my small pistol into my purse, congratulating myself on remembering to take it with me. After the events of the last couple of years, Todd had insisted that I get a concealed-carry permit. I still didn't like the thought of it, but I wasn't going to be foolhardy, either. Particularly with a murderer on the loose in the neighborhood.

Ack. I hadn't exactly thought of it like that until now.

Wayne had promised he would patrol the neighborhood more than usual for the next few days, but still.

"What time I am afraid, I will trust in You." I said the verse from Psalms out loud as I opened my van door. Thankfully, I had gotten it back from the police yesterday, and after Harry tinkered with the wires and undid whatever someone did to it to make it not start, it was as good as new.

Annie hopped in, and I backed down my driveway,

shivering in the pre-dawn dampness. What if I had left the stupid kettle on, and my business had burned to the ground? What if—

"God, you are my refuge. A very strong help in time of need." I continued to pray as I sped through the deserted streets, barely touching my brakes at our one blinking stoplight.

We pulled up in front of C. Willikers a minute or two later, my heart in my throat. In the glare of my headlights, nothing seemed amiss.

Thank God.

At least the building was still intact.

"Come on, Annie!" I threw open the van door and sprinted toward my shop.

Did I smell smoke?

I fumbled with the lock, then threw the door open and flicked on the small lamp by the front door. Nothing.

Annie plunged past me into the shop, growling.

I froze in the doorway.

Was someone in my store?

My purse—with my pistol in it—was in the van. My breath coming in gasps, I crept backwards onto the porch then turned and fled through the dark yard to the vehicle. Thank God I had left it unlocked!

I jumped in and closed the door as quietly as I could, then locked it. I wanted to drive away, but I couldn't leave Annie in there with...with...a bad person. My hands shaking, I pressed Todd's number.

He answered on the first ring; his voice more alert than anyone's should be at four o'clock in the morning. "Sweetheart, what's wrong? Where are you?"

"In my v-van. At my shop. Annie's in there and I th-think someone's in there and they might hurt her. Hurry, Todd! I thought I smelled smoke, but I didn't and so I c-came to check the shop and Annie s-started growling and—"

"Drive down to the sheriff's office, Callie. Now." Todd's command jerked me back to my senses.

"But Annie is in there!" I tried to fit the key into the

ignition, but my hands wouldn't cooperate. Was that someone peeking out the shop window at me?

"Go now."

I finally got the van started. Thank God the sheriff's office was right down the street.

"Are you driving?" Todd demanded.

I glanced back at the shop as I pulled away, my teeth chattering and my heart breaking. I couldn't lose a furry family member too. Not right now. Please, God.

"Y-yes, but Annie—"

"I'll get her. I'm on my way. A couple of the volunteer fire fighters should be at the station even if Wayne isn't. Stay there until I get there, please."

I obediently pulled into the gravel parking lot of the sheriff's office, then rested my head against the steering wheel, every ounce of strength gone.

"I'm so sorry, Annie," I whispered. It felt like the ultimate betrayal to leave her. I would never be able to forgive myself if something happened to her in there. *Oh, God. Please have mercy.* I moaned, fighting back the urge to wail. How much could one person take?

"Callie. Sweetheart." Todd's voice roused me again. "We'll take care of it. Promise me you'll stay with the guys until we can check this out."

"Okay." I let my phone slip from my ear and onto the floor, too weary to care. I closed my eyes in the silent darkness of the parking lot and sobbed.

I awoke to an insistent tapping on the windshield, my senses immediately on alert. What now? Why was I sleeping in my van?

Early morning sunlight pierced through the fog in my brain, and I straightened up to see Todd, arms crossed, leaning against my driver's side window. His face was haggard, but he grinned down at me and I sagged in relief.

"Is Annie okay?" I yelled through the glass.

He laughed. "Why don't you open your door and find out?"

Oh, yeah. I guess that would make sense. My brain still felt like mush, but I unlocked the door and pushed it open. "Hey, girl. How are you?"

Annie pinned me in my seat, whining and licking, her bushy tail thumping against the open door.

"Yes, and I love you." I endured the onslaught, then pushed her away gently. "She's trying to tell me something."

"She's talking to you, that's for sure." Todd waited until I stood, then pulled me into his arms. "What in the world were you doing at C. Willikers at four in the morning?"

"It's a long story." I pressed my cheek against his chest and listened to his heartbeat for a minute. "I take it there were no bad guys?"

He sighed. "Nothing. No signs of anyone being in the store. Not sure what set Annie off. We checked it out very thoroughly."

"And no fire?"

He pushed me away from him to look into my face. "No fire?"

"Yeah. That's why I went to check on the shop. Because I smelled smoke."

His brow wrinkled. "You smelled smoke where?"

"At my house." I grabbed his hand and tugged him toward the sheriff's office. It was already getting hot out here. "At first I thought my house was on fire."

"Wait. What?" He stopped me before I could reach for the door.

I shrugged. "I was sleeping, and I woke up smelling smoke. Really strong. I thought the house was on fire, but I checked everything out and it wasn't. Then when I was outside, I thought I smelled it again and decided maybe I forgot to turn the tea kettle off at the store and maybe the store was on fire. But it wasn't." It sounded crazy now when I talked about it, but at the time it had made perfect sense.

"And you didn't call me. Or anyone else." Todd shook his head. "What am I going to do with you, woman?"

"Marry me?" Oops. I glanced up at him, amused to see the shock in his eyes. "Sorry, I must be more tired than I thought."

"Callie Erickson." He ran the back of his hand down my cheek, his voice deepening. "You do have rotten timing, you know that?"

"Lack of sleep." I grinned up at him. "You can kiss me now."

He laughed out loud. "If sleep deprivation makes you flirt with me like this, I might deprive you of sleep more often."

"I'd like to see you try." I planted a fist on my hip sassily, realizing only then what I must look like in clothes I'd worn for more than twenty-four hours. Not to mention running around tracking down fires and escaping from bad guys in the middle of the night in said clothing.

But apparently, Todd was unfazed by such trivial matters, because it was only when the sheriff whipped into his parking spot a foot away from us that I came back to earth.

Wayne walked by with a paper coffee cup pressed to his mouth. "Got yer hands full with that one," he grunted. "She's a trouble-magnet."

A trouble-magnet?

I glowered at Wayne as Todd laughed. *Men.*

"Y'all heard the good news, I take it?" Wayne turned back toward us.

My heart leapt. "My parents?"

"Not that good of news. But good." He hawked and spat. "Ginger Slayton's toxicology report came back this mornin'."

Todd gripped my hand.

"Seems Miz Slayton's death was accidental after all. Anaphylaxis from peanut allergy." He jerked his chin at me. "Seems I was wrong to jump to conclusions about you, Miz Erikson."

His half-apology was probably the best I'd ever get, but I still had questions. "You mean she accidentally ate something with peanuts in it? And died? That fast?"

"Unfortunately, some people have severe enough peanut allergies that even the tiniest bit will do it." Todd shook his head. "But surely she was aware of her condition?"

"Yeah, Jim says she always checked everything out before

she ate it." Wayne shrugged. "Musta come in contact with it somehow. Maybe she went to a different restaurant or somethin'."

"Soo...that's it? The investigation is over?" Of course, I was happy to finally have an answer about Ginger Slayton's death, but what about all the other crazy events surrounding it, like the roses? "But what about—"

"That is awesome news," Todd said heartily, while steering me toward his truck. "Thanks for letting us know, Wayne. I'll give you a call later," he called over his shoulder.

I climbed in the truck and waited until he slid into the driver's seat. "What was that all about? I wanted to ask him more questions." I frowned at him. "And what about my van?"

"We'll get it later." He started the engine and pulled out of the parking lot. "I know you want more information. But at this moment, you need to be focusing your energies elsewhere, not getting all upset again about Ginger. I'm sure there are still unanswered questions, but—"

"It seems suspiciously easy for all of this angst and then all of a sudden—poof—it's an accident. 'Oops! Sorry, Callie, for accusing you of murder. Have a nice life.'" I blew out an aggravated sigh. "Do you think it was truly an accident?"

He sighed. "Wayne told us the results five minute ago. I haven't had time to think about it."

I crossed my arms, feeling out of sorts. "I don't think it was an accident. For one thing, what was Ginger doing in Sherm's yard if she was going into anaphylactic shock? Why didn't it happen at the restaurant or wherever she was eating whatever she ate? And why was she holding one of my roses?" I sat up straighter as we neared my shop. "Will you stop at C. Willikers? I know you guys checked everything, but I'd like to make sure for myself. That dream or whatever it was, was too vivid."

"At your service, madam." He grinned at me, no doubt grateful I had stopped the barrage of questions.

I lifted my eyebrows. He knew me well enough by now to know he hadn't heard the end of it.

I unlocked the door to my little shop, breathing in the

familiar scent of flowers and old books. Could Ginger's death really have been an accident? That would be sad, but not nearly as terrible as the thought of someone killing her in cold blood.

I shuddered, trying not to think about it. Or that my parents—no, I couldn't go there.

I flicked on the lights and opened the blinds, running my hand across the bookshelf by the door. "Definitely time to dust."

That was a trivial thing to be concerned about in the midst of a crisis. But I knew myself well enough to recognize that I was trying to focus on small, normal everyday details to help me deal with the larger situation that felt out of control.

Todd and Annie followed me in, both heading straight for the old leather loveseat in the book nook. "Long night." Todd slung himself onto the loveseat, hands behind his head, feet hanging over the armrest. "Want me to take you home later? I have today off. Maybe we can get lunch?"

I pulled my small watering can out from under the counter. Lunch? I hadn't had breakfast. Not that my stomach was up for much lately. "Sure."

I turned on the water at my utility sink in the back room and dumped fertilizer in the watering can. Obviously, we were both giving the topic of what to do about my parents a break, but that didn't stop my mind from going a million miles an hour. Were they alive? Were they being held captive somewhere? Why? By whom?

Water the philodendrons. Water the ferns. Water Aunt Dot's Christmas cactus.

Wait a minute. Where was the Christmas cactus?

I pivoted slowly, gazing around the main room. Had Sharlene moved it somewhere? If so, why?

Odd. I frowned and glanced in Todd's direction.

He and Annie were both snoring softly.

Where had Aunt Dot's plant gone? Had Sharlene sold it to someone? The thought horrified me. I thought I had made very clear to her from day one that that was a special plant and was not for sale.

But it was nowhere to be seen. My heart felt as bare as the empty plant stand in front of the main window. A lump rose in my throat. The Christmas cactus had been in our family for over a century. How many losses could I take? And how would I ever tell Aunt Dot?

CHAPTER TWENTY-FOUR

Focus, Callie. Maybe there's a reasonable explanation. I swallowed back my tears and I refilled the watering can, this time adding the special African violet food. Not many folks purchased African violets, but I loved them and enjoyed the challenge of encouraging them to bloom.

I stepped over to the display, admiring the many hues of purples, blues and pinks. Mom always loved the pink ones. I sighed, running my finger down one fuzzy leaf. Would my life ever be normal again? What if my parents were already in Heaven? What if I never found out what happened to them? What if—

"Stop it!" This was not helping. I had to bring my thoughts into captivity and not allow fear to control me. I stomped over to the sink to grab the watering can. It wasn't doing any good to—

I froze.

A book lay open on the counter.

I hadn't left a book open on the counter.

Especially a book that belonged to my mom. A book I would know anywhere.

I tiptoed over to it. Surely not.

But it was. My mom's worn, highlighted and underlined copy of the classic devotional, *Streams in the Desert.* I had seen the blue, hardback book along with her Bible every day of my life as a child. So, why was it here? Now? I ran my finger down the page as if the book could tell me where its owner was.

Could someone have put it here for a cruel joke? Who would do such a thing? And why?

My blood ran cold. Maybe someone really had been in my shop this morning. Maybe Annie had known what she was barking about. "Todd."

No answer.

I picked up the book, my hands shaking, and hugged it to my chest. At this moment, it didn't matter where the book came from. Even if someone had meant to terrify me, their plan wasn't working. To have a physical object that Mom had loved so much was like a gift from heaven itself.

I squeezed onto the edge of the loveseat, laid my head on Todd's chest and just breathed. Somehow, something so precious had come to be in my hands, right when I didn't think I could take the pain any more. True, the book induced its own kind of pain; the pain of those lost days of family love and unity, but it also brought hope. A stanza from Wordsworth's "To a Butterfly" skittered around in my tired brain:

> *Stay near me—do not take thy flight!*
> *A little longer stay in sight!*
> *Much converse do I find in thee,*
> *Historian of my infancy!*
> *Float near me; do not yet depart!*
> *Dead times revive in thee:*
> *Thou bring'st, gay creature as thou art!*
> *A solemn image to my heart,*
> *My father's family!*

Todd roused slightly, stroking my hair, his eyes still closed. "Hangin' in there, sweetheart?" he mumbled.

I nodded against his chest, inhaling the warm scent of his skin, my slow, hot tears soaking his shirt. Somehow, in that moment, I knew my parents were still alive. Deep in my spirit, I knew this wasn't over. *God, what are You showing me?*

A few minutes later, I struggled to a sitting position, my arm asleep from the awkward angle. I slid to the floor and rested my hand on Annie's side, then patted Todd's arm. "I found something you need to see."

"Hmm?" He rubbed one hand down the side of his face, then opened his eyes. "Sorry, love. Not much sleep lately."

I nodded. He had been going nonstop for a couple of days now, trying to do his own job and support me in my crisis at the same time. And then the loss of his friend. It was a lot for anyone to handle.

I held the book up. "I found this on the counter."

He raised his eyebrows. "And?"

"It's my mom's." I thrust it into his hands. "I found it on the counter a few minutes ago."

"Like, it wasn't here before?"

I nodded my head. "Like, I'm sure she had it in Zambia with her. My mom reads this devotional every single year. Starts in January and goes through December."

Todd sat up, suddenly alert. "Where did you say you found it?"

"On the counter by the cash register. It was lying there open."

"And it wasn't there when you closed up last night."

"Nope."

He stared at me. "You're certain."

"Positive."

"And it's not another copy of it? I mean, like a customer could have picked it up off the shelf and left it there?"

I shook my head. "Nope. I often have a copy of this book on the shelf, but this is hers. Look." I opened the book to the first page and read it out loud. "Presented to Bettina Williamson on December 25, 1962. From Lola and Mitch McGuire. How in the world did it get in my store?"

"I don't know, but it was a pretty bold move. Someone is trying to get your attention." He pursed his lips. "That makes me nervous."

I hugged the book to my chest again. "Do you think I should be worried?"

Todd looked at me like I was nuts. "We need to take this seriously, Callie. We're going to let the investigator know as soon as possible. Even small things are sometimes what we need to get a break in a case, and in your parents' case..."

I wasn't listening. What if the book itself wasn't the message? What if there was a note hidden in the pages? Or a secret code or something? I hadn't read all the Nancy Drew books for nothing. Surely there was a clue within this book. "Maybe I'm supposed to read something in here," I mumbled. What page had it been opened to when I found it? Oh, no. Maybe that was the page I was supposed to read.

I flipped through the pages, blowing out a sigh of relief

when I realized the ribbon marker was still between the pages. I pulled the frayed strand out, scanning the entry for June 2nd.

I sucked in my breath. The wedding. Aunt Dot and Harry's wedding was set for June 2nd. And today was May 25th. Was someone threatening to do something terrible at the wedding?

My hands started shaking. Surely not. Maybe the clue was in the entry itself?

"For Abraham, when hope was gone, hoped on in faith, His faith never quailed. Romans 4:18-19." I read the scripture text for June 2nd out loud. "Is that supposed to be some sort of clue?"

"Come up here by me." Todd pulled me up on the couch beside him, bending his head down to study the book with me. "Are you sure the marker was in this page?"

"Yes, it had to have been. The book was lying open, and at first I didn't even touch it." I thought back. I was sure I hadn't moved the marker. "Once I realized it really was my mom's, I grabbed it up." Uh-oh. "I probably shouldn't have touched it. Maybe there were fingerprints or something on it."

Todd sighed. "Maybe. But what if it's a coincidence? Sharlene has a key, right? Maybe she decided to do some devotional reading and accidentally left the book out."

I frowned at him. "How could it be a coincidence that my mom's devotional ended up on the counter of my shop while she is missing?"

"I don't know. Could she have sent it to Dot for safekeeping?"

"I can't imagine her sending it separately for any reason." I laid my head against his arm, thinking. "But still. Even if she had, how did it get here? Into my store? In the middle of the night?" I leaned down to rub Annie's ears. "I wish you could talk, girl. You'd tell us what you saw last night, wouldn't you?"

Annie whined and lifted a paw.

"She's smart, but not smart enough to talk, unfortunately." Todd stood and stretched. "I don't know what to think, Callie. We can't leave any stone unturned, but on the other hand, I don't know what motive someone would have for leaving your mom's book where you would find it. If it had been accompanied by a threat of some sort, that would be different." He rubbed his hand across the back of his neck. "Still. If someone really was in here last night..." He grasped my hand. "Promise me that you will call me the next time you feel the need to be traipsing around in the middle of the night."

"Okay."

He growled. "That didn't sound very convincing."

I shrugged. "I thought about calling you, but it was the middle of the night. And you'd been on duty for so many hours. Besides, Annie was with me and—"

He grasped me by the shoulders and gave me a gentle shake. "Callie. We've been through all of this before. I don't care what time of the day or night it is. If you need me, call me. Please."

"I will. But—"

"No. No excuses." His gaze deepened. "I can't imagine my future without you. We're going to get through this, I promise." He pulled me into his embrace.

"I know." Somehow, we would make it through. One day at a time. Sometimes one breath at the time, but the sun would come out again. "How do you think He's going to do it this time?" I murmured. I knew from experience that though some days it felt like the storm would never break, God had a way of calming me in the midst of it. Maybe that's all I was supposed to get from finding Mom's devotional. However it had gotten there, maybe it was a sign from God to trust Him and stop trying so hard to figure things out on my own.

CHAPTER TWENTY-FIVE

"I just wish—" I pulled away from Todd as the door opened. "Hey, Houston."

He grinned at us. "Hope I'm not interrupting anything."

"Nothing you haven't seen before." Todd slung his arm over my shoulders. "How are you, man?"

"I think I should be asking y'all that question."

I shrugged. "One day at a time, for sure."

"I get that." He glanced at his watch. "I couldn't get you to answer my texts, so I thought I'd run by and let you know a stack of boxes were delivered for you at the church. Not sure why."

A stack of boxes? I wasn't expecting a large shipment of yarn until next we—wait a minute. I ran toward the door.

"Where are you going, sweetheart?"

"They might be my parents' boxes!" I yelled over my shoulder to Todd. "Where are the boxes, Houston?"

The men caught up with me in the parking lot, Annie dancing around our legs.

"In the side hallway. I didn't know you were expecting something important or I would have come over sooner." Houston pushed the glass door open for us.

"I wasn't. I mean, I didn't know I was." I examined the first box. Yep, definitely my mother's handwriting.

Oh, Mom, where are you? The fear stabbed my heart anew and I blinked to hold back the sudden urge to cry. "She said they were going to ship a few things down here."

"A few?" Todd surveyed the small mountain of boxes.

I laughed in spite of myself. "My parents believe in being prepared."

"Then I guess we can deduce that they were still planning to come to Short Creek, at least as of—" He squinted at the postmark. "Two months ago."

"That's not super helpful." Anything they would have shipped two months ago wouldn't have any bearing on their current situation, would it?

Houston cleared his throat. "Am I missing something?"

Todd glanced at me before answering Houston. "It appears Callie's parents might be...missing. For real, this time."

"Oh, no. No one told me." Houston cracked his knuckles. "Callie, I'm so sorry. Weren't they supposed to arrive a couple of days ago?

"Yeah." My throat tightened.

"Apparently there's been no contact with them. Going on three days now." Todd pulled me to his side.

"Oh, Lord help us. Why are we standing around deliberating about boxes? We need to pray about this. Right now." Houston reached for both of our hands.

I gaped at him. The old Houston would never have been comfortable with leading an impromptu prayer session.

"Callie, you pray first," he commanded. "Todd and I will agree with you."

"Yes, sir." I bowed my head, conscious of the strong grip of the men's hands as they supported me, the stillness of the musty hallway, my own pulse beating in my throat. Until this moment, I had done a pretty good job of holding my thoughts and fears in check. But now, in the abrupt quiet and with people I loved, I imagined my parents in danger somewhere...where? God, where? Are they alive? Vague visions of guns, dark, empty rooms... Cold. Evil. Threats. My chest constricted.

"Jesus," I whispered.

The fear cracked, but held.

"Jesus, Jesus."

Todd and Houston began to pray, low notes in harmony with my plea.

King Jehoshaphat's prayer in 2 Chronicles 20 flitted into my mind. Surrounded by a great army, the king of Judah and all the people cried out to God for rescue. "God, we don't know what to do, but our eyes are on you."

I said it again, louder. "God, we don't know what to do, but our eyes are on you. Please show us what we should pray."

The fear retreated.

We waited.

"God, I pray Your protection on Jerry and Bettina right now. I pray that You will hide them under the shadow of your wings." Todd's voice grew stronger. "They are not lost to You, oh God. You know right where they are."

"Yes, Lord. Your will be done." I squeezed Todd's hand.

We waited again. I sensed the comforting presence of the Holy Spirit blanketing us, filling the room...capturing my soul with peace.

"They are alive." The sudden assurance was so strong, I blurted it out loud.

Houston nodded. "Yes. I have a strong sense of that as well."

Sensing that God had something more to show me, I closed my eyes.

The minutes ticked by. I could hear Todd and Houston's murmured prayers as I focused on listening to the voice of the Holy Spirit.

An image flooded my mind. I could see my parents sitting in a vast, open room, like an old gymnasium. The high, square windows were barred, the space crowded with people. My parents huddled on a mat near a wide-open door, their gazes riveted on a large chess board that lie between them. What?

God, what does this mean? God often used dreams and what people might call "visions" to communicate with me, but this particular scene puzzled me.

I shared it with Todd and Houston.

Todd stroked his chin. "That would seem to confirm our guess that they are being held somewhere against their will."

"I don't know. If I just go by the 'feel' of it, I would say yes. But then why would the door be standing wide open?" I bit the inside of my cheek, thinking.

"And what about the chess board? Do your parents play chess?" Houston loosened the knot of his tie and slipped it off.

"Not that I know of. But..."

Lord, show me what we need to know.

"My parents are with other people. In charge of other people? Playing a game?"

"What would playing chess have to do with anything?"

Todd's question interrupted my train of thought.

I blinked, then refocused on him. "The chess board may be symbolic of something else. God likes details, so I'm sure it has some significance. I'll have to pray about it more."

I was still thinking about it while Todd and I stacked the boxes in the workroom at C. Willikers. As we opened each one to find clothing, books, and housewares—but nothing that seemed even remotely a clue to anything out of the ordinary. As we drove to lunch. As we ordered our food.

"Or maybe..." I stared at Todd across the table at Italiano's. "Maybe my parents really did leave the airport by themselves." Maybe my mom, herself, had gone to my store last night and left the book for me to find. My heart leapt. Maybe my parents were right here in Short Creek but couldn't get in touch with me for some reason.

He shook his head. "I know there's been speculation on that, but until we can get the footage from the airport security cameras, I don't think I'd place too much credence on that theory."

I poked at my manicotti. "Why not?"

"I hate to be a pessimist, but what reason would your parents possibly have for letting you know they were coming, then purposely sneaking away from the airport, knowing you were there to pick them up? And what about your dad's stolen duffel bag?"

I pursed my lips. "I know. But what if there was a reason? What if they were involved in some big international scandal or something, and they're trying to throw someone off track?"

"Nothing is off the table right now, Callie." He took a sip of his iced tea. "I'm simply saying it's not probable."

"Why not?" I wasn't trying to be stubborn, but I had heard of a lot stranger things happening. Even watching the evening news, you heard some pretty weird stuff.

"It's simply too far-fetched, sweetheart. I know you're trying to hold out hope, but..." He stared down at his plate, but not before I glimpsed the look in his eyes.

My heart sank. "You know something you're not telling me."

He didn't answer.

"Todd."

He raised his head to look me in the eyes. "I don't know, know. But with Carly's death, we're on high alert. If she was somehow involved in what's going on with your parents—or Ginger, then we're in deep, Callie."

"Like what?" I whispered.

He shrugged. "I don't know. But we should have enough manpower with Bell County in on the case now. I'm going to ask Wayne to assign someone to you."

"Like, to protect me?"

He nodded. "If—and I'm emphasizing if—someone was in your shop last night, then things have turned another corner."

"What do you mean?"

"Up until now, except for the incident with your van, this case has been focused on finding Ginger's killer and more recently, your parents and their disappearance. If someone is now after you, that changes things."

I shook my head. "I don't want anyone following me around. I'll go spend the night at Willowbough tonight. Aunt Dot will love it."

"That's fine for tonight. But we're going to discuss this again tomorrow after you get some sleep."

CHAPTER TWENTY-SIX

"I don't want anyone following me around all day." I slammed my dryer door rebelliously, rankled that Todd had even suggested such a thing. "I'm not going to let some evil person wreck my entire—"

The doorbell rang, and I stomped to the door. It better not be Wayne again, because I was in no mood to talk with him. I stood on tiptoe to peer out the peephole but couldn't see who it was.

"Callie."

I froze.

It couldn't be, but—I jerked open the door to find my mother standing on my doorstep.

"Mom!" I pulled her into a hug, and she collapsed against me. Her blouse was damp against my cheek, and I could feel her trembling. I had forgotten how small she was. I held her like a child for a long moment, stroking her back. "Are you okay? Where's Dad?"

She shuddered against my chest, then pulled away to gaze up at me. "Bad person...took him, Callie. Tried to stop them...but I couldn't."

A bad person?

"Who took Dad? Took him where?" I noted her tear-swollen eyes behind her out-of-style glasses and the bruise on her cheek. She looked a lot older than I remembered. And more confused. Annie snuffled her hand, whining.

"Come into the house, Mom. It's too hot out here." I led my mom into the house, though she knew the way herself. Our family had spent many happy hours at this house over the years before Uncle Garth passed away while he and Aunt Dot still lived here. My hands shaking, I closed the door behind her as she plopped down into the rocking chair, clutching her purse. I couldn't think what to ask her first. How had she shown up at my door? It's at least a forty-five-minute drive from the Austin airport to our little town of Short Creek. How had she gotten here? Where had she been the last three days?

"Are you okay? Are you hurt?" I didn't see any blood anywhere, thank God.

She wrung her hands, staring at me, then dropped her gaze. Her voice came out in a whisper. "I don't know...I don't know... took your dad and I...I don't know...what happened. I'm ...sad lady. A sad lady."

Oh, boy. What in the world was going on? Jesus, please help.

"You'll be fine, Mom. I love you." I hugged her again, holding back my tears, then drew away and grasped her hands. They were clammy. "I'm going to make you a cup of tea, all right? Then we'll figure out what we need to do." My mother always made tea when there was a crisis. "Okay? Mom?" I knelt in front of her, trying to make eye contact. Annie pushed in next to me, almost knocking me off balance.

Mom plucked at a non-existent spot on her white capris, her eyes focused on the floor, her breathing rapid.

Was she in shock? I stood, feeling kind of shocky myself. I stumbled toward the kitchen to put the tea kettle on while I called Todd at his emergency number. I listened to it ring. Once. Twice.

Come on, Todd. I need you.

"Whitney here."

"My mom is here," I blurted as soon as he answered.

"Callie? Your number didn't come up. She's at your house right now? Is your dad there, too? Is she hurt?" I could tell he was in full cop mode.

"No. I don't know." I could feel my teeth start chattering. "I th-think she's in shock. She said something about s-someone taking my dad, but she's acting really weird. Breathing hard and she won't look at me now."

"I'm sending the EMTs over. I'm about ten miles out but I'll be there as soon as I can. Melanie and Junior are on duty, so you'll be in good hands."

I relaxed a little bit, picturing the burly Junior. I knew all of Todd's friends at the volunteer fire department. "Please hurry."

"I'm on my way, sweetheart. Take a deep breath for me." He lowered his voice. "This is a good thing, right? Your mom is found."

The tea kettle whistled, and I pulled it off the burner, sucking in a long breath as Todd suggested. I poured the boiling water over the tea bag into my favorite floral mug and watched the steam rise, then dissipate. Such a normal, everyday act. The familiar scent of Earl Gray tea nudged me toward calmness. *This is a good thing, Todd had reminded me. Yes. Mom is here. But what is wrong with her? And where is Dad?*

I leaned against the counter, waiting for the tea to steep, and glanced out into the living room. Annie sat with her chin on my mother's lap, one huge paw on Mom's knee. Tears streamed down my mom's face as she stroked the dog's head.

What had happened?

I fished the tea bag out and added half and half, with a little honey, the way Mom liked it. Setting it down on the end table near her elbow, I laid my hands on her bowed head.

"Holy Spirit, You are the great Comforter. I don't know what's going on in Mom's heart and her body, but I pray You will be very near her right now. Give us your peace as we go forward. Lead us to the knowledge we need to take care of this situation. God, I pray that You will release warrior angels to surround Dad, wherever he is. He belongs to You, Father. He is Your faithful servant. Reveal to us—"

A bang on the door sent Annie into orbit as the EMTs tromped into my small living room.

"Whoa, there, Annie." Junior ruffled Annie's ears as Melanie knelt in front of my mom. "What's going on, Callie? I didn't get much from Todd." He folded his arms across his hefty chest, his muscles bulging, and peered at me.

"I'm not sure. I—"

A third uniformed paramedic squeezed through my front door with an enormous yellow duffel bag, leaving a gurney parked on the walkway in front of my porch. He thumped the bag down and started yanking equipment out of it.

I couldn't remember the tall, blond guy's name, but I didn't miss the air of tension between him and Junior.

"My mom is..." I gestured toward her where she sat with a blood pressure cuff on, shaking her head at Melanie's questions. She looked so pale. "I think she might be in shock.

She's been missing for three days and—"

"Missing?" Junior frowned. "This the lady everybody's been lookin' for?"

"Yeah. It's a long story." One that I didn't feel like discussing with him while we were in the middle of this. I stepped around him to stand next to Mom, where the blond guy was already sticking electrodes on her chest.

Melanie glanced up at me, brushing her long brown ponytail over her shoulder with a gloved hand. "We're going to do a quick EKG. She doesn't have a history of heart issues? No heart attacks?"

"Not that I'm aware of." I frowned. Could Mom have a serious health thing going on and my parents hadn't told me? I squeezed Mom's shoulder. "They have been out of the country for three years, though, so it's probably been a while since she's had a full checkup of any sort."

"Ma'am, are you hurt anywhere?" Junior crouched to look in Mom's eyes.

Mom stared through him.

He tried again, his voice gentler this time. "Ma'am, can you tell me what happened?" He waited for a response, then stood to face me, shaking his head. "I'm thinkin' she suffered some kind of trauma. Seen it before."

Trauma? I gripped Mom's limp hand. "Like what?"

"Let's get her loaded up, folks." The blond guy ripped the EKG printout out of the machine and turned to me, hitching his thumb in his belt loop. "No signs of cardiac arrest. Does she take any medications on a regular basis?"

Wait a minute. Why were they taking her to the hospital if they hadn't found anything wrong? "Not that I know of. Like I said, she's been living in Central Africa for three years. I don't—"

A quick knock on the door preceded the sheriff's entry. Todd crowded close behind him, and I watched him assess the scenario in one quick sweep as he hurried toward me.

He pulled me close against his side but looked at Junior. I knew he had to tread a fine line between professionalism and personal involvement at times like this. "How is she?"

"Taking her in for an assessment. No visible signs of trauma except a bruise on her face. EKG is fine."

Todd nodded. "I'm riding with you."

The intensity in Todd's voice alarmed me. Why would he need to accompany my mom to the hospital? He'd never even met her. Shouldn't I go with her?

Junior raised his eyebrows. "It'll be a little crowded back there, since we got Wilcox training with us today."

"We'll make it work. Give me one sec." Todd grabbed my hand and tugged me toward the kitchen, Annie on our heels. Once we were out of sight of the others, he drew me into a quick hug, then pushed me away to look into my eyes. "I'm not at liberty to give you any specifics, but we've gotten some credible intel in the last hour that is prompting us to take your parents' situation very seriously."

I thought they already were taking it seriously. My mouth went dry. "What do you mean?"

He looped my hair back over my ear. "You're going to have to trust me on this until I can give you more information, sweetheart."

"I trust *you*, but I don't know about the other people. What are you saying? What does 'serious' mean?" I forced myself to stop wringing my hands.

"I'm saying we need to know where your mom is at all times until we figure out what's going on." He sighed. "I wish I could give you more than that right now, but I can't."

"We're heading out, Whitney!" Junior yelled from the front door.

Todd half-turned toward the living room. "One sec."

"Like, she's in danger from someone?" I stared at him. What was he trying to tell me? "What about my dad?"

He shook his head, and my heart dropped at the flare of pain I glimpsed in his dark blue eyes before he hid it away again.

"Do you know where he is? Is he alive?" I whispered. *Please, please God. Let my dad be alive.* I listened to the ambulance idling outside my house. Was this a nightmare?

"Callie, I can't." Todd grasped my hands. "I'm sorry, honey.

Follow us to the hospital, okay? Your mom needs you to be there with her. I'll see you in a few minutes."

He brushed my cheek with a kiss and was gone, leaving me alone in the sudden quiet, with only the familiar cinnamon-gum scent of his breath left to comfort me. The dogs milled around my legs as I shut the front door and leaned against it. I needed to talk to Aunt Dot.

"Auntie, I'm on my way to the hospital. Mom showed up at my door a little while ago." Thank God for speakerphone function. I slammed on my brakes at the red light on 31st and the Loop, my cell phone flying off the passenger seat and onto the floor.

"Oh, my. Is she injured? Why are you going to the hospital? What about Jerry?"

I leaned to snag the phone while the light was still red. "I don't know where Dad is. Mom didn't seem hurt physically, except for a nasty bruise on her cheek, but she was not herself." The light turned green and I sped the last two blocks to the hospital. "I'm pulling into the parking lot of the ER right now. Can Harry bring you over?"

"Oh, Callie. I'm praying. We'll be there as soon as we can. Please give Bettina a squeeze for me. I'll call Jason and let him know."

"Thanks." My brother would flip when he heard that Mom had shown up at my house. "Tell him I'll call when I know more details." I locked my car and strode through the parking lot, finding myself scrutinizing each vehicle as I walked past it. Where was my dad? Could he be in one of these cars? And why would Todd need to ride with my mom, unless he was afraid something bad was going to happen to her on the way?

The automatic doors whooshed open as I neared them, and I walked through, letting my eyes adjust to the extra-bright artificial lighting. I scanned the rows of black vinyl chairs, then turned toward the front desk. I hadn't been to the emergency room since the time I got clunked in the head with a rock a year or so ago, and that time I had come in by ambulance. I stepped toward the window at the desk.

"Hi, my mom was brought in a few minutes ago. Bettina Williamson."

"Hmm. Looks like she's in C12." The woman wrote the number on a name tag and handed it to me. "But you can't go back there yet. They're still assessing her." She looked around me to focus her gaze on the person behind me. "Yes, sir. How may I help you?"

I stuck the name tag on my shirt and stepped closer to the window. "So, when can I see her?"

"We'll call you, ma'am. We're very busy right now, as you can see. Please have a seat."

In other words, go away. Seems I had heard that before, from the snippy airport information woman. Didn't anyone care that this was my mom? My life? I gritted my teeth and headed toward the nearest seat, resigning myself to the inevitable wait.

I tried to sit, but I was too keyed up. I wandered around the waiting room, half in shock. Where had my mom come from? And where was Dad?

After my fourth circuit around the room, I stopped to shuffle through the magazines in the wall rack. I might as well settle down. It could be a while.

I wasn't interested in reading about movie stars, fitness or car racing, but maybe a National Geographic...I snatched up the magazine, staring at the image on the cover. Charms. Exactly like the one I had found in Ginger's garage and was wearing around my neck. Except that instead of a big eye, these charms pictured arms, legs, crosses, hearts—what in the world?

"Myth or Miracle?" I read the title out loud.

Hmm.

I flipped open to the article. "Milagros are small metal religious charms. The word milagro means 'miracle' in Spanish. These small charms, often depicting arms, legs, praying people, farm animals and a wide range of other subjects are typically nailed or pinned to crosses or wooden statues of various saints like the Virgin Mary or Christ, sacred objects, pinned on the clothing of saint statues, or hung with little red ribbons or threads from altars and shrines. They are also carried for protection and good luck."

Double hmm.

But what was the significance of the eye? And why would Ginger have a milagro?

I skimmed the next page. "People also might carry a milagro with them in order to get its benefit. For instance, a curandera—a spiritual healer—might bless a milagro and recommend that the person carry it in her pocketbook or on her person, in order to cure a physical ailment or to ward off evil, or bring about a change of fortune. Various body parts, such as kidneys, livers, lungs, ears, noses, breasts, lips/mouth as well as the better-known arms and legs are usually used when asking for help with a particular ailment of the identified part or in thanks for healing of the ailment."

Weird.

So, Ginger had a problem with her eye?

"Some believe milagros are pretty literal and there are no special meanings for the individual pieces other than what is visually evident, while others claim more representative or spiritual meanings. For example, eyes can represent the concept of watching, while a leg or a foot may represent some condition associated with it, such as an injury or arthritic condition. It might also represent one's strength, and the concept of travel, such as not only walking, but a journey, or even the idea that one might be safe driving back and forth from work every day."

I sank down with the magazine into the nearest vinyl chair and glanced at my watch. What was taking so long back there?

"How long have you been waiting?" I asked the frazzled-looking woman next to me.

She snorted. "Longer than I should have been, and it doesn't seem like they're super busy today. But you know Scott and White Hospital. They're never in a hurry for—"

"Callie!" Harry strode toward me, his energetic step belying his silver hair. He held his arms out to me. "What's going on, darlin'?"

I stepped into his embrace for a moment, catching a whiff of his spicy aftershave. I pulled away and sighed. "I don't know.

They haven't allowed me to see her yet. Where's Auntie?"

He stuck a hand in the pocket of his neatly-pressed jeans. "Thought I'd get the lay of the land first before I brought Dot over. What do you mean, they haven't *allowed* you?"

I shrugged. "They said the docs were assessing her and they would call me."

"That's nonsense. Follow me."

I stuck the magazine in my purse and obediently trotted after him toward the back of the waiting room.

We waited beside the automatic doors until someone came out, then Harry grasped my arm and we darted through. "See, you're in. Now let's find her."

"They said she's in C12." We strode down the hallway. I was such a rule-follower. Was someone going to come and nab me for disobeying the receptionist? "I don't care," I said out loud.

"There's the C hallway." Harry took a sharp right, dragging me along with him. "Sometimes, a person needs to take charge. These people don't know what they're doing."

"There's Todd." I rushed toward him where he paced like a palace guard in front of Room C12, talking on his phone.

He noticed me and smiled but held his hand up to stop me from entering. "Give me one sec, Callie."

Harry and I skidded to a stop. Why all the mystery? I needed to see my mom. I put my hand on the doorknob.

Todd moved in front of me, blocking my way. "They need another minute, sweetheart." He shoved his phone into the front pocket of his jeans. "I know you're anxious to see her, but you need to give her time to talk to them. We need all the information she can give us."

I leaned my head against his chest and sighed as Todd's arms encircled me. "Is she going to be okay? Is she remembering anything about my dad?"

He shifted his position against the doorframe, and I sensed him looking at Harry. "Not that I know of, but we're working on it. She's apparently fine physically, but she has been traumatized. We have to go slowly with things like this."

"Who's in there with her?" Harry tapped his booted foot

on the tile floor. "They brought the psych folks in, didn't they?"

I pulled back to see Todd's face.

"Yeah, and the victim assistance workers."

Victim assistance? I winced. "At least she's not physically injured."

Both men looked at me, and I read the concern in their gazes. "We're in for a long road, aren't we?" My throat tightened. I was afraid to imagine what might have happened.

Todd brushed my hair away from my cheek. "She will need a lot of rest. The counselor—do you know Susannah Hammons?"

The name sounded familiar, but I couldn't pull up a face to go with it.

"Anyway, you'll like her. She'll be able to tell you more in the coming days. She's kind of our unofficial department counselor."

Harry snorted. "*The* Counselor has far more to say than Ms. Hammons in there."

The Counselor. The sweet Holy Spirit. Yes. I blew out my breath. "What is He saying, Harry?"

Harry smiled at me. "It's going to be all right. He is shielding her right now in His arms. He's got this."

Father God? I clung to Todd's hand and closed my eyes, allowing my spirit to rest for a minute in that knowledge. I could hear the low murmuring voices beyond the wooden hospital door, but I blocked them out, letting His comfort wash over me. I pictured myself as a scared baby bird, hiding under the warm, protecting wings of the Father. My heart still ached, but my spirit took in a deep draught of peace. He was still in control. He loved me and my parents. He cared that my heart hurt and that I was scared of what I'd have to hear in the next few hours and days. He was already there... He was in my future. He had it covered.

Todd squeezed my hand, and I knew both of these men were crying out to God on my behalf at that moment. Asking for His wisdom. His strength.

"Whew." I opened my eyes and wiped a tear with a shaky hand, straightening my shoulders. *It's going to be all right.*

"We're going to be okay."

Well, at least for a minute.

Todd's phone rang. "Whitney. Yes, she's right here." His gaze met mine and he grimaced.

What now? I forced myself to breathe. Had they found my dad? Was he alive?

Harry threw his arm around my shoulder and squeezed tight as we both watched Todd stuff his phone back in his pocket, his jaw tight.

"We need to head to Austin ASAP."

CHAPTER TWENTY-SEVEN

I stared at Todd. "Austin? Why? Did they find my dad?"

"No, not yet. But that's where the incident occurred. At the airport." He took off his Texas A&M baseball cap to run his fingers through his dark hair, then resettled the hat on his head. "In an investigation, you are required to talk to the authorities in the precinct where it happened. Also, they're the ones holding your mom's suitcase. Maybe they'll release it to you."

"Now?"

"I hope they'll give it to you today. But sometimes they hold—"

"No, I mean, do I have to go now? What about my mom?" I felt the panic rising,

threatening to strangle me. "Where do I need to go? To the police station?" I hated driving in Austin traffic to begin with, and I hated even more that I had to go today. And I didn't know where the police station was. I pulled in a deep breath through my nostrils and clutched Todd's sleeve, the cotton fabric smooth to my touch. "Nothing else about my dad?"

Come on, Todd. Throw me a lifeline, here. I searched the blue eyes I knew so well, finding deep compassion and tears to match my own.

But no answers.

I gripped my elbows, holding myself tight against the pain.

Really. All I wanted was for Todd to offer me some hope. But apparently, he was unable or unwilling to do that. I clenched my teeth against an unexpected rush of anger and glued my gaze to my phone screen.

Even if Todd didn't care about me, God could do this. He could work a miracle. He could make my dad text me right now, saying everything was fine. He could make the craziness stop. He could fix it this very minute. Or maybe God wasn't willing to do that, either.

I spun away, resisting the urge to throw my phone as hard as I could.

Come on, Dad. Please be alive. Hot tears stood in my eyes as I stared unseeingly at the blank, white hospital wall.

I felt the warmth of Todd's body behind me before he pulled me into his strong arms, my back pressed against his chest.

"Aww, Callie. I'm sorry, honey. I know this is hard." He nuzzled his whiskery cheek against the side of my face as he cuddled me close.

I held myself rigid for a long moment, then sagged against him, my momentary anger trickling out of me like water from a pricked blister...slowly, bringing relief. His heart beat against my shoulder blade, a sure, steady rhythm that comforted me. I breathed in his familiar cinnamon-gum-and-aftershave scent and swallowed hard. I could fuss and fight against reality all I wanted, but in the long run, there was nothing for it except to put one foot in front of the other and do what I needed to do. As Jason, my brother, often reminded me, "Acceptance brings peace."

I pushed out of Todd's embrace and dug in my purse for a tissue, not meeting his gaze. Maybe that's what I needed. A 12-step program. Do this, then do that, and then you're magically better. Or free. Or fixed. Whatever.

My brother would be quick to tell me that's not how it works, but that part didn't matter right now. What I wanted was for somebody to give me answers. Or at least a plan. Was that too much to ask?

Stop it, Callie. I despised my own sudden cynicism. Where had it come from?

Jesus, please help me.

I had to get a grip. This, too, would pass. One day, I would reflect on this season of my life and remember His faithfulness as I stumbled through valley, flood and fire. I would be able to discern His hand. I would praise Him for bringing me out into the sunshine again, to a place where I could breathe. A fragment of Psalm 66 floated into my thoughts: *We went through fire and water, but you have led us out to a wide space to breathe again.*

Yes. Somehow, He would deliver me from even this. I had

to believe that, or I was sunk.

I forced air into my lungs and raised my eyes to Todd's. "What about Mom? I can't leave her here all by herself."

Harry shifted. "I'll go get your aunt. We'll sit with Bettina for as long as we need to. Dot's chomping at the bit to see her, anyway."

Five hours later, Todd dropped me off at Mona's with a dull headache, and without my mom's suitcase. Mom had been moved out of the ER cubicle and into a real room by the time Mona and I made it to the hospital.

We ran into Harry in the hallway outside the room. "They decided to keep her overnight? How is she?" I asked.

His brow creased. "She's been asking for you."

"Do you know who I'd talk to about her situation? I mean, other than the doctors? I didn't think I'd be gone the entire day today."

Harry gestured toward Mom's door. "They all left their contact information for you, and Dot can fill you in. I'm headed down to the truck to grab Dot's sweater."

I waved at Harry as he headed toward the elevator at the end of the hall. Hoping my mom was resting, I slipped into her room without knocking, Mona close on my heels.

Aunt Dot sat in her wheelchair, holding my mom's hand in the dim, cool room. Mom didn't move.

"Is she awake?" I whispered.

My aunt shook her head and cut her gaze to the side.

Mona, never one for picking up on social cues, hustled over to kiss my aunt, while I followed Aunt Dot's gaze to a uniformed cop hunkered in the corner near the bathroom.

I started, then sighed. What could my parents be involved in that required round-the-clock police presence? Good grief.

I knew a lot of the local cops because of Todd, but I didn't recognize this guy. He lifted his chin in greeting and I nodded back, then raised my eyebrows in Aunt Dot's direction.

She rolled her eyes at him, sliding her hand from my mom's grip and pushing her chair away from the bed to make room for me. "She just fell asleep. They about talked her to death with all their questions."

"She looks pale." I tucked the covers under her chin, then pulled a chair closer to the bed and patted my aunt's hand. It was ice cold. "Thank you for staying with her for so long. You must be exhausted."

"I'm all right. Did you get any answers at the police station?" She pulled her glasses off and yawned.

"No. Only more questions." I glanced at the deputy, then back at Aunt Dot. Was the guy there to guard my mother? Or to eavesdrop on our conversation? Or both?

She shrugged. "I think Todd asked him to stay," she whispered.

"That would make sense." Apparently, Todd wasn't taking any chances with either my mom or me. I appreciated his concern, but still.

I sighed, watching Mona dig around in her red leather purse. The thing was as big as a duffel bag, and I idly noticed that the enormous rhinestone cross on the front matched her earrings.

She stood, clutching her phone. "I'm not getting any phone service up here and Rob'll be wantin' his supper. I'm goin' to grab me a cup of coffee while I call him. What do y'all want?"

Aunt Dot yawned again. "A cup of decaf would be nice."

"What I need is food." A wave of fatigue rolled over me, making me feel slightly dizzy. "And sleep." And my dad to be found unharmed, please. Now that would be awesome.

Mona winked at me. "I'll do my best."

I groaned. "Nothing fried, please. And no donuts. You know I can't stomach donuts, even on good days. Maybe soup. Or chocolate."

Silence reigned after Mona left. I leaned my head back and closed my eyes, my head whirling. "This all seems surreal. How could we go from normal life to this in the span of three days?" And I hadn't even told Aunt Dot about seeing Jim with my dad's duffel bag. Or that my parents' boxes had arrived from Zambia. Or that I found Mom's devotional book in my store. Why did things have to be so complicated?

Aunt Dot stayed quiet, probably knowing I needed time to process.

I opened my eyes to stare at my mother. She breathed evenly and peacefully, but the lines of strain on her face remained, even in her sleep. What had she been through?

"They said she appears to have suffered emotional trauma, Callie." Aunt Dot spoke in a low tone. "But she couldn't seem to tell them what happened."

"Does she remember anything at all?" I fingered the edge of Mom's blanket, trying to ignore the cop in the corner.

"She remembers boarding the plane in Kansas City, but that's it. Until she showed up at your house."

"How can she just not remember whole chunks of time? I don't understand." But I did recall the same thing happening to several of the sex-trafficking victims whom I had talked to recently. Apparently, a lot of their experiences were so painful or horrible that their brains blocked the memory. I shuddered, praying that nothing like that had happened to my mom. "If only she could tell us what happened. Or where Dad is."

Aunt Dot nodded. "The psychologist said that sometimes this type of memory loss is temporary, but it can also last for months. Or even longer." She lowered her voice. "But I'm not sure it's only that. Haven't you noticed her sounding a little confused the last few months when you talked to her on the phone? She hasn't been herself."

I gulped. "I haven't talked to her much lately." Sadly. But now that Aunt Dot mentioned it... "She did seem a little off when I talked to her on her birthday. But I didn't think much of it." Birthday. Hmm. "And she called me instead of Jason on his birthday. Oh, no. Do you think—"

We stared at each other.

"God will see us through, darlin'." Aunt Dot rubbed her eyes. "He's brought her back to us alive, and He knows what He's doing. If she found her way to your house, then maybe your dad is somewhere nearby, too."

"I hope so. When I was in the garden at Willowbough the other day, I thought I heard—" No, I didn't want to tell her about thinking I heard my name. It was too far-fetched. "Oh, my gosh. I forgot to tell you something crazy. Wayne told Todd and me that he is ruling Ginger Slayton's death an accident."

"What? That's wonderful." She put her glasses on and peered at me. "Isn't it?"

I shrugged. "Kind of. Apparently, she had a life-threatening peanut allergy and that's what killed her."

"She ate something with peanuts in it?"

"I guess that's the story."

Aunt Dot steepled her hands under her chin and regarded me for a long moment. "But you're not buying it."

I shrugged again. "Just seems too easy." I yawned so wide my jaw almost popped. "But I'm too weary to think about it anymore right now. At least Wayne is off my case." I had almost dozed off when I remembered where I had previously seen the Willowbough employee from the other day. He was the one who stole my dad's duffel bag.

CHAPTER TWENTY-EIGHT

But it wasn't until the next morning that everything made sense.

I wandered out into the side yard in my robe and slippers, nursing my second cup of tea. It was quiet back here in the humid spring day, everything covered in dew. The dogs milled around me, then trotted across the yard to do their business while I moseyed around, inspecting the almost-opened buds on the climbing rosebush and listening to the birds singing their morning songs. The sun, barely peeking over the horizon, brought to mind a few of my favorite lines from *The Uncelestial City*.

"It is the season of larks. They will be flinging the bright seed of song in the furrows of grey light, till the East is gold with the smooth sheaves of singing."

I'm not sure if I grasped the full meaning of the words, really, but their imagery caught my fancy every time I read them. *The bright seed of song.* I leaned over to sniff the honeysuckle, then straightened and stretched my back. It was a new day. And my mom, at least, was alive. And safe. My own song of thanksgiving arose in my heart.

"Good thing Your mercies are new every morning, Lord," I murmured. "I think I used up all of yesterday's and then some."

The sunrise was glorious, and I could hardly bear the thought of going back in the house. "I'll bring my Bible out here and sit, dogs." They glanced at me as I headed toward the side door.

Something dropped on my head.

"Aaah!" I slapped at it, hoping it wasn't a huge bug of some sort.

It wasn't a bug.

But...what in the world? I picked up the object. It was another milagro, this one shaped like a little house. I craned my neck to look up into the peach tree. My friend, the crow, hopped up and down on a small limb and fluttered his wings.

"Did you drop this on my head?" I stared at the crow, the

tiniest shadow of an idea forming in my mind. It was common knowledge that crows were attracted to shiny objects, but...had this crow dropped this down for me on purpose?

I had heard about how intelligent crows were, but really. What were the odds that a bird would drop a—wait a minute.

I ran into the house and rummaged around for the magazine I had "borrowed" from the ER. The magazine with the article about milagros. I re-read it. Yep, exactly as I remembered.

I snatched my phone and called Todd, my entire body trembling. "I know who has my dad."

"What?"

"I know who it is. I was thinking and praying half the night and then this morning, all the pieces came together."

"Who?"

I didn't dare say it out loud, just told him where to meet me. "I'll be there in ten minutes."

I pulled into the trailer park—the one Sharlene had moved to a few weeks ago—right as Todd flew in from the opposite direction, pulling up next to me.

"Callie. Are you sure about this?"

"Yes. I'll tell you why later, but for now, we need to hurry."

He grabbed my arm. "You are not going in there."

"But—"

"No. I am trained to handle situations like this. And we don't know if they are in there. Anyway, I have backup coming soon."

I could tell from his face that I wasn't going to win this one. "What if you need help before they get here?"

He shook his head. "I'm not going in yet, anyway. I'm going to take a quick peek around the exterior. Please stay out of sight and don't come inside until I give you the all-clear. And pray."

We slunk along the side of Sharlene's trailer and around

a row of scraggly shrubs until we stood behind the dilapidated single-wide next to Sharlene's. This had to be the one. Faded blue siding and a fake owl sitting on the roof, Sharlene had said. She hadn't mentioned the dripping air conditioner unit that was wedged precariously in one of the back windows.

Was my dad looking at me through one of those windows? I knew he was in there. It was all I could do not to bolt through the flimsy-looking back door.

"Stay here. Please, Callie." Todd pulled me into a quick embrace. "God's got this," he said, pushing me away. "Hopefully it won't take long."

I watched as he stealthily approached the back of the house then held my breath when he disappeared around the corner. A few minutes later, he slipped back into the yard and shook his head, then tried the "garage" door.

My heart pounded as he disappeared.

I paced and prayed. Where were the other officers who were supposed to be coming? Had they pulled up in front of the trailer? I stretched my neck but couldn't see past the overgrown bushes. Maybe if I squeezed into the little space between the fence and the back of the trailer house, I could see better without being seen.

I stuck my toe in the fence and clambered over, thankful I had thought to wear my tennis shoes. My heart thudding, I waited with my ear against the metal exterior. I couldn't hear anything.

Maybe that was good.

Maybe that wasn't good.

What if Todd was in trouble?

I glanced at my watch. He'd been in there at least five minutes now. That seemed like long enough to figure out what was going on. It wasn't like he had to search lots of rooms. Of course, if my dad was tied up or something and Todd had to untie him—

I heard something crash inside the house.

Oh, no. I squeezed my hands together tightly. I couldn't

stay out here. I had to help. I took a deep breath and double-checked the pistol in my pocket. *God, please send angels to watch over us. Let evil be destroyed and my dad set free in the name of Jesus.*

I stole from my hiding spot and rushed for the back door, not caring anymore if anyone saw me. I tripped over an old tire and fell, hitting my knee, hard. As I scrambled to my feet, I heard another crash.

Oh, no.

I sucked in a deep breath and reached for the back doorknob.

"Take the net, Callie."

The voice was so commanding, I obeyed without thinking, grabbing the large fishing net that hung on the wall next to the door. I soundlessly opened the door into the house and crept into the kitchen. Dirty dishes were piled in the sink, and I wrinkled my nose at the smell of weeks-old trash.

I flattened myself behind the kitchen door as I heard a groan. Then, praise be to God, my dad's voice. I edged out from behind the door and peeked into the living room. Dad, pale but alive, was sitting in a kitchen chair, his hands and feet bound. I gripped the handle of the net tightly, restraining myself from crying out or running to him.

Todd lay white and unmoving on the floor at Dad's feet, blood flowing from a gash in the side of his head.

Oh, no.

No, no, no.

Veronica Mears, the housekeeper from Willowbough, stood over him, a heavy-looking lamp in her hand. "So, you thought you'd help your little girlfriend out and rescue her parents, huh, tough guy?"

Todd groaned. Thank God he was still alive.

I stayed still, considering. If she dropped that thing on Todd's head, he'd be a goner. At least she didn't have a gun. And I did.

But—

The net, child.

Ah, the net.

Veronica's back was to me, her attention on Todd. I risked stepping a little further out from behind the door, hoping Dad would notice me. I watched his eyes flick over to me and widen before he schooled his features and looked away. But it was enough. Even in that brief moment, I sensed his love for me.

I calculated the distance between myself and the crazy woman. Would I have time to get close enough behind her to trap her in the net before she heard me? And what if she smashed Todd's head with the lamp while I was trying to take her down?

"Now!" The voice speaking to my spirit was gentle but firm.

I rushed forward and swung the net over Veronica's head and torso, yanking her backward at the same time. The lamp fell on my foot and I collapsed on top of my captive.

"Ha! I got you!" I yelled. "Yes! Thank you, Jesus!"

Veronica writhed and screamed, trying to claw at me. "Let me go. I didn't do anything on purpose."

I pulled the net tighter around her head. "Be quiet, Veronica. We don't want to hear it."

"Actually, I'd love to hear it." Todd rolled to a sitting position and scooched himself over to lean against the threadbare couch, pressing the front of his shirt to his head. He grinned at me, then winced. "Nice catch, sweetheart."

"Why do I always lose?" Veronica wailed. "I hated her. She stole Jim from me."

What?

I straddled her, pinning her arms tightly between my legs as I glanced around the dingy room. My eyes widened at the large, framed picture of Jim Slayton ensconced on the end table next to a vase of Eden roses. Another framed picture of a young, high-school-aged Jim hung on the wall, a bunch of dry, ancient-looking roses resting on top of it like a funeral arrangement on a casket. Photos of smiling children circled the arrangement. Jim and *Ginger's* children. The photos recently stolen from Ginger's house, no doubt.

Wow. The truth dawned on me slowly as Veronica began to sob. "All I ever wanted was someone to love me. She stole

Jim. She stole my job. I hated her."

"You killed Ginger because of Jim?" I almost felt sorry for her. Out of the corner of my eye, I noticed Todd edging closer to my dad. "How did you think killing Ginger would help? You still don't have Jim."

"Yeah, thanks to you." Veronica twisted her head back and forth, her sobs turning to a snarl. "Ginger was my best friend. She betrayed me. She always said she was sorry, but she wasn't. Jimmy loved me before he loved her."

A sudden thought struck me. This woman's whole life was a lie. She lived in a run-down single-wide trailer house, not in a ranch-style brick home. She didn't have a husband. She didn't have a garden. I guessed she probably hadn't ever done much of anything except work at low-paying jobs. "You don't have children, do you? Or a dog?" I asked gently.

"I don't need to answer any of your questions. You and your fancy aunt think you know it all, don't you?" She glared at me. "Her with all her 'God loves you' stuff. If He loved me, He would have helped me way before now."

My eyes welled at the misery etched onto her face. How much had unforgiveness cost her? And how much God must grieve over sin and all the pain it causes. "He does love you, Veronica. More than you know."

"Shut up. I hate you. It didn't take you long to move in on Jim, did it? As soon as Ginger kicked the bucket."

My jaw dropped. What was she talking about?

"I could have made Jim love me again. But you had to butt in. I saw the way he looked at you." She turned her face toward the wall as the Temple PD SWAT team burst through the front door and swarmed into the room, then whipped back to pierce me with her parting shot. "How did it feel to have someone you loved stolen from you?"

I slid off her onto the floor, speechless, as a police officer snapped handcuffs on the cursing captive.

My dad cleared his throat. "Well, you all sure know how to welcome folks down here in Texas. Would someone please let me out of this chair?"

CHAPTER TWENTY-NINE

"So she started screaming and crying and saying she didn't do anything and nothing was her fault and blah, blah, blah." A couple of hours later, we all sat squeezed into Aunt Dot's tiny living room. I tucked my legs up under me on Aunt Dot's couch, my parents on either side of me. Aunt Dot's beloved Christmas cactus plant that I had recovered from Veronica's trailer sat on the side table, lovingly watered by Harry.

My dad rested his arm around my shoulders, and I leaned in to him, hardly believing my parents were here, safe, and sitting with me in this room. It had been so good to reconnect with them both this afternoon before Mom was released from the hospital—nothing like the awkward reunion I had expected and dreaded after many years of not-so-great communication.

Somehow, in light of almost losing them, it was easy for me to hold them, weep with them, and yes, repent to them. I also realized how some of the stuff I had thought would stand between us had disappeared in the light of my more mature perspective on life. I saw where I had erred in my judgment of them as we wept together over those difficult years when my brother's terrible choices had affected us all.

I also saw what Dad had apparently been unable to bring himself tell me or Aunt Dot over the phone—that Mom was indeed in the early stages of a particularly fast-moving type of dementia.

"I didn't know what to do, Callie," he had whispered against my cheek, my hair sticking to his tears. "I first started suspecting something like this about six months ago, but I told myself we'd visit a doctor once we got stateside."

"It's going to be all right," I murmured now, squeezing both of their hands.

Mom turned to give me a small smile, and I grinned back at her, careful to conceal my sorrow.

Fortunately, at the moment, she was experiencing one

of her more lucid days, according to Dad. The doctors at Scott and White had started her on meds that they told Dad would help slow down the progression, thank God.

And now we had time to get to know one another again. I squeezed my mom's hand again, thankful for the opportunity that I had feared lost. I vowed I would make the most of the time we had together while she still knew me.

Harry stood behind Aunt Dot, while Todd leaned against the doorway to the kitchen, holding an ice pack to his neatly-stitched up head.

"I still can't believe it. Why would Veronica Mears, of all people, want to kill Ginger?" Aunt Dot's glasses were slightly askew.

I glanced at Todd. "Well, I'm sure more will come out, but it's a pretty sad story. Apparently, she and Jim Slayton, Ginger's ex-husband, dated in high school and college. She told the detective that they had even been engaged at some point."

"And Jim dumped her for Ginger?" Harry asked.

"Yes, that's the gist of it. But to make matters worse, she and Ginger were best friends at the time. And then, to add insult to injury, Ginger beat her out for a scholarship that Veronica was counting on to finish college. Veronica ended up dropping out and never finished."

"That's so sad." Aunt Dot pursed her lips. "So that was her motive."

"What we know of it so far, at least." Todd flipped his ice pack over. "The part I can't figure out is why she felt she had to involve Callie and her parents in the whole situation."

I shrugged. "I don't think she planned to, at first. She happened to be there at the Donut Hut that day I talked to Ginger about my roses, and later decided to try to frame me."

"Why do you say 'at first'?" Harry asked.

Todd and I exchanged glances. "After Ginger's death, Veronica thought Callie was moving in on Jim," Todd said. "Evidently, the woman is somewhat deluded. She apparently held out hope all these years that she might still have a relationship with Jim if only Ginger were out of the way. Then, when she saw Callie talking to Jim that day out in front of his office, that pushed her over the edge, and she came up with the plan of kidnapping Jerry and Bettina to get revenge on Callie. And hopefully distract Callie from her supposed relationship with Jim so Veronica could get on with her plan to win him back."

"Unbelievable." Harry shook his head. "Completely unbelievable."

"Yes, and she was the one who was in my shop that night and left Mom's devotional on the counter, trying to spook me."

Aunt Dot appeared to be lost in thought. "Oh, my word. Callie." She reached for her laptop. "Do you remember that letter I received for the advice column? The one I read to you from the woman who said she was lonely and no one ever brought her roses?"

We stared at each other. "That had to have been from Veronica. But why would she send it to you?"

"A cry for help...mixed-up, sad woman." My mom murmured, rubbing her cheek. "Sad lady."

"Yes, Mom. Very sad." I patted her arm.

Wait.

Sad lady.

Those were the same words Mom had said to me the day she showed up at my house. But I thought she had meant herself. Oh, man.

"You were trying to tell me about Veronica when you came to my house, weren't you, Mom?"

She shrugged.

"You were. I just didn't understand." I hugged her. "I'm sorry I didn't figure it out sooner." I glanced at Todd. "I think that's what my dream of the chessboard was. God was showing me that there would be many different 'moves' before the puzzle was solved."

"But how did you ever figure it out at all, Callie? I mean,

I've always known you were smart, but, wow." My dad smoothed his graying mustache.

"Yes, Detective Erickson. How did you figure that out?" Todd's teasing tone coaxed a chuckle from Harry.

"The crow. Remember I told you about an old crow that's been hanging out in my yard?"

"A crow? Like, a bird?" Dad asked.

"Yes. I first saw him a few weeks ago, and he seemed to be injured. I felt sorry for him, so I fed him dog food." I laughed. "Apparently, he decided I was his new best friend."

"Anyway...?" Todd encouraged.

"I've been finding odd objects in the backyard. A bead; a fishing lure kind of thing. Anyway, this morning I was out there thinking and praying and the crow dropped this on my head." I held out my hand to show everyone the house-shaped milagro.

"I still don't understand." Aunt Dot wrinkled her brow. "Another charm? It kind of looks like the 'eye' charm."

I shrugged. "Yeah, that's what helped me make the connection to Veronica, because they're not regular charms. They're called milagros, and some people use them kind of like good luck charms. I'll explain later. I feel like all of the pieces of this puzzle have been floating around in my brain for days now, but I couldn't figure out how they all fit together until this morning when I saw the milagro and started thinking about houses."

"Tell on, Nancy." The smile Todd sent me across the room made my heart skip a beat.

"Well, when I looked at this milagro, I thought back to the article I read about them yesterday that said a house milagro could stand for one's own house, or for—here, let me read it. I took a picture of it this morning." I pulled out my phone. "Houses represent, normally, one's own home, and the blessings that might be made on it and on the family that dwells there. It can also represent the hope of having one's home, or it can represent someone else's home. It might also represent one's workplace or school. When traveling, it can be a charm to ensure that one will arrive safely home again, or it can establish a connection between the traveler and the loved ones at home."

I looked around at everyone's puzzled faces. "I remembered seeing this same house charm—or one exactly like it—on Veronica's key ring that day she came into C. Willikers to show me her soaps and lotions. And then I thought of the 'eye' milagro I found in Ginger's garage and concluded that if Veronica was into milagros, maybe she was the one who had dropped the 'eye' in Ginger's garage."

"The more I thought about the possibilities, the more I started seeing how it could be Veronica behind everything. And as far as the 'eye,' Veronica had probably either given it to Ginger at some point while Ginger was still alive, or had hidden it in Ginger's car or home without Ginger's knowledge."

"Why?" Aunt Dot wrinkled her forehead.

"Because the 'eye' milagro carries the idea of watching someone, though usually in a positive context, like a deceased loved one watching over a person or something weird like that."

"So strange."

"But how did you connect Veronica with your mom and me?" Dad asked.

"An educated guess?" I shrugged. "Once I started thinking back on all my interactions with her, I realized she had given me a couple of clues, but I hadn't recognized them. For one thing, that day she came into C. Willikers, she apologized for what she said that day here at Willowbough, but then when she left the shop, she looked at me again and said she was really sorry. I assumed she was buttering me up so I'd carry her soaps and stuff in the store." I sipped my tea. "And then there were the pictures of her house. Or what she claimed was her house."

"Did she show you pictures of her house too?" Aunt Dot raised her eyebrows. "She was always showing me pictures of her house and kids and going on and on about her redecorating projects and her garden. She seemed like a pretty normal person, except she was so sad all the time."

"Yeah. One day when I came to see you, she showed me a picture of 'her' kids with a dog, in front of a house. At the time, I was like, 'Oh, that's nice.' But now I'm sure it was Jim and Ginger's kids in front of the house."

"Still don't...understand." My mom wrinkled her brow.

"It was Ginger's house, Mom."

Aunt Dot gasped. "She had a picture of Ginger's house that she said was her house?"

I nodded. "And I didn't recognize it as Ginger's house when I saw it, partially because it must have been an older photo before Ginger had done some exterior remodeling and put in the landscaping, but also because I had no idea that I shouldn't believe it was Veronica's own house and kids." I shook my head. "Veronica was apparently living in a fantasy world, pretending Ginger's house was hers, Jim and Ginger's kids were hers...even her hang-up with gardening was make-believe." I took a breath. "Oh, and that was another thing. That day she came into C. Willikers, she said she wanted to buy a plant to give to Aunt Dot and Harry for their wedding, but she didn't want to take it right then, because she didn't know anything about plants."

"You know, when she kidnapped us from the airport, she first took us to a house where we stayed for a night," Dad said.

"What?" Could Veronica have taken my parents to Ginger's house? "Dad. Did you have your duffel bag there?"

He nodded. "Yeah, but then she made us run out the back door when she heard someone in the morning. I guess it got left there. Nothing super important other than my Bible. I'm sure sad to lose that."

"I have it." I explained the whole duffel bag situation. "Who knows why Veronica had her co-worker from Willowbough steal it to begin with?"

"To instill more fear," Todd said. "Let's face it, the woman is a nut job."

"That's for sure. She said all kinds of crazy things in those couple of days. She about went out of her mind when your mother wandered away, but she must have decided it wasn't worth it to track her down since she still had me for collateral. And, maybe she counted on Bettina not really, uh..." He glanced at my mom and she smiled at him vaguely. "Not really being able to get the details accurate enough to make a difference."

The grief in his eyes hurt my heart. "We'll be all right, Dad."

He nodded and cleared his throat. "So how did you find out where Veronica really lived?"

"I ran a search online." I shrugged. "Then when I realized she lived in the trailer park right down Main Street, I was like, 'duh'. Because Sharlene just moved into the trailer park a few weeks ago and kept talking about this lady named 'Roni' who she had been praying for."

"Wow. So 'Roni' was really Veronica." Harry leaned his shoulder against the kitchen doorway. "So how did she actually kill Ginger? Did you come up with that answer, Nancy?"

"Yes, she did." Todd made his way across the room to me. "This girl is something else."

I grinned at him. "That part wasn't so hard, once I realized how obsessed Veronica was with Ginger. I figured she had to know how allergic Ginger was to peanuts, so then it was a pretty easy jump to guessing Veronica had somehow managed to bring Ginger into contact with a peanut product."

"Ah. So then it would look like an accident and no one would suspect it was murder." Aunt Dot nodded. "Very clever."

"In a gruesome kind of way." I made a face.

"Do they know yet how she did it?"

"My guess is that it was something in the gift basket the Garden Club ladies gave Ginger for her birthday that day at Donut Hut. After Veronica tried to sell me her lotions and lip balms, I remember thinking how it seemed like everyone was making and selling that kind of stuff right now. That got me wondering if the club members ordered the gift basket from Veronica. What if Veronica made a batch of lip balm or lotion with peanut oil instead of coconut oil, knowing it was to be a gift for Ginger and also knowing Ginger's severe allergy to peanuts?"

"Ah." Harry stuck his hands in his pockets and jingled his change. "But that would be pretty risky, wouldn't it? Since so many people know Veronica makes those things and sells them?"

"In a way. But it would also be a pretty good cover-up. So many people know and have likely used her stuff, who would suspect her of intentionally swapping out the ingredients to kill Ginger?"

"But what if Ginger didn't like lip balm and never used it?" Aunt Dot fingered her ring.

"I suppose Veronica thought it was worth trying." I looked up at Todd, and he nodded his agreement with my theory. "And if it didn't work this time, maybe she would have tried something more overt. Who knows?"

"Unfortunately for Ginger, it did work how Veronica hoped it would." Todd lowered himself to sit on the floor in front of me.

"But what was Ginger's body doing in Sherm's yard? Did she die there or did Veronica take her there for some reason?" Harry raised his eyebrows. "Doesn't seem like it would make sense for Veronica to purposely leave the body where it would be found, unless she wanted to make it look like murder."

Hmm. I hadn't thought of that.

What had Veronica shouted at me this morning?

I knew you and Jim had somethin' going before poor Ginger even died.

Where would she have gotten that idea? I'd never met Jim personally until after Ginger's death. Unless...unless she had seen him drop by C. Willikers. That time I met him at TemBel Landscaping and we talked about his donation to Hope House, he had said he stopped by C. Willikers a couple of times but

214 I To Err is Human

never caught me in. I grimaced, more than a little creeped out at the thought of the woman being so obsessed with Jim that she was following him around and watching everything he did.

"Maybe framing me for the murder was pre-planned after all." Yikes.

"Why do you think that, Callie?" Aunt Dot stared at me over the top of her reading glasses.

"This morning while she was slinging accusations at me—"

"While you were sitting on top of her." My dad chuckled.

"Yes." I rolled my eyes. "She screamed something like she knew Jim and I had something going even before Ginger died. Because the woman was paranoid and creepy, even innocent interactions fueled her ridiculous fantasies. How could she act completely normal the rest of the time?"

We all stared at each other. No one had an answer for that.

And, I hated to ask Todd this, but at this point, everything needed to be out in the open. "Did you ever learn more about your friend Carly?"

He ran his fingers through his hair and worked his jaw for a minute. "Apparently Jim hired her as a PI."

Really. I hadn't seen that one coming.

"Dear God. Veronica messed with her too? Did she do something to her car to cause the accident? How much evil is one woman capable of?" Harry's voice was aghast.

"No." Todd rolled his shoulders. "It appears it was truly an accident. She took that curve out there near Brenham's barn too fast and crashed into one of the utility poles. Might have made it, but the vehicle caught on fire."

I leaned over to wrap my arms around his neck and pressed my cheek against his. "I'm so sorry, honey," I murmured.

He leaned into my embrace for a moment, then straightened up. "What I want to know is how the roses fit in."

I squeezed his shoulder, respecting his need to change the subject. "That I don't know. Maybe Veronica didn't have anything to do with digging up my roses after all."

"But she sure capitalized on it by making everyone think

all of this had to do with your missing rose bushes. And she had to keep getting more fresh roses from somewhere. Oh, from Jim's nursery, of course, right?" Harry stroked his chin and looked at my parents. "Thank God y'all are okay. Dot spent many hours in prayer for you."

"Not just me, Harry." She smiled up at him.

"I don't know about Jerry, but I could...feel everyone's prayers. I knew God was going to...deliver us." Mom leaned her cheek against mine for a moment, then rose unsteadily to hug Aunt Dot. "We're here...in time for the...wedding. That's the...best part."

Todd cleared his throat. "Both weddings, you mean?"

What?

I gulped as he stood.

He knelt in front of me and grasped both my hands in his, his dark hair tumbling down over the bandage on his forehead. "Callie, I love you with all of my heart. Will you marry me?"

My throat tightened. Was I ready for this? Were we ready for this? "Are you sure?" I croaked out.

"You're supposed to say yes, darlin'," Harry drawled. "Put the poor man out of his misery."

I looked around the room at the dear faces gathered around us and released my fear of the future. There was only one way to find out what it would hold.

"I would be honored to marry you, Todd." I stared into his gorgeous blue eyes and smiled. "Under one condition."

He froze.

"It has to be a double wedding. This weekend." I framed his dear face with my hands and let my love shine through my eyes. "Deal?"

He whooshed out his breath. "Deal." He tugged me to my feet amidst the applause of our family and drew me into his embrace, leaning down to whisper in my ear. "But after that, Detective, you're all mine."

I rested my head against his chest and just breathed. "Deal."

EPILOGUE

Three days later, I stood in the tiny bathroom at C. Willikers, wearing *the* dress, Mona hovering at my side. I stared at myself in the mirror. Between Sharlene and Mona's ministrations, I barely recognized myself in an elegant updo and subtle makeup. I trailed my fingers over the beaded bodice, swallowing against the lump in my throat. "I can't believe this is finally happening."

A couple of years ago, I never would have dreamed that God would bless me with a second chance at marriage to an amazing man...and the courage to go through with it.

"It's the real deal, girlfriend. At least it will be, once we finish this photo shoot." Mona pushed past me and held up her phone. "Move out here and let me take a few more pictures before we go outside. Todd is going to die when he sees you later. The silvery shoes are perfect."

I held up my short lacy train and squeezed out of the bathroom. It had been Aunt Dot's idea to have pre-wedding pictures taken in my garden at C. Willikers. I struck a pose for Mona. "How does my veil look?"

Sharlene stuck her head in the front door of the shop. "The photographer's here!"

"We'll be out in a sec." Mona stretched up on tip-toe to smooth my veil back, then took my hand and squeezed it. She tried to speak, then stopped, her eyes filling.

I squeezed back, my throat tight and my eyes hot. "Don't make me cry." I laughed shakily.

She grabbed me into a bear hug, and I breathed in her familiar scent. She released me after a long minute and blew her nose. "I heard it straight from the cow's mouth that y'all didn't have time to decide where you're going on your honeymoon."

Straight from the cow's... I refocused. "No, but that's okay.

We'll figure something—"

She drew herself up and grabbed both of my hands again. "So me an' Rob decided to give y'all our timeshare down at the coast. We were gonna go in August with the grans, but we got to talkin' last night and Rob, he's got such a big heart, you know, he says, 'Sugar, why don't we give our week to Callie and Todd? We can go to Arkansas instead and see that big ol' motorcycle store we been wanting to visit.' So I said, 'Honey-pie, that's the best idea you had in a long, long time.' And he said—"

I laughed as the front door banged open. "You're the best, Mona. Please tell Rob thank you. We'd love to—"

"Are y'all coming? The photographer's getting antsy." Sharlene stepped inside. "Whew, it's getting warm out there."

I hugged Mona to my side and we made our way out onto the front porch, arm in arm.

She sniffed and hugged me again, then pulled away. "You go, girl," she said. "You're the most beautiful bride I've ever seen."

A few minutes later, I posed in front of my newly-planted Eden rosebushes, generously provided by Jim Slayton and sheepishly replanted by Jake Haskell.

"I'm sorry I dug them out to begin with, Ms. Erickson," Jake had said. "I misread the address of the yard I was supposed to do. By the time I realized my mistake, Ginger was dead and you had already been accused of the murder." He hung his head. "I figured it served you right to have your rosebushes destroyed if you were that bad of a person."

But all that was behind us now. I touched my gauzy veil, still wondering if I was dreaming. I could only stand amazed at what God had done in my life in these last few years.

Todd.

Dot and Harry.

My relationship with my parents.

Hope House.

Peace.

Protection.

Forgiveness.

A honeymoon at Mona's timeshare condo.

What more could a girl want? I plucked a rose, stuck it in my hair and smiled at my future.

"Let's get this party started!"

Author Note

Dear Readers,

I hope you were cheering for Callie and Todd at the end of this book...and for Callie's reunion with her parents! Both events were a long time coming and neither one turned out as Callie might have imagined.

Isn't life like that? Many of us walk through our days both dreaming about and dreading the future, yet if we stop to think about it, much of life doesn't turn out as we'd hoped—or feared—it would. Sometimes they're much, much better. Sometimes, they're worse. Often, they're simply different. So why do we spend so much energy trying to figure out our future, when God says not to worry, but to trust?

God has been teaching me about trusting and resting during this season of my life. I'm learning to still my soul and sit at His feet. I'm learning that He would rather I "be" with Him than do for Him. Jesus said, "Come to me, all you who are weary and burdened, and I will give you rest. Take my yoke upon you and learn from me, for I am gentle and humble in heart, and you will find rest for your souls. For my yoke is easy and my burden is light." (Matthew 11:28-30, NIV)

If you're struggling today, you can find rest for your soul in God. But if you're not in the habit of quieting yourself, it might be more difficult at first than you imagine. Keep at it! God always loves a heart that is seeking His.
"My heart is not proud, Lord, my eyes are not haughty; I do not concern myself with great matters or things too wonderful for me. But I have calmed and quieted myself, I am like a weaned child with its mother; like a weaned child I am content." (Psalm 131:1-2, NIV)

So find a quiet place. Take a deep breath. Read His word. Still your thoughts and ask Him to speak to your heart. He will.

Book Club Questions

1. To err is human; to forgive, divine. What does this famous quotation by Alexander Pope bring to your mind? Why do you think Callie was wrestling with unforgiveness for her parents throughout the Short Creek books? Why do we need to forgive others? Ourselves? How is God's forgiveness greater than ours? To whom do you need to extend forgiveness today?

2. At several points in the story, Callie recognizes that she is focusing on herself and her own wants and needs more than she should. What does she do to change this? Why do we as humans tend to be self-centered? Why must we examine ourselves and our motives on a regular basis?

3. Callie's employee and friend, Sharlene, a fairly new follower of Christ, is longing to get married. What advice would you give Sharlene?

4. After being introduced to Houston and Nicole in the first Short Creek book, we follow their story through the three books until Houston is ready to propose to Nicole at the end of the third book. We watch (mostly through Houston's eyes) as Nicole's journey through inner healing takes her from drug addict and sex-trafficking victim to counselor at Hope House and soon-to-be wife of a minister. Do you know anyone who has a similar story? How can you encourage someone who is just beginning his or her journey to restoration, sobriety, and freedom? Or someone who has been walking that path for a long time?

5. At one point in the story, Callie has a vivid dream about her parents. What are some biblical instances of God speaking to people through dreams? Do you believe God reveals information to us or gives guidance in dreams? Have you had a dream you know was from God?

CPSIA information can be obtained
at www.ICGtesting.com
Printed in the USA
FSHW020956050421
80161FS

9 781943 959747